The Awakening of Dr. Brown

KATHLEEN CREIGHTON

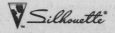

Silhouette®

INTIMATE MOMENTS™

Published by Silhouette Books

America's Publisher of Contemporary Romance

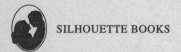 SILHOUETTE BOOKS

ISBN 0-373-27127-1

THE AWAKENING OF DR. BROWN

Visit Silhouette at www.eHarlequin.com

Printed in U.S.A.

"What did you want...before all this happened? What kind of life did you see yourself having?"

Ethan took his time answering. "I saw myself opening up my medical practice in a little town straight out of Norman Rockwell, some little town that really needed a doctor. I'd have a wife and some kids, and I'd spend my life helping other people feel better."

"And now?" Joanna asked. Why was there an ache in her throat, and a lump the size of Kansas? She looked over at him and saw him shrug.

"That hasn't changed." He glanced at her, his eyes quiet and dark. *Shaman's eyes.* Joanna's inner voice mocked her as she realized, *Not for me. Me, a wife? A mother? Who am I kidding?*

But then her inner voice was back, louder than ever, as it said, *Why not me?*

Dear Reader,

Valentine's Day is here this month, and what better way to celebrate the spirit of romance than with six fabulous novels from Silhouette Intimate Moments? Kathleen Creighton's *The Awakening of Dr. Brown* is one of those emotional tours de force that will stay in your mind and your heart long after you've turned the last page. With talent like this, it's no wonder Kathleen has won so many awards for her writing. Join Ethan Brown and Joanna Dunn on their journey into the heart. You'll be glad you did.

A YEAR OF LOVING DANGEROUSLY continues with *Someone To Watch Over Her,* a suspenseful and sensuous Caribbean adventure by Margaret Watson. Award winner Marie Ferrarella adds another installment to her CHILDFINDERS, INC. miniseries with *A Hero in Her Eyes,* a real page-turner of a romance. Meet the second of bestselling author Ruth Langan's THE SULLIVAN SISTERS in *Loving Lizbeth*—and look forward to third sister Celeste's appearance next month. Reader favorite Rebecca Daniels is finally back with *Rain Dance,* a gripping amnesia story. And finally, check out *Renegade Father* by RaeAnne Thayne, the stirring tale of an irresistible Native American hero and a lady rancher.

All six of this month's books are guaranteed to keep you turning pages long into the night, so don't miss a single one. And be sure to come back next month for more of the best and most exciting romantic reading around—right here in Silhouette Intimate Moments.

Enjoy!

Leslie J. Wainger
Executive Senior Editor

Please address questions and book requests to:
Silhouette Reader Service
U.S.: 3010 Walden Ave., P.O. Box 1325, Buffalo, NY 14269
Canadian: P.O. Box 609, Fort Erie, Ont. L2A 5X3

Books by Kathleen Creighton

Silhouette Intimate Moments

Demon Lover #84
Double Dealings #157
Gypsy Dancer #196
In Defense of Love #216
Rogue's Valley #240
Tiger Dawn #289
Love and Other Surprises #322
Wolf and the Angel #417
*A Wanted Man #547
Eyewitness #616
*One Good Man #639
*Man of Steel #677
Never Trust a Lady #800
†One Christmas Knight #825
One More Knight #890
†One Summer's Knight #944
†Eve's Wedding Knight #963
*The Cowboy's Hidden Agenda #1004
*The Awakening of Dr. Brown #1057

*Into the Heartland
†The Sisters Waskowitz

Silhouette Desire

The Heart Mender #584
In From the Cold #654

Silhouette Books

Silhouette Christmas Stories 1990
"The Mysterious Gift"

KATHLEEN CREIGHTON

has roots deep in the California soil but has relocated to South Carolina. As a child, she enjoyed listening to old timers' tales, and her fascination with the past only deepened as she grew older. Today she says she is interested in everything—art, music, gardening, zoology, anthropology and history—but people are at the top of her list. She also has a lifelong passion for writing, and now combines her two loves in romance novels.

Prologue

The nightmare came as it always did, borne on wings of music. Heavenly music; joyful, happy music. Music that filled her heart with delight and tumbled from her throat in ribbons of song. Music that poured into her feet and made them want to dance.

Then...as it always did, everything changed.

In her dream, one minute she was laughing and dancing, singing for the pure, unbridled joy of it. In the next moment, the music became an undulating wail that replaced joy with terror and her legs with lead.

No longer dancing, now she was running, running, running, while around her the world turned violent shades of fire—orange and red and yellow white and the wail grew to a shriek that filled all the spaces inside her head. The air was thick and black with smoke and choked her when she tried to breathe it. She wanted to scream, tried to scream, but there was no air, no breath for screaming.

Still...still she tried, until her throat was raw and the pain inside became too terrible to bear.

Then, as always, she woke up.

Awake, she could still smell smoke, but strangely, now it seemed to comfort rather than terrify. And there were cool fingers stroking the damp hair from her forehead, and a voice steeped in bourbon and cigarettes crooning, "Hush, baby-girl, hush now, don't you cry. You gonna be fine now. The Doveman's got you under his wings...."

Little by little the fear and pain subsided. Her throat relaxed, her breathing slowed, and she drifted into sleep on the whiskey-sweet notes of the Doveman's song:

"Hush little baby, don't say a word,
    Papa's gonna buy you a mockin'bird..."

Chapter 1

"**W**ho you gonna be this time?" Doveman turned on the piano bench as a final riff of music dropped from his gnarled but still-nimble fingers, effortlessly as raindrops from the sky.

The rock-and-roll legend known as Phoenix pulled her gaze away from the window to look past him, tilting her head slightly as she replayed the music inside her head, then tried it again paired with the lyric *Who am I this time?* A smile played across her lips and her heart quickened; together in just such a way, she and Rupert Dove had created more hit songs over the years than she could count.

She tossed away the question with a shrug, and the smile grew wry. "Hey—I'm open to suggestion. I've done vamp and virgin, waif and glamour queen—"

"Don't forget punk." Doveman's voice was even drier than his usual Black Jack-and-Camels rasp.

"I try to, daily," Phoenix replied, mimicking both tone and manner.

Doveman's cackle of laughter was affectionate. "You was *young,* girl. Cut y'self some slack. You done traveled a long, long road since those days."

He swiveled back to the keyboard, his fingers finding their way so surely the sounds they produced seemed to come from the air itself rather than human hands. And so clever and intricate was the variation, even Phoenix didn't recognize for a moment the main theme from "Pretty Mary," the biggest hit single from her last album, *Fire and Ice.* The song that had won them both multiple Grammys, the one that had prompted critics to say of the album and the subsequent world tour that "Phoenix has entered a new dimension of sophistication and maturity."

But that had been four long years ago. An eon measured in pop culture time.

Phoenix turned back to the window, feeling chilled in spite of the heat haze that shrouded the city like fog.

Behind her, Doveman's voice rode gently on the current of his music. "That one—that *Fire and Ice* tour, now—that was a good one. Done real good with that one. But the river rolls on, girl, it don't go back. You got to go on to somethin' new."

The river rolls on.... But I *have* gone back, Phoenix thought, her gaze skipping past the city's redbrick jumble to the tiny sliver of harbor waters sparkling in the sun like a diamond in a rubbish heap.

Down there, between the newly renovated harbor with its tourist havens and pricey high-rise apartment buildings, and the converted loft on the edge of a newly renovated warehouse district in which she stood, blocks and blocks of dingy, dilapidated row houses straggled like defeated soldiers to the water's edge. Down there, hopeless people still passed empty days on sagging stoops and street corners and children played and skinned their knees on crumbling sidewalks with broken curbs.

This she knew. Oh, yes, she—and only one other—knew that it was on one of those same streets that multimillionaire rock icon Phoenix had played as a child. But she still had the scars on her knees to prove it.

"The Phoenix shall rise again," she intoned.

Doveman chuckled, missing—or ignoring—the irony. He nodded without turning. "That's right. Phoenix is gonna rise up again. Question is, who she gonna be this time? You got to decide, child."

Who am I? Standing at the window with her back to the old piano man, Phoenix drew a catching breath.

"Here's an idea for you." Doveman's voice had softened. And she realized the melody hidden in the blues variations that tumbled so easily from the piano keys wasn't "Pretty Mary" any longer, but something slow and sweet and hauntingly familiar.

An indefinable sadness clutched at her throat. In response to it, her voice hardened. "Shoot."

"How about for this tour, for this album, you just be yourself? Joanna Dunn?"

Doveman's music faded with his last word, so her laugh gusted into silence. The emotion gripping her now wasn't sadness, nor was it indefinable. What it was, she knew full well, was fear—raw and unreasoning fear. The fear of a small child abandoned in the darkness.

Jerking around to face him, she said, "Get real!" in a brittle voice that sounded like anger.

Not the least bit perturbed by her fit of temper, Doveman shrugged. "Why not? Girl, it's who you are. Time you let folks see who Phoenix is."

She shook her head; a derisive sound puffed softly from her lips. But as she gazed at the coffee-brown face of the man who'd been like a father to her for more than twenty years, she felt her anger drain away. When it did, only the fear remained.

With her voice still hard as stone she said, "Doveman, I haven't been that person for so long, I wouldn't even know who she is now."

Unwillingly, her glance went back to the window, pulled inexorably by its view of row houses, tenements and despair. "Besides—" and now suddenly her voice had gone sharp and bright, pain disguised as laughter "—who in their right mind is going to pay money to listen to somebody named Joanna Dunn?"

She didn't wait for the answer to that, didn't expect or want one. She jerked herself away from the window and announced, "I'm going out," as she snatched up a pair of sunglasses and a New York Yankees baseball cap that were lying on the white leather sofa.

Rupert Dove only said mildly, "If you're walkin', better take one of the boys with you. This ain't exactly a strollin'-around neighborhood."

And he watched as the rock star's famous lips curved with a small, sardonic smile. He said nothing more, knowing it would fall on deaf ears; in all except music matters, Phoenix listened to no one but herself.

He watched silently, then, as she twisted her long black hair and stuffed it beneath the baseball cap, as unforgettable silvery eyes vanished behind mirrored sunglasses. "Be careful out there," he drawled by way of a farewell. She threw him a wave, went out the door and left him shaking his head and chuckling to himself.

He doubted she'd have heard the sadness in his laughter, even if she'd stayed.

Doveman's heart was heavy with concern for the girl-child he'd raised and loved as his own for more than twenty years. Not for the sake of her physical safety—he knew she was capable of handling anything those mean streets might throw at her. Nor was he afraid she might be recognized, even on the streets of the city of her birth. Phoenix had always been a master of the art of disguise.

It was the part hidden away beneath all the layers of her disguises he worried about, the part only one old black piano man even knew existed. The part named Joanna Dunn.

Swiveling once more to the keyboard, Doveman reached into the bowels of the baby grand and drew out his hidden stash—a crumpled pack of Camels and a half-used up book of matches from the convenience store down on the corner. He preferred matches over a lighter, always had; liked listening to the sound of the matchhead scraping grit, liked the flowering flame, the faint smell of sulfur. Now, touching the flame to the tip of the cigarette, he closed his eyes and drew the forbidden smoke deep into his lungs. His body reacted to the abuse with a violent fit of coughing, which he accepted philosophically. His lungs were shot to hell anyway; the way he saw it, he might as well enjoy what life there was left to him.

But that was another reason why he worried.

"Doctor? I put that otitus media in exam three, when you're ready." Ruthie Mendoza, casually dressed in jeans and a pink cotton smock with *kitty-cats* printed on it, waved a clipboard from the opposite end of the counter.

"Thanks, Ruthie." Dr. Ethan Brown returned his pen to its customary place in the pocket of his lab coat and tried to sneak a glance at his watch as he laid the chart he'd just completed back on the pile.

Bibi Schmidt, whose mild gray eyes missed little, glanced at him over the tops of her half glasses as she reached for it. "You gonna try and get some shut-eye this afternoon, Doctor? It is your night to ride-along, isn't it?"

"It is, and I'd hoped to." The smile Ethan gave the clinic's volunteer administrator/receptionist was wry. "I don't know what it is with this sudden epidemic of ear in-

fections. Lord, it's June—cold and flu season should be over
with by now.''

"Swimming," said Mrs. Schmidt, returning to her paperwork. "School's out, it's hot, these poor kids are out there
trying to cool off in that filthy river." Bibi had been a school
administrator in a former life, and Ethan didn't doubt she
knew whereof she spoke.

After a moment, the bookkeeper glanced up again. "Who
are you going to be riding with tonight?" Her expression
was bland, her tone casual but with a particular undertone.

Ethan had come to know that look and that tone well in
the six months or so he'd been serving at the South Church
Street Free Clinic; behind Mrs. Schmidt's stern and stony
schoolmarm's demeanor lurked the soul of a schoolboy
prankster.

Playing along, he replied in a similarly casual tone, "Oh,
I don't know. Most likely be Kenny." He slid a sidelong
glance toward the other end of the counter, where Ruthie
was poring over an upside-down chart and pretending complete disinterest in their conversation.

"Baumgartner?" Behind the half glasses, Mrs. Schmidt's
eyes were now openly twinkling. "Why, that's that nice
Jewish boy, isn't it? The one that has such a crush on our
Ruthie."

"I wouldn't go so far as to call it a *crush*," Ethan mused.
Then, following a pause, "More like…the hots."

"He does not!" That brought a rich, warm color to
Ruthie's cheeks. "And even if he did, so what? I'm not
interested." She dropped the clipboard with a clatter and
went flouncing off.

"A good thing she isn't," said Mrs. Schmidt in a dry
undertone, watching the nurse walk away toward the back
of the cavernous room that had once been a fire station's
engine bay. "What kind of a future can there be for those

two—a nice Jewish boy in love with a sweet Catholic girl whose twin brother just happens to be a priest?''

For a moment Ethan allowed his own gaze to follow Mrs. Schmidt's, before he jerked it back to the counter and its pile of charts. Ruthie was a sweet girl and he was fond of her, in a way. But the fact was, there was simply no place in his life for entanglements—not now, and not for the foreseeable future. At least for the next year and a half, while Everett Charlton Brown was still in residence at 1600 Pennsylvania Avenue and his entire family under a constant media microscope and his son's future in limbo as a consequence.

Ethan didn't resent the notoriety his father's choice of careers had forced upon him—he truly didn't. At least, not anymore. Rhett Brown was a good man and a great president, and he'd done some wonderful things for the country—the world, even. But to be honest, there were times when Ethan thought about his childhood back in Iowa, thought about holidays spent on his aunt Lucy's farm, or building a tree house in the backyard in Des Moines with his sister Lolly....

He thought about Lauren, and how she'd managed to escape the limelight practically on the eve of their father's presidency. And yes, he envied her sometimes, with her law practice and her two kids and her Native American lawman husband, living out there on an Apache reservation in the wilds of Arizona, far from the glare of TV cameras.

Back then, while struggling through med school and internship out in California, he'd mostly been too busy to think about his own future...about personal relationships, anyway. A family, a wife, children...it had all seemed too far off to worry about. Lately, though, he had begun to think about it—something to do with being on the verge of turning thirty, he imagined—and whether it would ever be possible for a man in his position to meet someone he could fall in love with. Someone who would love him back, for the right reasons. Ethan didn't consider himself to be shy—although others might disagree with him, and he supposed he might have been shy, as a child. Now, as far as he was concerned, he was just a very private person. And one thing he knew for certain: if and when he did meet someone, there was no way in hell he was going to risk having his personal life, his emotional affairs turned into public entertainment like some huge Hollywood production!

Another thing. If he ever did decide to brave the media attention over a woman, it was going to have to be something pretty compelling—the real thing, nothing less—which was a long way from the kind of gentle affection he felt for Ruthie. The truth was, he thought of her as…well, a younger sister.

Of course, part of the reason for that attitude may have been the fact that Ruthie's twin brother, the priest, happened to be Ethan's former college roommate and best friend.

Also, both the Mendoza twins and Mrs. Schmidt were among the very few in town who were fully aware of Ethan's identity. Not that he could have kept it a secret, even with the well-trimmed beard and longish hair he'd tried to cultivate in an attempt to disguise his all-too-familiar face, given the presence of the pair of Secret Service agents who passed their days in vigilant boredom upstairs in what had once been the firehouse's kitchen. Not to mention the news crews that showed up on the clinic's doorstep from time to time in defiance of the unspoken agreement between the media and the White House that the president's children were to be strictly off-limits. There'd been more than one occasion when Ruthie, Father Frank or Mrs. Schmidt had been called upon to run interference with a camera crew while their quarry escaped out the back door.

Ethan's sense of gratitude toward the three was therefore deep and heartfelt, not only for their loyalty and discretion, but for refusing to allow the unfortunate accident of his parentage to stand in the way of genuine friendship. He'd learned the hard way, during the six and a half years his father and stepmother had occupied the White House, how rare and valuable such friendships were.

So it was for that reason he took advantage of every opportunity to promote EMT Kenny Baumgartner's cause. Tonight's ride-along, which was part of the arrangement with the city that allowed him to put in his hours at the clinic free of charge, he devoutly hoped would provide him with a few more of those chances.

Ethan gave Mrs. Schmidt a wink and a wave as he picked up the clipboard Ruthie had abandoned, and turned to confront the unhappy patient in the curtained cubicle designated as exam room three.

The patient—a boy about seven or eight years old, dressed in the standard urban uniform of baggy jeans and oversized T-shirt and a baseball cap turned backward—sat slumped on the paper-covered exam table. The boy's mother had been sitting beside him, but she slid off the table at the doctor's entrance and now faced him, one nervous and protective hand resting on her son's knee.

"Hi, I'm Dr. Brown," said Ethan in a brisk but friendly tone designed to put them both at ease, offering his hand first to the mother, then the boy. He glanced down at the chart in his hand. "And you are..."

"This is Michael," the boy's mother offered, and in a fiercely whispered aside to her son, accompanied by a glancing swat on his denim-draped leg, "What you doin', boy? Get that hat *offa* your head."

"Okay, Mike—"

"It's *Michael*." Obeying his mother while at the same time thrusting his chin defiantly upward, the boy slid proud amber eyes toward Ethan. "Like Michael Jordan. Ain't nobody ever called Michael Jordan *Mike*."

"You're right about that," Ethan agreed, instantly charmed. He gave the boy's mother a wink and was gratified to see her relax, if only slightly. "Michael it is, then. So, I understand you've been having earaches?"

"Maybe I shouldn't of brought him for such a little thing," the boy's mother said, tense and defensive again. "But, my sister Tamara? A woman where she works told her her boy had earaches, and they was so bad his eardrums busted. Said they had to operate on him, put tubes in his ears. I don't want my baby to have to have no operation. Don't want him to have no tubes in his ears. So I thought—"

"No, it's good you brought him in." Ear scope at the ready, Ethan leaned toward the child, who, predictably, pulled away with a sharp *"Ow!"* Ethan eyed him sternly. "Come on, now, you think Michael Jordan would raise a fuss about such a little thing?" Again the amber eyes slid toward him with that look of proud disdain. "Hey, I just want to take a look inside your ears, see what's going on in there. Okay?"

Michael nodded, but grudgingly. But he sat perfectly still for the duration of Ethan's exam.

"How is he?" Hugging herself, the boy's mother hovered at his side, all hunched-up shoulders and worried eyes. Dark eyes, Ethan noticed, rather exotic, tilted, almond shaped and much darker than her son's. "His eardrums—they ain't busted, are they? Maybe I shoulda brought him in sooner, but I couldn't get offa work—"

Ethan assured her the boy's eardrums were still intact. "Looks pretty red and angry in there, though. We're going to get him started right away on some antibiotics—"

"Am I gonna hafta get a shot?" Chin cocked, Michael regarded him with his brave golden glare.

Ethan laughed and squeezed the thin shoulder. "Nah— you just get to take some nasty orange medicine. You take it all, though, every time your mama tells you to, no arguing, okay? Otherwise you're just gonna make those germs that're causing your earaches good and mad, and then they'll come back twice as mean next time. You understand?''

Trying not to look relieved, Michael nodded. Ethan scribbled a prescription for the antibiotic and handed it to the mother, explaining in an undertone the procedure for getting it filled free of charge at a nearby pharmacy and securing her promise to bring her son back for a checkup in three days.

Then, remembering what Mrs. Schmidt had told him about the most likely cause of the current rash of ear infections, he turned back to Michael, who had already hopped down from the exam table and was looking much happier now that he no longer felt the need to keep up a macho front worthy of his namesake and hero. "And no swimming, you hear me? Not until those ears are completely cleared up."

At that, his mother gave a gasp and dusted her son's shoulder with her glancing swat. "Michael! You been swimming in that filthy river again? After I done *told* you? Didn't I tell you stay away from that filthy water? What am I gonna do with you, boy?'' She turned eyes glistening with hopelessness to Ethan. "I'm sorry, Doctor, but I got to work, I can't watch him all the time. My sister Tamara, she supposed to watch him days, but she got the baby... It wasn't so bad when he was in school, but now, with summer vacation and him home all day...''

Ethan nodded in automatic sympathy as he drew aside the exam room curtain; it was a story he'd heard many times before, one that unfortunately he had no answer for.

Just outside the curtain the woman stopped, turned abruptly and asked, "So, how much I owe you?''

It caught Ethan by surprise; he was already moving on, his mind leaping ahead to other things—the afternoon's schedule, Ruthie's lovelife, the evening's four-to-midnight

EMS ride-along. He turned back with a frown, poking absently at his lab coat pocket. "There's no charge, ma'am, this is a free clinic."

But the woman—Ethan glanced now at the chart, searching for her name…Louise, that was it, Louise Parker—drew herself up, somehow seeming inches taller. And in the proud lifting of her chin, reminded Ethan suddenly and for the first time of her son.

"Uh-uh—I got me a job, I been offa welfare for a year, now. I ain't no freeloader. Michael and me, we pay our own way."

Ethan glanced imploringly at Mrs. Schmidt, who had heard the exchange and was watching with great interest from her cubbyhole behind the reception counter. The woman drew a folded bill from the pocket of her faded jeans and thrust it at him. "Here—it's all I got right now. If it's not enough I'll give you the rest next time I come. Let's go, Michael."

Speechless, Ethan watched Louise Parker and her son until the clinic's front door had closed with a click behind them. Then he unfolded the bill. "My God," he whispered, showing it to Mrs. Schmidt. "Twenty dollars—I'll bet that's a lot of money to her."

"Probably." As she went back to her books Mrs. Schmidt added in a musing tone, "That is one lucky little boy, you know that? With a mother like that, he might actually have a chance."

Across the street from what had once been the South Church Street Fire Station, a thin black woman hurried along the sweltering sidewalk. So preoccupied was she with the scolding she was administering to the small boy dressed in baggy clothes and a backward baseball cap shuffling along beside her that she failed to notice a similarly dressed

youth—this one Caucasian and of indeterminable gender—
until they had all but collided.

"Michael!" The woman's sharp whisper accompanied a
light swat to the sagging seat of the boy's trousers. "What
you doin', boy? Mind your manners! Say 'excuse me.'"

"'Scuse me," the boy dutifully mumbled, just as the
"youth" was muttering, in a voice several tones deeper than
her own distinctive contralto, "No, no, that's okay—my
fault. I wasn't looking where I was going."

The woman had done a double take and was now regarding the youth with an appraising stare, taking in the pale
hue of her skin, the mirrored sunglasses, the New York Yankees logo on her baseball cap. "Hey," she demanded on a
rising note of incredulity, "you *lost?*"

Safe in her disguise, Phoenix reached out to give the bill
of the little boy's baseball cap a tug—why, she didn't know,
she normally had little use for children. "Nah," she said
with a wry smile, "not exactly. I was just looking for something...a place I used to know."

"Yeah, well..." Looking extremely doubtful, the woman
was edging away from her now, hands protectively on the
child's shoulders. "If I was you, I'd be askin' Father
Frank."

"Who?"

"You know—the priest? Over there at St Jude's." She
pointed, then hurried off in the opposite direction, calling
back over her shoulder, "He can probably help you." But
she sounded, Joanna thought, as if in her opinion any white
person dumb enough to be walking around alone in that
neighborhood was most likely beyond help. She wondered
if the woman knew St. Jude was the patron saint of lost
causes.

Half a block down the street in the direction the woman
had indicated squatted the ugly redbrick pile trimmed in
white that housed the rectory of St. Jude's Catholic Church.

Next to it on the corner, the church itself—for which the street had been named nearly a century before—was only a slightly more graceful edifice, brightened somewhat by a Victorian abundance of stone trim and stained glass windows. On a tiny patch of grass tucked between the two, a stocky man dressed in black bermuda shorts and a white T-shirt had paused in his task of manhandling an old-fashioned push lawn mower in order to watch the exchange. Now he came toward Joanna, wiping sweat from his face with the sleeve of his T-shirt.

"Can I help you?"

Joanna hesitated. Normally she had no more use for priests than she did for children. But the man's eyes were kind. "Maybe," she said grudgingly, and jerked her head toward the street. "Didn't there used to be a firehouse around here somewhere?"

The priest smiled. "That's right—that's it over there, across the street. Used to be the old Church Street station. They moved it a few years ago—three blocks over, on Franklin. Got too small, the street too crowded, I guess. Anyway, they've got a big new station over there—police, fire and EMS, all in one building. Go back down a block, then over three—you can't miss it." He paused, liquid dark eyes narrowing with concern. "Is everything okay? Anything I can do for you? You need to use the phone—"

Joanna shook her head. Then, for reasons she couldn't begin to understand, heard herself explain, "I used to live around here—years ago. I was just wondering..." She paused and drew a careful breath, released it in a soft laugh. "I guess things have changed quite a bit."

"Yes, I guess they have." The priest's eyes rested on her now with gentle appraisal. She felt herself tense under their scrutiny, and was instantly annoyed. Priest or not, the man was probably younger than she was; what right had he to make her feel like a truant?

But instead of turning her back and walking away, for some reason she hesitated still, her eyes going once more to the narrow redbrick building across the street. A man was just emerging from the arched front entrance, pausing the way people do when they come from air-conditioning into the heat, as if he'd just missed bumping into something solid. A young man, he appeared to be, with a tall, healthy, well-built body dressed in blue jeans and a short-sleeved shirt with a collar, open at the neck. Sort of preppy looking, in spite of a neatly trimmed beard. Definitely not from this neighborhood. Even from this distance—just something about the way he moved, maybe, the way he carried himself—she could tell he was good-looking, even handsome in a wholesome, blond, shredded wheat sort of way. *Nice.*

Memories crowded in, filling her chest with a treacherous sadness. Nice voices…kind faces, smudged with soot. *Your momma's gone, honey, you come with me now…it's gonna be okay. It's gonna be okay…*

"It's a free clinic now," the priest was saying, and his eyes were friendly and young once again. "Staffed by volunteers, mostly. My sister works there part-time—she's a nurse over at Community Med. Hey, if you happen to drop in over there, tell Ruthie Mendoza her brother Frankie said hello."

But the rock icon known as Phoenix barely heard him. She was already moving away down the cracked and dirty sidewalk, walking quickly, one hand going to her mirrored sunglasses as if to reassure herself the disguise was still in place.

Ethan could hear a stereo thumping before he'd even reached the door of the EMS station. Classic light rock—so he'd guessed right about Kenny Baumgartner being his ride-along partner. Kenny was thirty-one, considered ancient for a paramedic, so his tastes in music tended to run pretty close to Ethan's, which made him a welcome relief from some of the younger EMT's and their mind-numbing, not to mention ear-deadening preferences. Ethan wondered if it was a sign of advancing middle-age, now that he was approaching thirty himself, to be finding fault with the younger generation's music.

"Ah…good song," he said as he walked into the EMT's lounge to a driving beat, the familiar and haunting chorus of "Pretty Mary."

"Classic," Kenny agreed without looking up. The paramedic was sprawled in a chrome and plastic kitchen chair poring over his latest sailing magazine, bobbing his head and whistling tunelessly in time to the beat. "One of the all-time top ten—right up there with the Boss, man. Might even beat out "Born To Run.""

That brought a snort from the lanky and obscenely young EMT who was lounging with one elbow propped against the countertop, waiting for something in the microwave. Any comment the paramedic had intended as a follow-up was preempted by the oven's prolonged beep, and he uttered instead a satisfied, "Ah!" as he popped open the door. The smells of pepperoni and processed cheese filled the off-duty room.

"Heard she's got a new CD coming out." Kenny tossed aside the magazine and tilted his chair back at an alarming angle. "Supposed to be starting a big worldwide tour, is what I heard."

Concentrating on separating mozzarella from cardboard, the young paramedic glanced up long enough to say, "Who?" just as Ethan was exclaiming, "No kidding?" So then both Ethan and Kenny had to pause to give the kid a look of incredulity.

"Phoenix—who the hell are we talking about?" Kenny said, shaking his head as if in profound disgust at such ignorance, as Ethan set his medical bag on the floor and sank into a chair, wiping sweat with his shirt sleeve.

"Oh, yeah, Phoenix…right." The EMT—Leon, according to the tag on his uniform pocket—shrugged, licked his fingers, then added, "Isn't she supposed to be in town?"

Again, both Kenny and Ethan stared at him. And again it was Kenny who asked, "Who? Phoenix? Here?"

Leon placed his pizza on the table and shrugged.

"Where'd you hear that?" Kenny demanded, clearly in disbelief.

"Hey," said Leon, looking offended, "I read *Rolling Stone*." He glanced from Kenny to Ethan and back again. "It's true. Supposed to be getting ready for some big new gig."

It was Kenny's turn to snort in derision. "Nobody kicks off a tour from this town, man. This town is where tours come to *die*."

Leon could only shrug, being totally committed to the lava-hot mozzarella he'd just bitten into. Presently he managed to mumble through the mouthful, "Just tellin' you what they said, man. It was like, she used to be from here or something."

Once again both Ethan and Kenny were struck momentarily dumb by that news, but the stunned silence lasted only a second or two before it was filled by the raucous blast of the alarm. It was a sound that never failed to send a bolt of electricity through Ethan, kick his heart rate into high and lift up the hairs on his forearms, and in that instant he lost all interest in the likely whereabouts of the rock-and-roll legend called Phoenix.

Kenny righted his chair with a thump. "We'll take it," he said to the younger paramedic, who was hunched over his pizza, desperately trying to sever the umbilical cord of cheese that bound him to it. Ethan was already on his feet and reaching for his medical bag. Kenny signaled to him with a jerk of his head. "Time to rock 'n' roll." He grinned at his own cleverness, then let the grin slide toward wryness as he added, "Starting in early tonight. Must be the heat."

Kenny's words proved prophetic. During the course of Ethan's four-to-midnight ride-along, he and Kenny had already handled two multi-injury MVAs, a jogger with chest pains, the combatants in a bar brawl, and a portly fellow who'd fallen off a ladder while attempting to install an air conditioner in a second-floor bedroom window. So, when the Klaxon sounded at eleven-forty-five, Leon and his partner, Scott, generously offered to take it.

"'Bout time for ol' Doc, there, to be headin' for the barn, anyways," was the way Leon put it, a blatant reference to Ethan's age. Which had been the source of a running, and in Ethan's opinion not very funny, joke among the younger EMTs for quite a while now.

Kenny, who had been listening to the dispatcher, shook his head. His face was grim as he gave Ethan the head-jerk signal to roll. "Balcony collapse over in The Gardens," he said, referring to one of the worst of the many slum neighborhoods in that part of the city, one well-known to police, fire and rescue squads who'd nicknamed it The Gardens because it was anything but. "Sounds like one for you, Doc. Do you mind?"

Ethan was already a step ahead of him going out the door, adrenaline pumping. "That's only a few blocks from here," he pointed out as he signaled to the driver of an anonymous dark sedan parked in the No Parking zone in front of the station. He climbed into the EMS wagon and pulled his safety belt across his shoulder as the wagon rolled down the drive. Watching in the side view mirror, he saw the sedan take up its customary position a couple of car-lengths behind as they sped down the dark street, lights whirling and siren wailing.

* * *

High in her converted loft, Phoenix heard sirens and woke from a restless sleep. It was not the first time; the sirens had been busy tonight. As all the times before, she woke with her heart racing and her body slick with sweat, and it was a minute or two before the chill of terror faded and her breathing grew quiet again.

But you're safe here…safe.

From somewhere a melody came to her and she sang it softly to herself in her mind. Yes, and she remembered now, remembered where she'd heard it most recently. It was the melody Doveman had played that afternoon, segueing from "Pretty Mary," except that he'd played it in a minor key and with a bluesy rhythm.

The words came to her, and she sang them to herself, too, finding in them a familiar comfort.

Hush little baby, don't say a word,
Papa's gonna buy you a mockin'bird…

Often, in times of dire emergency, Ethan's mind entered a zone of quiet, a place from which it could operate calmly and efficiently, protected from the distractions, the fear, the sights, sounds and smells of crisis that surrounded him. He didn't know when it had begun; it just seemed that it had always been so, and he was grateful for the gift.

It stood him well now, as the EMS wagon screeched to a halt at a curbside crowded with people, in a shadowy darkness noisy with panic, anger, shock and uncertainty.

"Paramedics—move aside, please, let us through. Step back please…."

From somewhere out beyond his zone of quiet he heard Kenny's voice, calm but loud, and weighty with authority. He heard sobbing, a woman's voice, many voices speaking rapidly in tones of panic, shock and fear, speaking all at once, explaining, imploring...praying.

"It was so hot, you know? The air conditioner don't work. The babies was in bed...she was just gonna sit for a while, out where it's cool..."

"There was this noise...and then the whole thing came down!"

"Just tore right out the wall!"

"Wasn't nothin' I could do...wasn't *nothin'* anybody could do..."

"Oh, Lord Jesus...Oh, God...somebody gotta help her!"
"Somebody..."

With that faraway part of his mind, Ethan felt himself climbing over rubble, kneeling on chunks of bricks and wrought iron that cut his knees even through his jeans. He could feel adrenaline pumping through his body, feel the sweat running in rivers down his face, feel his hands moving swiftly and surely, exploring crushed and mangled flesh. He heard his own voice shouting orders, firing instructions, heard himself calling for the equipment, the fluids, the tubes and lines and wraps that could and so often did salvage lives that seemed beyond saving. With the distant part of his mind he felt and heard those things...even while the quiet, protected part knew it was hopeless.

"Hey, Doc, there was nothing you could do." Kenny's gravelly voice came from somewhere behind him, heavy with regret, gentle with acceptance. "The femoral artery was cut clean through. She bled out in a matter of minutes."

"Yeah," Ethan muttered, "I know." Emerging from his quiet place, he now felt shaken, exposed and vulnerable. He tore off a glove and drew the hand across his eyes, and then as his gaze shifted to the face of the body sprawled like a broken doll in the rubble before him, swore with vehement surprise. Dark eyes stared up at him, almond-shaped eyes with a familiar exotic tilt.

"What?" Kenny asked. "You know her?"

Ethan nodded. His stomach clenched, and then his teeth. "She was in the clinic. Just this afternoon. She's got a kid."

At that moment, just as if he'd been waiting for his cue, a small boy tore free from the arms that had held him safely away from the circle of tragedy and pushed his way to Ethan's side.

"Hey, Doc—you gonna fix my momma. She gonna be okay, right?"

Jostled off-balance, Ethan looked up into Michael Parker's amber eyes. Oh, how he wished he could lie. He desperately wanted to; his mind searched for the comforting words. But instead, he only shook his head.

For one endless moment the boy stared back at him with frightened, angry eyes...bravely lifted chin. Then he pushed at Ethan, struck him hard with both doubled-up fists before he turned. Blindly. Then waiting hands reached for him and pulled him away.

Somewhere, someone was sobbing.

Only when he was sure the boy was safely away did Ethan lift his hand and gently close Louise Parker's unseeing eyes.

Chapter 2

The day after the tragedy in The Gardens, Ethan was in the rectory of St. Jude's Catholic Church monitoring the progress of a hastily convened meeting of the Citizens' Alliance for Community Action from his hiding place in the rectory kitchen. Such skulking and hiding seemed cowardly to him but was actually a compromise of sorts. Father Frank had tried his best to dissuade him from coming at all.

"Bad idea," the priest had insisted that afternoon on the phone. "The news media's got their teeth in this in a big way. When word gets out—and it will—that the ride-along doctor on the scene was the president's son…"

"Maybe that's not such a bad thing," Ethan said heavily. He'd thought about it a lot, during the course of a difficult day and worse night. "Something needs to be done. If we use my name, my dad's influence—"

"We'll be sitting in the middle of a three-ring circus. Ethan, my friend—my naive friend—I know you mean well, but do you have any idea what will happen down here—

what will happen to these people once the various government agencies and the media get involved in this?''

Ethan's jaw tightened. ''Well, I expect my work at the clinic would be history, but at least something would be done about improving conditions in The Gardens. Those tenements—''

The priest's snort interrupted him. ''The Gardens will become a political football, everybody fighting over what to do and how to pay for it and who gets the credit, and the media will be egging them on, and while the struggle goes back and forth, what do these people who actually live down here do? After an appearance or two on national network television, they go on as before—only with less privacy. No, my friend…'' a sigh gusted over the line ''…and perhaps it is shortsighted and God forgive me, but I don't much care about what new legislation gets passed, or what new ordinances, or what new development projects get proposed for sometime in the far-distant future. I care about these people, and what they need is some changes to be made *now*. Before somebody else dies.''

Before somebody else dies.

Safely out of view of those attending the meeting in the next room, Ethan leaned his forehead against the wall and closed his eyes. In his mind, as in a darkened movie theater, he saw again the body in the rubble, the blood, the blind dead eyes. And another pair of eyes, very much alive. Angry amber eyes. Proud, frightened eyes. He felt again the frustrated blow from a pair of small, clenched fists. He heard poignant echoes of Mrs. Schmidt's voice: *With a mother like that, he has a chance.* What will become of Michael Parker, he wondered, now that his mother is dead?

Ethan knew what it was like to be a small boy left suddenly without a mother. Those memories came to him, not as images on a movie screen, but as a cold, sick feeling in his stomach, a yawning emptiness in his heart. Almost a quarter of a century later, oh, how well he remembered it— the fear, the desolation, the terrible sense of abandonment. Back then, part of him had wanted to lash out in anger; part had tried to retreat into the remembered security of baby- hood. Every part of him had felt utterly bereft.

But he'd had his sister, Lauren. He didn't know what he'd have done without Lolly, even though most of the time she'd treated him the way older sisters generally treat younger brothers. Still, she'd been there for him when it counted.

And then…there'd been the miracle. Dixie had come. Dixie, with her gifts of music and laughter and breezy Texas ways. Starved for a mother's love, six-year-old Ethan had fallen for her immediately, long before his father had made her officially his stepmother. Long before the entire country had fallen in love with her casual, down-home charm and embraced her as its most unconventional First Lady. As his father the president was fond of saying, both in public and in private, God Bless Dixie.

Ethan had been lucky. He'd had Lolly to keep him on his toes and Dixie to love and care for him. Who would Michael Parker have?

Beside him the crack in the kitchen door cautiously wid- ened, and he straightened hurriedly as Ruthie Mendoza slipped through and sidled past him. From the parlor, which also served the church as an informal meeting room, he could hear a rising level of noise and activity. He wondered what he'd missed while his mind had been wandering in his own distant past.

"What's going on?" he asked Ruthie in a whisper.

"Wrapping up." Ruthie didn't bother to lower her voice. Nor did she look at him, but went on making unnecessary adjustments to the platters of oatmeal-chocolate-chip cook- ies that were spread across the kitchen table. From the way she'd been pushing them on him all evening, Ethan suspected she'd made them herself. "I'm just going to take these in…"

She swept toward him with a plate of cookies in each hand and a spot of color in each cheek. All Ethan could do was pull the door open for her and shrink back behind it, well out of the line of sight of anyone in the parlor. As Ruthie sailed out the door, her brother, wearing a short-sleeved black shirt and his clerical collar, for once, side-stepped around her and into the kitchen. Ethan all but pounced on him.

"What happened? What did they decide? Are they going to the mayor? What about—"

"No city, state or federal officials—not yet," Father Frank said with the contained satisfaction of someone who's had things go exactly his way. He picked up a cookie and bit into it, glancing down at his rounded shirtfront as he did so; apparently Ruthie had been nagging him again about putting on weight. He shrugged and picked up another cookie. "First thing we have to do is find out who owns that building—or block of buildings. Then we decide where to go from there. Lawsuits, like government agencies, take too long. What we're hoping is that the threat of bad publicity will be enough to squeeze these slumlords into bringing their buildings up to standard."

"You want me—"

The priest shook his head. "Mrs. Schmidt's volunteered to go down to city hall tomorrow morning. She's got a friend who works in the…I forget what department, the one where they issue permits, fire and safety inspections, things like that. Anyway, she'll—" He broke off with a muttered, "Oops" as someone bumped the door from the outside. He lunged to block unauthorized entry while Ethan once again flattened himself against the wall.

Through the partly open door he could hear the unmistakeably carrying voice of a television news reporter:

"Oh—Father Mendoza—Father, I wonder if you could take just a moment to tell us—" The door closed, cutting off the rest.

After a moment, swearing softly and feeling utterly powerless, Ethan adjusted a Chicago Cubs baseball cap to hide his blond hair and let himself out of the rectory through the side door, where a Secret Service agent waited unobtrusively for him in the shadows.

Mrs. Schmidt arrived at the clinic shortly after noon the next day, four hours late and with Father Frank Mendoza close on her heels. Ethan didn't have to ask if the trip to city hall had been successful; both looked ready to burst.

Whatever the import of the news they'd brought, it had to wait while Ethan finished suturing a toddler's badly mangled lip—from falling off the steps, his mother claimed. Ethan devoutly hoped it was true.

He was on his own, since Ruthie wasn't due in until two o'clock and Clair, the morning nurse, was accompanying a compound fracture to Memorial Hospital for emergency surgery. He did his best to comfort the hysterical child and just barely managed to shove the mother into a nearby wheelchair before she passed out in a heap beside her son's gurney. Meanwhile, Mrs. Schmidt and Father Frank fidgeted, reminding Ethan of leashed hunting dogs eager to be off after their quarry, whining and quivering and licking their chops.

"You're never going to believe it," they both said at once, leaping into the lull after the still-sniffling toddler and his mother had departed. Folding his arms across his barrel chest as if to physically contain himself, the priest yielded the floor to Mrs. Schmidt with a nod.

She took over eagerly, breathless as a girl. "It wasn't easy. Thank goodness my friend Clair knew what to look for. I don't think we'd have found it—at least not so quickly—if it hadn't been for her. Not to mention the computer. Aren't they just the most amazing things, though? You just punch in—''

Anticipating a major sidetrack, Ethan interrupted. "So, did you find out who owns those buildings?"

Mrs. Schmidt opened her mouth, but Father Frank—self-control apparently exhausted—got there first. "It's an investments firm. They own all sorts of things, real estate, mostly. That firm in turn is owned by a corporation. The name of the corporation is…Phoenix Enterprises, Inc." And he and Mrs. Schmidt said the last together then paused, once again looking fit to burst.

Ethan waited. A long five seconds or so ticked by before he made the connection. "Phoenix…what, you don't mean—''

Mrs. Schmidt and Father Frank both nodded happily. Ethan groped for the wheelchair recently vacated by the toddler's mother and lowered himself into it.

In an office in a downtown high-rise—situated almost directly across the harbor from the rehearsal studio and temporary living quarters of the rock icon known as Phoenix—Doveman sat on a leather sofa and watched his girl-child pace. *Like an angry panther.* Some critic had said that, he remembered, talking about the way she'd pace back and forth across the stage—he'd forgotten which concert tour it was, now. Didn't matter. That critic had been right on. A panther was what she looked like, and right now, angry was what she was.

"How did this happen?" she asked as she about-faced, in a voice like a panther's snarl. "Explain that to me, Patrick. I want to know how *I* became the owner of a *tenement*. A tenement in which somebody *died*."

Doveman had often thought Patrick Kaufman resembled a great big rabbit with that overbite and those pale buggy

eyes, especially like he was now, sitting upright and alert
with his skinny forearms braced on his desktop. Which
Doveman knew was a misleading impression; no man as
meek and mild as Kaufman appeared to be could have sur-
vived twenty or so years as Phoenix's business manager.

"It was a sound investment," Patrick said, in the pleas-
antly deep voice that always seemed a surprise coming out
of that Don Knotts body. "Those old row house neighborhoods are right in line with this whole wave of renovation
that began back in the eighties with the yuppie invasion—
block by block, they're taking over the city. It's only a matter of time—"

"A matter of *time?*" Phoenix's soft, whiskey voice
cracked on the last word, like the crunch of broken glass.
Only Doveman heard the pain in it. "There're people living
in those buildings. What did you think they were going to
do while you're waiting around for the yuppies?" She
paused, one hand going briefly to her forehead, then suddenly whirled and slapped both hands down on the business
manager's desktop. Knowing what was coming, Doveman
winced and closed one eye. "You know what, Patrick?"
she snapped, leaning across it, her face barely inches from
Kaufman's. "You're *fired.*"

Kaufman merely sighed and shook his head; Phoenix was
notorious for firing people. Over the past twenty years,
Doveman figured the business manager had probably been
fired six or seven times, at least. This time, though, he
wasn't all that sure she didn't mean it.

"You never told me not to invest in apartment buildings—"

"Tenements, Patrick—*tenements.* I…am…a *slumlord.*"

She pushed herself away from the desk and in turning,
caught Doveman's eye. Just for an instant, but that flash of
blue cut into his heart like a steely knife. *Easy, baby-girl,*
his old whiskey-burned eyes said back to her, singing the

song he'd sung to her for so many years. *Doveman knows how you're hurtin'. Doveman understands.*

But she pivoted away from his eyes, body still tense, not ready to hear him yet. "Well. So now somebody's died." Her voice was hard, harsh, trying so hard not to show any emotion at all. "What now? Am I being sued?"

Kaufman shook his head. "No, not yet, anyway. This citizens group—apparently they just want you to meet with them, talk about what needs to be done. They said—"

"So do it." Phoenix waved a regal hand in Patrick's direction, apparently forgetting already that he was by her own decree no longer hers to command. "Meet with whoever you need to meet with. Find out what they want and give it to them. And *no publicity,* do you understand? Whatever it takes— *What?*" Kaufman was slowly but firmly shaking his head.

"I said *you.* It's you they want to meet with. They made that very clear. They want you to meet them at the building where—" Now Phoenix's head was going back and forth like a mechanical doll's.

"No. No way José. Not even if Hell freezes over."

"Then there will be publicity," Kaufman said flatly. "That they've promised, and I think you'd be wise to believe them. The media has already been all over this. Be thankful it's not an election year, or it would probably be worse. As it is, it's a five-minute wonder—Young Ghetto Mom Seeks Relief From Heatwave, Dies in Balcony Collapse; Slumlord Sought. Film At Eleven! Tomorrow it'll be old news." He paused, rocking slightly in his swivel chair. "Unless, of course, somebody gets hold of the juicy little factoid that the slumlord in question is none other than the rock icon known as Phoenix. Who, by the way, currently happens to be in town preparing to launch a career comeback with a new album and world tour...."

"Tell them here," Phoenix whispered, after a tense and

prolonged silence. Perhaps only Doveman could see that she was trembling. "I'll meet with them here, in this office—that's it, or nothing. Let them go to the media if they want. Then they can sue me. And see how long it takes before they get one dime out of me!"

With her panther's stride she crossed the office and was out the door. While Kaufman let go a hiss of breath, Doveman gave a shrug, picked up his stained and crumpled fedora and followed.

In the elevator, Phoenix leaned like an exhausted marathoner against the back wall. She heard Doveman step on just before the door closed, but he didn't speak and neither did she. Behind her usual pair of mirrored sunglasses, her eyes were shut tight. There was a brassy taste in her mouth, and a sickening lurch in her stomach that had nothing to do with the elevator's controlled plunge.

Tenements. Dear God, she owned tenements. She—Joanna Dunn—was a slumlord.

Somewhere God—no, not God. Somewhere the *Devil* must be laughing.

Momma, we're cold. Can me and Jonathan and Chrissy get in bed with you?

That was what she remembered most—the cold. But it wasn't cold that had killed this woman...this Louise Parker. It was the heat. All she'd wanted was a little breath of air.

"Doveman," she said in a raggedy croak, "I didn't know."

He replied, his voice husky with more than the lifelong effects of whiskey and cigarettes, "I know, child. I know."

Father Frank had tried his best once again to convince Ethan to skip the meeting.

"We promised her no publicity," the priest had argued. "What if somebody spots you and follows you? The cat will be out of the bag for sure, and there goes any hope we have of a quick resolution."

Ethan promised to keep a low profile. He was confident he could—he'd gotten very good at eluding reporters over the years. Now and then even his Secret Service agents—to their extreme dismay—found themselves guarding an empty nest.

"I know why you want to go so bad," Father Frank teased him. "You just want a chance to see Phoenix up close and personal. Hey—you think I don't know? Whose picture do you think was taped inside *my* locker door all through high school?"

"Sure, I want to see her," Ethan said, not smiling back. "I want to see her face."

He couldn't have said why it shocked him so profoundly to learn that one of his all-time favorite singer-songwriters—the one responsible for the music that had fueled his idealistic fervor all through college—was, in fact, a slumlord and the person responsible for Louise Parker's death. Or what he hoped to see in her face—the face that had filled his adolescent dreams—as she confronted Louise Parker's neighbors. Repudiation, maybe? *Say it ain't so, Joe.* He only knew that thinking of his favorite Phoenix songs, like "Fire On The Water" and "City Woman"—more poignant and gut-wrenching than "Pretty Mary" as far as he was concerned—now left him with a bitter taste in his throat, and a very personal sense of betrayal and loss.

So, while wild horses couldn't have prevented Ethan from attending the meeting in Phoenix's business manager's high-rise office, in keeping with his promise to Father Frank, he was doing his best to keep from being noticed. Which was proving to be more difficult than he'd anticipated.

He supposed he couldn't really blame Phoenix for not wanting to confront the delegation of citizens in the intimate confines of her business manager's office. Instead, she'd

chosen to hold the meeting in one of the building's conference rooms. Designed for corporate business meetings, its
furnishings consisted of a huge expanse of polished tabletop
surrounded by sumptuous leather-upholstered chairs. At the
head of the table, a polished wooden lectern flanked by pot-
ted dracaena plants loomed before a screen worthy of a
small multiplex. It was a room designed to intimidate corporate vice presidents; it would have taken much less to awe
the small group of people that stood shifting their feet on
the plush burgundy carpeting.

Having been shown into the room by an aloof secretary
and left to their own devices, the delegates—Father Frank
and Ruthie Mendoza, Mrs. Schmidt, Kenny Baumgartner
from EMS and six residents from The Gardens, eleven in
all including Ethan—rather tentatively selected seats around
the huge table. No one spoke; the only sounds were some
rustlings and scrapings, nervous throat-clearing, a subaudible hum of tension.

A door, cleverly hidden in the design of the paneling to
the left of the movie screen, swished silently open. There
was a collective intake of breath, followed by a disappointed
exhalation as a tall but slightly built, rather stoop-shouldered
man came into the room. He moved without hurry, pausing
just short of the lectern to make eye contact with those
seated around the table and to introduce himself as Phoenix's business manager, Patrick Kaufman.

"We come to see Phoenix," one of the tenants, a balding,
heavyset black man in his early sixties said in a loud, bel-
ligerent voice, which prompted several of the other delegates
to nod and mutter in agreement, much like an evangelical
congregation murmuring "Amen."

The business manager held up a long, pale hand. "She'll
be along very shortly. As I'm sure you're aware, she is
currently in the midst of preparations for a new world tour.
She has rearranged her schedule in order to meet with you

today, so I hope you will be patient—'' He broke off as Father Frank rose to his feet on a wave of more rustlings and angry murmurs.

"Yes, and as I'm sure *you're* aware, a woman has died." The priest spoke quietly, but even his customary poise was betrayed by a slight tremor of nervousness. "And many of these people have taken time off from work in order to come here today—time they can ill-afford. I would hope—''

"Hi—I'm so sorry to have kept you waiting." The husky voice, instantly recognized and unmistakable, spoke from the back of the room. And every head in the room snapped toward the sound as if pulled by the same invisible thread.

Later, when he'd had a chance to think about it, Ethan was able to convince himself that she probably hadn't meant to make such a dramatic entrance. It was just that, with Phoenix, there couldn't be any other kind. The woman had only to step onto a stage, or walk into a room, he thought, and you could hear the thud of bass guitars and the zap-zap of laser lights, taste the tension, smell the excitement. It seemed as if she carried the spotlight with her wherever she went, like some kind of personal energy field. And yet…and yet… For the life of him, he could not put his finger on the reason why.

It couldn't have had anything to do with the way she was dressed. In jeans—fashionably low-slung on hips as slender and lithe as a girl's—and a pale blue knit top with a square-cut neckline that clung to her supple body like a stocking and stopped just where the waistband of the jeans began, she could have passed for one of the delegates seated around the conference table—or one of their children. But for the mirrored sunglasses, of course. And the hair—that famous hair, now the irridescent blue-black of a crow's wing—that fell from a haphazard center part, rippled down her back and slapped gently against her buttocks when she walked.

"Traffic was murder," the world famous rock star said

as she crossed the room with the same long-legged stride
that would carry her the width of a concert stage in a few
pounding beats. Her voice was breathless, her smile wry,
inviting those seated around the table to commiserate.
"They've got Fremont all torn up—what are they doing,
fixing potholes? Anyway, I got lost in all those one-way
streets they've got downtown now. Whose idea were
those?" Having reached the head of the table, she whirled
and addressed those seated around it as if she truly wanted
to know.

The delegates shifted uncomfortably, awestruck but unwilling just yet to relinquish the angry baggage they'd come
with. Father Frank, apparently only just remembering that
he was still on his feet, slowly lowered himself into his
chair. Someone—Kenny, maybe—cleared his throat too
loudly. Ethan wasn't surprised to find that his own heart
was beating hard and fast. He could hear its echo, like distant drumbeats, inside his own head.

Phoenix stepped behind the lectern and slowly took off
her sunglasses. Then, for long, unmeasurable moments she
said nothing, while her unshielded eyes—those remarkable,
trademark eyes, electric, heart-stopping blue and fringed
with sooty-black—traveled around the table, touching each
person there in turn.

With his own confrontation with those famous eyes fast
approaching and his frequent and futile wish for invisibility
strong within him, Ethan was surprised to find himself smiling. Laughing, actually—silently, with a schoolboy's dry
mouth and sweaty palms, deafened by his own heartbeat—
laughing with pure chagrin at his own childish vulnerability.

And it happened to be just that moment that the eyes
touched his. They slid past the laughter and moved on...
Then jerked back suddenly, flared with something he
couldn't fathom, and abruptly lost all expression, as if a
curtain had fallen behind them. But in the instant before they

moved on, for good this time, Ethan felt a strange jolt of recognition. They reminded him of someone, those eyes. Someone or something he'd seen just recently.

It was a few moments more before it came to him exactly where. With the shutters down, devoid of all life and expression, Phoenix's eyes—the almond shape, the exotic tilt, not the color—reminded him of Louise Parker's eyes.

The realization made his throat tighten and his body go chill with the cold wash of memory. And he no longer felt the slightest urge to laugh.

Her eyeball-to-eyeball circuit complete, Phoenix spoke softly, in her trademark rusty croak. "First, I'd like to thank you for agreeing to meet me here." Her smile was quick—not too much, for this was a somber occasion. "I thought we'd all be more comfortable here, on such a hot day."

Ethan winced as a low mutter rose from those seated around the table. Could the woman not know how it was, exactly, that Louise Parker had come to die?

"Got no AC in The Gardens," someone growled.

"Maybe if we did, Louise Parker still be alive." That was echoed by a rumbling chorus of Amens.

Phoenix waited, her face impassive, until the last grumble had died. It occurred to Ethan then—irrelevently, he thought—that she wasn't wearing any makeup at all. Or it was so skillfully applied that it appeared as if she wasn't. The eyes, of course, needed no enhancement, but the matte texture and soft color of her lips could only have been natural, with a slight sheen on the lower one as if she'd recently wet it with her tongue. Her skin showed telltale flaws—a hint of a flush, faint traces of freckles across her cheekbones, thumbprint smudges beneath her eyes. Something about the smudges touched Ethan, before it occurred to him to wonder if she might have deliberately gone without makeup—or even enhanced those shadows—for just that very purpose.

"I want you to know how deeply we regret this terrible

accident.'' She spoke stiffly now, without her customary charisma, as though she were reading from a prepared statement. ''Of course we intend—''

''Accident? Wasn't no accident killed Louise—it was negligence, pure and simple!''

''Negligent *homicide*.''

''Murder, that's what it was!''

''Yeah, out-and-out *murder*.''

At that outburst, Kenny Baumgartner came alert in his chair and placed a protective arm across the back of Ruthie's. Mrs. Schmidt shifted and made distressed noises, while Father Frank leaped to his feet, arms upraised to quiet the angry delegates.

''Ladies and gentlemen, please—this isn't what we came here for. We came here to talk—and listen. Let's listen to what she has to say.''

Patrick Kaufman, who had moved to his client's side at the first angry shout, was now urgently whispering in her ear. Phoenix listened, nodded almost imperceptibly, then faced the room once more. This time her eyes stabbed at the seated delegates, cold blue slashes from out of a face so set and pale it seemed frozen.

''Until yesterday,'' she said in a tight, harsh voice completely unlike her famous tiger's purr, ''I had no idea I even owned these buildings, much less what condition they were in. Now that the…situation has been brought to my attention, obviously I'm going to see to it that any existing problems are taken care of. If you people will submit a list of needed repairs, Mr. Kaufman will—''

''What's wrong in The Gardens ain't no paint and plaster gonna fix,'' said the older man who'd first spoken. Once again his neighbors muttered and nodded, apparently approving of the job he was doing as their spokesman. Until he added, ''Those buildings shoulda been condemned a long time ago.''

Now the murmurs of approval broke off in a collective double take, followed by a few uncertain little cries of protest. Father Frank and Mrs. Schmidt both turned toward the speaker in alarm. Directly across the table from the outspoken man, a black woman with caramel-colored hair sculpted into a tower of braids and curls half rose and leaned toward him on her hands. ''What you talkin' about, *condemned?* Then where am I gonna go, huh? You tell me that, Jerome Wilkins! Ain't nothin' else around here I can afford.''

Jerome shifted his focus from the head of the table to this new protagonist. ''You rather stay and have the place fall down on your head? What's wrong with you, Neva? You just got done telling me you got chunks falling outa your ceiling, came near to hitting the baby's bed. Now you're telling me—''

''Chunks of plaster? That ain't nothin'. I got rats big as cats climbin' in bed with my kids. You want to see—''

And suddenly everyone was talking at once, shouting back and forth across the conference table, some even whacking its polished surface with open palms or fists to make their point. Father Frank was on his feet again, pleading for calm to absolutely no effect. Kenny Baumgartner had his body shifted clear around to form a barrier between Ruthie and the other delegates, as if he expected missiles to start flying at any moment. Mrs. Schmidt had her hand over her mouth and her eyes closed and was slowly shaking her head.

So it was that, for a moment at least, no one but Ethan noticed that Phoenix had left the lectern. Only he watched her business manager dither briefly, then step out of her way...watched as she strode the length of the room, back the way she'd come, moving so quickly her passing left a breeze. By the time she reached the door, though, every eye in the room was on her, and the bickering and shouting had died into abashed silence.

Phoenix turned, one hand on the doorknob, and spoke to the shocked assembly in a voice barely above a whisper. "I will not deal with a mob. One person...I'll talk to one person. You—" and she pointed a finger directly at Ethan "—the quiet one—what's your name?"

Ethan probably couldn't have answered if his life had depended on it. Fortunately, Father Frank stepped in and did it for him. "Uh...this is Dr. Brown," the priest said hoarsely, so flustered he actually stammered. "He's the doctor that—"

"Fine," snapped Phoenix. "Doc, I'll meet with you. Patrick, set it up."

And she was gone, leaving a room filled with frustrated silence behind her.

Leaving Ethan with an image burned into his mind like a sun-shape branded on his retinas: the image of a set, pale face and a pair of eyes that no longer reminded him even remotely of a dead woman's...eyes so charged with emotion they left him feeling as though he'd received a jolt of electricity. He felt shocked and confused...and no longer certain the emotion he'd seen in those violent eyes was anger.

Chapter 3

"Why does it have to be me?" Ethan said to Father Frank in a low voice, half grumbling, half honest bewilderment. "You're the one who should be doing this. You're the group's organizer and spokesman. I never said a word. What in the hell made her pick me?"

The two of them were alone in the conference room; the other delegates of Citizens' Alliance had long since been herded away by the relentlessly frosty secretary, and Patrick Kaufman had gone to consult with his client about arrangements for meeting with her chosen delegate. Father Frank was sitting in one of the conference chairs, leaning back with his arms folded across his belly, looking remarkably at ease and cheery, Ethan thought, for a man who'd just had a meeting of critical importance blow up in his face.

He, on the other hand, found it impossible to sit still. At the same time restless and wary, he paced with the slow and tentative edginess of a cat exploring unfamiliar territory. When he got no immediate answer to his question Ethan threw the priest a glance and found him smiling.

"What?" he demanded with a small uplift of shoulders and hands. For Ethan, who prided himself on his easygoing and unflappable nature, it was a gesture of extreme annoyance.

Father Frank shook his head, in the maddeningly smug way of someone who knows the solution to a particularly vexing riddle. "To answer your first question, simply, it has to be you because you're who Phoenix picked. She's calling the shots right now, in case you haven't noticed. It appears she's called our bluff. Maybe she knows we don't want publicity over this any more than she does—that it won't get us what we're after, which is action, *fast*. We're lucky she's at least willing to work with us—with you, anyway. As for why you—" He broke off, once more shaking his head, though his smile was more wry, now, than smug. "You really don't have a clue, do you?"

Ethan did have a clue, actually, but it embarrassed him to say it. He waited, scowling, for his former college roommate to do so instead.

The priest obliged with a sigh. "You're a *guy*. As in, young, impressionable, and above all, the opposite gender."

Ethan snorted in a wholly ineffective attempt to disguise his discomfort. "You're a guy, Kenny's a guy, half the tenants are guys."

"I'm a *priest*, in case you've forgotten. And it's pretty obvious to anyone with half a brain that Kenny's only got eyes for Ruthie. The tenants are after her blood, so that leaves you. Besides, as I said, you're young, good-looking—"

"Impressionable. You said impressionable."

"Yeah, I did." Father Frank was silent for a moment. "I think it's pretty safe to say Phoenix is someone who's accustomed to having her way. She's used to being the one in control. That's why she walked out just now. Things had gotten out of hand—she wasn't in control. She thinks—"

"She thinks that with me, she will be." Ethan pulled out

the chair next to the priest's and sank into it. After a moment he said in a soft, chagrined growl, half to himself, "I'm not sure she isn't right. She's *Phoenix,* for God's sake." He leaned forward earnestly; he and Frank Mendoza went back a long way, and he'd long since gotten over the impulse to apologize for his language lapses. "You think you're the only one who had a crush on her all through high school? She was..." He lifted his hand and waved it helplessly, unable to find the words.

"She was the classic rebel, the Bad Girl," Father Frank said, in the gentle tone of reminiscence. "But there was something untouched—and untouchable—about her, too. Every girl wanted to be her, every guy wanted to have her, but nobody ever could. A potent recipe for an icon."

Ethan nodded. But he didn't feel comfortable explaining, even to his closest friend, that with him, where Phoenix was concerned it hadn't ever just been about sex appeal. That had been part of it, of course; he'd been a normal adolescent male. But raging hormones couldn't have accounted for the way he felt when he listened to her music. The stirrings in his soul that even now he couldn't give a name to. The hours he'd spent with his guitar and a Walkman portable stereo, softly playing and singing along.

"I gotta tell you," he said ruefully, leaning toward his friend, the priest, in the classic manner of a confessing sinner, forearms on his knees, hands clasped together between them, "she still has it. You know? When she walked in, I have to tell you, my pulse rate shot up."

Father Frank laughed and clapped him on the shoulder, more like college roommate than priest to sinner. "Just means you're alive, my friend. And about the rest—" He broke off momentarily as the conference room door opened to frame the secretary's patrician form, then continued in a hurried aside as they both rose to follow her. "Don't underestimate yourself. That woman may not know it yet, but

I think this time Phoenix may have bitten off more than she bargained for.''

"Are you sure you want to do that?'' Patrick Kaufman asked in a neutral tone.

Phoenix ignored him while she carefully selected a cheroot from the rosewood humidor on the bookcase shelf behind his desk and lit it with the matching rosewood-and-silver desk lighter that sat beside it. She puffed out a cloud of fragrant smoke before she said with an audible hiss, *"Yess."*

Patrick shrugged. "Suit yourself." He glanced at his watch and murmured, without even a hint of sarcasm, "I suppose you'd like me to leave you two alone?''

That was the great thing about Patrick, Phoenix thought. She could browbeat him all she wanted, even usurp his private office in the middle of a working day, and it never had the slightest effect. She wondered sometimes what went on behind those pale, rabbity eyes, whether a real heart pumped inside that narrow chest.

"Yes, thank you, Patrick,'' she said with exaggerated sweetness. "And while you're at it, tell Miss Freeze to turn on the voice mail machine and get lost, too, would you please?'' She let her voice drop an octave to its customary purr. "In situations such as this I find it's best to work in...privacy.'' Around the cigar her lips formed a seductive smile.

Which, naturally, had no effect whatsoever on Patrick. "I'll suggest to Mrs. *Fitzhugh* that she take an extended lunch,'' he said dryly, punctuating that with the snap of his briefcase lock.

Alone in the lushness of burgundy, brass and mahogany, Phoenix took the cheroot from her lips and gazed at it with satisfaction. She didn't smoke—had given it up years ago, in fact, with reasonable ease, never having been all that serious about it to begin with. But, she thought, it was amazing what a prop like that did for her self-confidence. Almost like having a microphone in her hands.

Well, hell yes—it is. It's the same. Just the same... She closed her eyes and concentrated on slowing her breathing. She inhaled the sweet, heavy perfume of cigar smoke...psyching herself...calming herself...preparing. Because it *was* the same, this moment, waiting here in the plush privacy of Kaufman's office for that young, gentle-looking doctor to join her. No different from all the moments before, so many of them, waiting in the wings for that moment when she would erupt onto a stage before a stadium filled with thousands of screaming fans. Same butterflies, same pounding heart, same adrenaline rush. Somehow, that made it easier—a familiar and therefore much more manageable fear. Whether of one or fifty thousand, an audience was an audience.

Ethan's first thought when he smelled cigar smoke was that Patrick Kaufman's meek and mild exterior hid some unexpected depths. Phoenix appeared to him only as a silhouette, standing behind Kaufman's big mahogany desk with her back to a bank of windows framing a pale noonday sky, so he didn't see, at first, that it was she who was responsible for the cigar smoke. Until she stepped forward, gesturing with what appeared to be a twig held between her thumb and forefinger, then lifted it and put it between her lips.

"Hey, Doc." Her rusty voice was muffled only slightly by the cigar. "Glad you decided to take me up on my offer. Have a seat."

Ethan nodded by way of a greeting, feeling about as uncomfortable as he'd ever been in his life. After a moment's hesitation he took the burgundy leather chair she'd indicated and settled himself into it, striving to appear relaxed and knowing he was fooling absolutely no one.

He waited for Phoenix to seat herself, either in the mate to his chair or the big one behind the desk. When she did neither but remained standing with her backside propped casually against the desk behind her, he remembered suddenly what Father Frank had said to him in the conference room. *She has to be the one in control.* By seating him and standing herself, he realized, she'd put herself in the familiar—and comfortable—position of performer, with him as her audience.

Oddly, he felt himself warming toward her then, actually admiring her cleverness. He almost smiled—before he remembered what her reaction had been the last time he'd done that. So he kept the smile inside and concentrated on keeping his outward demeanor somber.

She made a breathy sound—soft, ironic laughter—and blew smoke toward the ceiling. "Come on, Doc, don't look so disapproving."

"Not disapproving," said Ethan. "Surprised, maybe."

"Surprised? Why?" Her lips curved, forming a smile around the slender shaft of the cigar. Ethan's stomach lurched oddly, as if the chair had just dropped out from under him.

He shrugged and leaned forward, elbows on the chair arms, hands clasped across the empty space in front of him. Trying to look—and think—more like a physician and less like a starstruck boy. "Oh, I don't know—I guess I thought you'd have a little more concern for your health—and your voice."

She took the cigar from her mouth, frowning critically at the glowing end. "I don't smoke, actually. Just wanted something to play with." She slid a sideways glance at him from under her lashes. "Looks kind of neat, though, doesn't it?"

"I think I saw one in a Clint Eastwood movie."

"Yeah," said Phoenix with a hint of a smile, "me too." She whistled a bar or two of haunting melody. When he recognized it as the theme from a famous spaghetti western, Ethan felt it was safe to return the smile. When he did, the whistling broke up into a husky chortle, the kind that provokes a similar one deep in the listener's own chest.

"There, you see? Not a bad little icebreaker." She looked around for an ashtray and seeing none, laid the cigar carefully on the glass desktop. "And now that we have—broken the ice, that is…" her eyes zeroed in on him with a directness that was, in an odd way, more seductive than flirting "…Dr. Brown seems kind of formal, doesn't it? Don't you have a first name?"

Ethan hesitated, wishing, not for the first time, that his parents had had the foresight to name him something like…Bobby, or James. As exhilarating as the idea was of being on a first-name basis with Phoenix, the combining of Ethan and Brown was just unusual enough to be recognizable. She hadn't recognized him yet, and for reasons he couldn't explain, even to himself, he wanted her to know him just as plain Dr. Brown for a little while longer. As long as possible, anyway. She'd have to know eventually, he supposed, but…not yet.

He cleared his throat and said quietly, "Under the circumstances, I think Dr. Brown is probably more appropriate." And watched her eyes flare with the same indefinable emotion he'd seen in the conference room, when she'd caught him smiling at her. The one he still wasn't sure was anger.

"Doc it is, then," Phoenix said with a smile she didn't allow to reach her voice or her eyes. Outwardly calm, she felt jittery inside, as if she'd missed a stage mark during a performance, or come in on the wrong beat. Nothing she couldn't cover, but it rattled her nonetheless. She straightened and moved unhurriedly around the desk, putting it and some distance between herself and the oh-so-arrogant *Dr. Brown.* Who the hell did he think he was? It astonished her to discover that she was disappointed. That she truly did want to know.

"So, Doctor…Patrick tells me you work at a free clinic down there in the…neighborhood."

Yes, and when Patrick had told her that, she'd remembered why the doc had seemed so familiar to her, remembered that she'd seen him before, coming out of the clinic that day, the day she'd gone for her little walk down memory lane. She wouldn't tell him that, though. He would wonder what the likes of Phoenix had been doing in that neighborhood. He would wonder why.

"That's right," he was saying, watching her with neither judgment nor speculation in his brown eyes. Just a curious intensity that she found unnerving.

She picked up the cheroot, stared at the still-smoldering tip and then, annoyed with herself, put it back down. How was it that she felt edgy and nervous as a teenager in the principal's office, while *he* sat there looking, as Doveman would have said, like butter wouldn't melt in his mouth? Transferring her annoyance to him, she said sharply, "Tell me, how is it that you're all the way over here with a group of concerned citizens during clinic hours, Doc?"

He shrugged, his eyes narrowing just slightly, as if from a sudden and brief flare of light. After a moment he said evenly, "I don't know, civic duty?"

She gave a soft snort of laughter. "Right. So, who's minding the store? Or do you just shut it down when you have…a civic duty to attend to?"

His gentle gaze made her feel vaguely ashamed. "I have another doctor covering for me."

What was it with this guy? Phoenix wondered. Her head was full of a million questions she wanted to ask him, a million things she wanted to know about him. Since when did she give a rip?

And where did he get off, this kid—younger than she was, he had to be—sitting there looking at her with such assurance...like some sort of shaman, as if he knew all the answers to the riddles of the universe? Who the hell did he think he was? Didn't he know who *she* was? She was *Phoenix,* for God's sake!

"Come on, Doc. Civic duty?" She threw it at him like an accusation. "Patrick told me you were there the night that woman—"

"Louise Parker."

"What?" He'd spoken so softly she'd barely heard him. Or perhaps didn't want to hear.

"The woman who died. Her name was Louise Parker. Yeah, I was with her when she died. I couldn't save her. I tried, but I...couldn't."

Well, she for sure didn't want to hear that—the pain in his voice. Suddenly claustrophobic, she paced to the edge of the desk, stopped with a jerk and turned to face him. Took a deep breath. "Look, I'm truly sorry about what happened. I am. I had no idea I owned those buildings. To tell you the truth, I own a bunch of things I don't know about. Look—handling my money is Patrick's job, and I don't get in his way. I trust his judgment. If he thinks it's a good investment, he goes ahead with it. That's the way we've always done things, that's the way I want it. Of course—" she paused, wondering why she felt a need to say it "—when I found out about this I fired him."

"Of course," the doctor said dryly, "I can see that."

"I'm always firing people," she said, shifting her shoulders as if that could get her out from under the burden of guilt he was dumping on her. Damn him. This doctor was making her feel defensive. And she hadn't done anything wrong to feel defensive about. She *hadn't.* Not this time.

What the hell right did he have to make her feel bad? "Ask anybody. Look, I can't help it if nobody believes me."

She was utterly mystified when he smiled. *Really* smiled. A smile of such warmth and blatant sex appeal it made her breath catch. My God, why hadn't she noticed before how gorgeous this guy was? Good-looking, sure—that had been the whole point, hadn't it?—but this…*this* was way beyond basic good looks. She found herself wondering what he'd look like without the beard, and whether he wore it to make himself look older, more doctorish. Lord, the man had the face of an angel—a completely *masculine,* incredibly sexy and extremely irritating angel. And, she suspected, underneath the casual slacks and short-sleeved shirt, the body of a Chippendale dancer….

Something—a noise, a slight movement—brought her back to her senses. Had he made that faint, embarrassed sound, or had she? How long had she been standing there staring at him? How long had she been smiling this goofy smile? She drew a shaken breath. The claustrophobia wrapped itself around her like a warm, wet blanket.

"Hey, Doc," she said in the slightly thickened voice that in her case was most often the accompaniment of sexual foreplay or way too many Bloody Marys. "How about if we get out of here—go somewhere and grab some lunch?"

"Lunch?" Ethan repeated the word as if he'd never heard it before. The truth was, food was just about the farthest thing from his mind just then. He was feeling lightheaded and queasy, a little off-balance—symptoms that might be indicative of a fever, perhaps an infection of the inner ear. Except that Dr. Brown knew there was nothing whatsoever wrong with him, nothing physical, anyway. What was "wrong" with him, he suspected, was nothing more complicated than a case of acute sexual desire. Which was not a terribly difficult diagnosis, given that he was sitting a couple of arm's lengths from one of the world's most desirable women, and the woman was smiling at him like…as if she—oh, come on, Ethan, say it!—as if she was coming on to him.

Good Lord—seducing him. Which, he reminded himself, according to Father Frank had probably been her intention to begin with. And which, he dimly recalled, he'd expressed concern about his ability to withstand. With good reason, it now appeared.

It occurred to him that no matter how he felt about food at that moment, going out for lunch was probably the best idea he'd heard in a while.

"Fine," he said, in a voice as viscous as hers. He had to remind himself to sit straight in his chair. He felt as though his body had begun leaning toward her of its own volition, as if she generated a magnetic field of some kind, something impossible to resist, like gravity.

It took a supreme effort of will to tear his eyes from her and focus them on his watch. Nearly one. He'd told the doctor standing in for him at the clinic that he'd be back at two. "I have an hour," he said. And then, hearing the unaccustomed sharpness in his voice, gruffly added, "If there's somewhere close by…"

"Perfect. Give me five minutes…." Already making for the door, she paused abruptly the way he'd seen her do so many times during performances, her body an incredible study in the dynamics of energy and motion, changing direction with the heart-stopping suddenness of birds in flight. "Just want to change into something…less comfortable." And she smiled, lowering her lashes to sultry half-mast, her sexuality cranked up to full wattage, now. It was classic Phoenix—the Phoenix whose music videos had fueled countless millions of erotic fantasies.

Ethan wondered what she would say if he told her that for all her efforts, the heat she was generating in him now was barely a flicker compared to the conflagration he'd experienced a few minutes ago, when she'd allowed him one brief glimpse into what he felt certain was the heart of the real Phoenix.

True to her word, she was back in less than five minutes, although it was a moment before Ethan realized it. For an instant, just a heartbeat, he actually mistook her for Kaufman's frosty secretary. Already half out of his chair when the double take kicked in, he smiled and self-consciously patted a nonexistant necktie. "Wow. I think I'm underdressed."

The "less comfortable" outfit she'd changed into was a formfitting dove-gray business suit, with a skirt that ended a good eight inches above her knees. Serviceable black high heels put her somewhere near Ethan's own six feet in height, and her glorious long black hair had all but disappeared into a sleek and tidy bun. A pair of tortoiseshell glasses and a black briefcase completed the ensemble.

At the look on his face, Phoenix laughed, a child's delighted chortle. "Protective coloring," she said, and pirouetted, showing off her costume as unselfconsciously as a child might. "I can lose myself in any crowd. It's so easy—you just have to dress like everybody else, walk like everybody else. Nobody looks at faces, don't you know that? People see what they expect to see. It's lunch hour in a downtown business district. Trust me—nobody'll look twice at one more gray flannel suit." She paused to squint critically at him, one long glance down…then up. "Too bad I don't have an extra one for you." But the way she said it, with a little half smile and a certain shimmer in her eyes, took most of the criticism out of it.

"Oh, well—" she shrugged as she turned, for some reason breathless "—just try and keep a low profile, okay?"

Weren't those almost exactly the same words Father Frank had said to him on the way in? Ethan was silently laughing as he followed Phoenix out of Kaufman's office.

And for the second time she happened to glance at him just in time to catch him in the act. "What?" she demanded, coming to a dead halt. "What is it with you, anyway? Or maybe I should say, what is it with *me* that you think is so damn funny?"

"Trust me," said Ethan quietly, "there's nothing about you I find even remotely funny." But all at once he was looking at her—*really* looking, and seeing not Phoenix the icon, but the woman behind the image. With eyes half-closed, as if through a filter he saw once again the woman—perhaps even the *girl*—he'd first caught a glimpse of when she'd told him about firing her business manager. Vulnerable and uncertain. "I was laughing at myself, actually. Don't you ever do that—laugh at yourself?" He reached around her to open the door she seemed to have forgotten.

She threw him a quick, startled look, and except for a breathy sound too subtle to ever be called a snort, didn't reply.

In the corridor, they almost collided. Ethan had made the turn he thought must take them to the elevators, but Phoenix, unexpectedly, had started in the opposite direction. For one dizzying moment he felt the brush of her body against his arm, an engulfing fireball of heat. Smelled her scent— unique, indescribable, but once encountered never to be forgotten—simply Phoenix.

"Uh-uh—this way," he heard her say through the ringing in his ears. "I have a secret exit. It's a service elevator, or something—goes straight down to a loading dock in the parking garage. Patrick got me a key. It's not fancy, but it saves hassles—you know."

Ethan *did* know—very well. What he didn't know was how he was going to get word to the Secret Service agent stationed in the lobby downstairs, patiently waiting for him to step off one of the building's three polished brass elevators. He did try to avoid putting his protectors' jobs and his own safety at risk unnecessarily. As he lengthened his stride to keep up with Phoenix's brisk pace, he wondered whether there might be a cell phone in that briefcase she was carrying, and what she'd think if he asked to use it. He reminded himself that he was a doctor, after all.

The freight elevator was large, utilitarian and slow, and smelled faintly of chemicals. As the doors rumbled shut behind her, Phoenix punched the button for the lowest parking level, then settled herself against a side wall a polite distance from Ethan, who was already stationed against the back. He angled a long look at her briefcase and thought again about asking for a cell phone. Instead it was she who broke the awkward elevator silence.

"*You* tell me, Doc—" and her voice seemed loud in that enclosed space "—what do these people want from me?"

The question caught Ethan off-guard. Playing for time, he cleared his throat then shrugged. "I don't think I should speak for them."

She laughed, a sharp, rude bark. "You're their spokesman. Isn't that what you're supposed to do?"

Ethan shook his head. "Spokesman? That was your idea, not mine." He studied her, wondering about the faint pink flush that had crept into her cheeks, just below the rims of the tortoiseshell glasses. "I was just here as an interested observer. I don't consider myself qualified to speak for anyone, much less the people who live in those buildings. I don't have any idea what their lives are like. I don't think anyone does."

"Yeah, well, I guess you'll have to find out, won't you," Phoenix snapped as the elevator bumped to a stop. She pushed through the gap in the opening doors, then halted, one hand on her hip, to look back. The doc was sure taking his sweet time, standing there looking around him with that funny little frown on his face. "I thought you said you were in a hurry." What was he waiting for, a *bus?*

"Sorry," he said as he joined her, looking guilty as sin, "but I really need to make a call. You don't happen to have a cell phone, do you?"

"What, in here?" Following the direction of his eyes, she glanced down at the briefcase in her hand and was half-surprised to see it there. "God, no—this is just for show."

Then it occurred to her—she'd all but forgotten he was a doctor, easy to do when he looked so little like one. It was hard to think of him that way even now, hard to imagine him actually saving people's lives... "I thought all you doctors had your own phones," she said, but in a friendly tone to show him she'd forgiven him. "Beepers and all that."

He pulled a hand from his pocket and showed her a small black object. "Just a beeper. No phone." He smiled wryly. "Maybe when I actually have a salary."

"Ah." She shrugged; financial concerns made her uncomfortable, which was why she employed Patrick. "Well, I think there might be one on the next level, next to the pay booth."

There was. Unaccustomed to waiting for anyone, Phoenix paced and fidgeted while he made his call. It wasn't that she minded waiting so much—although admittedly it was a whole new experience for her to have to adjust to someone else's schedule—but much of the success of her protective coloring depended on staying in motion, not giving anyone a chance to look too long or too hard. Standing still made her nervous—another of Doveman's sayings—as a cat in a roomful of rocking chairs.

"Done?" Thank God, she thought when she saw him turn from the pay phone at last. But no, now he had to stop and punch buttons on his beeper, check his watch, punch more buttons. Then...good Lord, *now* what was he doing, tying his *shoe?*

"Sorry," he said when he finally joined her, looking anything but. Looking, in fact, maddeningly serene. "I wasn't exactly prepared for this."

"We can skip it if you want to." She said it offhandedly; it was no big deal to her, was it? She was Phoenix; these people wanted something from *her*. Why should she bend over backward to accommodate them? But she was surprised to find her heart beating faster as she waited for his answer, astounded to discover that she cared what the answer might be.

"No, that's okay—I think I'm ready now." He smiled.

And because she couldn't control the urge to smile back at him, she turned her head so he wouldn't see it and rasped a brusque reply. "Well, okay, then—let's go."

Out on the sidewalk, she paused for her usual paparazzi sweep. All seemed clear, except—her heart gave a lurch as, down at the end of the block, a very tall black man in a dark business suit came flying around the corner of the building as if in hot pursuit of someone or something.

But...no, it was okay. The man lurched to a halt—apparently the cab he'd been trying to wave down was already in service—and resumed a more normal pace, heading their way but without any obvious signs of interest. He seemed to be avidly watching the street, in fact, probably hoping for another cab. Good luck. Anyway, Phoenix told herself, he was too well-dressed to be paparazzi. And she'd seen no sign whatsoever of a camera.

Still, on the two-block walk to the restaurant a few heads did turn their way. More than a few. Phoenix was beginning to worry that she was losing her touch, until she realized the stares weren't directed at her at all.

"People are looking at you, Doc," she said in an undertone. "I think I'm being upstaged." But she felt amused rather than resentful. Even, in an odd way, proud.

The doc, however, was definitely embarrassed. He gave an uneasy laugh and said, "Nah—it's just because I'm dressed all wrong. Like you said—should have worn a suit and tie.''

Lord, was the guy adorable, or what? He actually looked guilty, as if he thought she might mind that people were paying attention to him and not to her. She didn't know what surprised her more—that, or the fact that she *didn't* mind.

Phoenix was still chuckling as they went together into the restaurant, the doc holding the door for her like a natural-born gentleman. But what she was thinking about was how odd it felt, being out with a man who made more heads turn than she did. A *doctor,* moreover, someone with a life—and responsibilities—more important than hers. It gave her a strange, unsettled feeling.

Dammit, she'd thought she had everything under control with this tenement fiasco, that she knew just where she was going. Now she was beginning to wonder if she'd made a wrong turn somewhere, because nothing where she was now felt familiar to her.

The restaurant was Bonelli's—basic Italian, not great food but popular with the downtown business lunch crowd and well off the tourist track. Phoenix had been there a couple of times with Patrick, as his client, and dressed as she was now, and no one had recognized her. Business people, Phoenix had found, were too involved with their own affairs to have much interest in who happened to be sitting at the table next to them.

The maitre'd remembered her, and even asked politely after Mr. Kaufman when he saw her unfamiliar companion. Then he did a huge double take and for some reason seemed to become quite flustered. Must be gay, Phoenix thought, amused at the man's reaction. Chalk up another conquest for the doc.

As she turned to follow the maitre'd, she noticed that the man in the dark suit, the one who'd tried unsuccessfully to flag down a cab, had come in just behind them. Moments later, she saw him being led to a table close to theirs. But he seated himself with his back to them, facing the entrance, and she stopped worrying about him.

"See?" she said smugly as she tucked the briefcase neatly beside her chair. "What'd I tell you? Nobody notices you when you look like everybody else. Works every time."

There was only a murmured response from her companion. The doc had already disappeared behind his menu, and looked up just long enough to order a glass of water from the waitress who had appeared to take their drink order. When Phoenix asked for the same, though, he lowered the menu and leveled his calm, shaman's gaze at her over its edge.

"If you want a drink, don't let me hold you back. I've got a long afternoon and evening ahead of me at the clinic, or I'd be tempted myself."

She shook her head, smiling a little. He said, "What?" in a mystified tone, his own smile hovering tentatively. When she didn't answer right away, he folded the menu and laid it aside, giving her his undivided attention.

She almost wished he hadn't. *Lord,* those eyes…

"Believe it or not, I'm a working girl, too, Doc." Her voice felt huskier than usual, but she didn't try to clear it. What *was* it about this man, that he could shake her confidence so, just with a look? "Maybe lives don't hang in the balance, but I do occasionally have some people depending on me to show up on time and sober."

For a moment he didn't answer. Then he said quietly, "I never thought you didn't." And in some indefinable way, she felt ashamed.

And so it was somewhat defensively that she asked, "What *do* you think, Doc? About me. Me as a person, I mean."

His eyes narrowed the way she'd seen them do before, as

if a bright light had flashed suddenly. Again he didn't answer right away, and in the silence she suddenly realized that her heart was beating way faster than it had any reason to.

It seemed an age before he said in his off hand way, "I'm not sure I ever have, to tell you the truth. Thought about you as a person. It's not an easy thing to do, you know, you being...who you are."

Phoenix made an impatient sound and leaned back abruptly, while he broke off to nod a thank-you to the waitress who'd just brought their water glasses. For some reason, when he did, the waitress flushed bright pink. And for some reason, Phoenix was beginning to find that not quite as amusing as before.

"It would probably help," the doc said after the waitress had fled, bringing his eyes back to her, "if I had something to call you besides Phoenix. Which I'm willing to bet money is not the name your parents gave you." He waited for her reply, and when it didn't come, nodded toward her. She felt his eyes briefly touch the gray flannel that covered her pounding heart. "You want to know what I think?"

She murmured, "Doc, I'm sure you're going to tell me."

His gaze was unwavering, his expression detached but kind—the doctor delivering his diagnosis. "What I think is, that name and everything that goes with it is like another disguise to you. *The Rock Star.* People see what they expect to see—isn't that what you told me? So, people look at you and all they see—all they know—is the rock star. And..." She caught her lip between her teeth and held it, waiting. "...I think that's the way you want it."

The silence this time was measured in heart-beats...drumbeats. Phoenix counted them off in her head like beats of music, one bar at a time...and when the timing seemed right she heard her own voice murmur the lyrics: "Well, Doc, if you tell me yours, I'll tell you mine."

And how long *that* silence might have lasted she would never know. Something intruded—a polite cough—and the world came crashing in on her in a torrent of sound. A waiter was there, ready to take their orders; beyond him, diners spoke in murmured conversations, dishes clattered and silver clinked. Somewhere out in the city a siren wailed. Phoenix shuddered.

The waiter took their orders and went away. Phoenix wasn't sure what she was having; she'd simply seconded the doc's choices. She devoutly hoped it wasn't the eggplant. Lord, she *hated* eggplant.

The cocktail waitress was back, hovering at the doc's elbow.

"Please," the girl whispered, so nervous and jittery that, if she'd been a character in a comic strip, Phoenix thought, she'd have those little drops of water flying off her. "I'm sorry to bother you…please don't tell anyone. I'll probably get fired for asking, but— Oh, God. I'm so nervous. I've never done this before. Please—" and she slapped her order pad down in front of him "—could I just have your autograph?"

Oh, Lord, it was too funny. Phoenix made a strangled sound and clapped a hand over her mouth to hold back the laughter. The doc threw her a desperate look.

The waitress was suddenly mortified. "Oh—God. You are him, aren't you? Ethan Brown? I was so sure… Oh, God, I feel really stupid…"

Ethan? Ethan Brown… Where had she heard that name?

The doc was smiling at the poor girl and saying in his quiet way, "No, no—that's all right. I mean, you're not wrong. And it's okay. Here—I'll sign that for you if you want me to…" He took the pen from the waitress's trembling fingers and scrawled something on her order pad, then handed both pen and pad back to her.

"Oh, God…*thank you.* Thank you *so much.*" The girl all

but dropped a curtsy. She was whispering as she scurried away, "Ethan Brown...my sister is just going to *flip out* when I tell her...."

And the doctor turned slowly back to Phoenix, wearing that same guilty look he'd had stepping out of the elevator in the parking garage. Very much like a little boy caught with his hand in the cookie jar.

"Ethan..." she purred, low in her throat, a smile hiding the shock, the cold, trembling anger that had come on the heels of revelation. "So...that's the name you didn't want me to know. Ethan Brown. Okay, my next question is— were you ever going to let me in on *your* little secret?"

Chapter 4

"It was never a secret," Ethan said, squirming in his chair. "I don't go around announcing it." But he felt completely fraudulent.

Phoenix made a soft breath sound that wasn't quite laughter. "You must think I've been living under a rock." She said it lightly, but Ethan didn't believe it for a minute.

She must feel like a fool, he thought. I've humiliated her. He had an idea that wasn't something this—or any—woman would easily forgive.

"Not really," he said, leaning toward her, eager to make amends for having deceived her. "It's understandable. I've tried pretty hard to—" he smiled wryly "—keep a low profile.'" He waited, but she didn't smile back. He cleared his throat and ploughed on. "It helps that the tabloids are easily bored, and the mainstream media know better than to intrude—if they want to keep on good terms with the White House, that is. So it's been a while since my picture's been in the papers or the six o'clock news...." He was babbling.

He forced himself to meet those incredible eyes…an incredible risk, he knew. For a moment he felt as if he were balanced on the very edge of a high diving board, and vertigo one scant breath away. He had the impression of something lurking beneath the shimmering surface of her eyes but didn't trust his balance enough to look closely to see what it was. Hoping it might be forgiveness, he gestured toward his beard and smiled.

"And then, I guess I have my own little ways of disguising myself. You said it—people see what they expect to see. And the president's son would have to be about the last person you'd have expected to run into in a meeting with a committee of slum tenants."

"True." But she was brittle, still. Unmollified. Her eyes shimmered through the curtain of her lashes like sunlit water through a forest. "All the more reason you should have warned me, don't you think?"

"I was trying to keep—"

"—a low profile. I know." She leaned sharply forward, like a cat pouncing on a mouse. "Tell me, Doc—or I guess I can call you Ethan, now—what else were you trying to do?"

"I beg your pardon?" The suddenness of her anger was as shocking to him as a slap.

"What is it you're after? Is it some kind of political thing?" She was braced on her forearms, shoulders hunched and eyes shooting cold blue fire. "If it's the publicity—"

"Publicity would be the last thing any of us want," Ethan countered in a voice as cold as her eyes, but much, much softer. Because it was his way, when faced with violence of any kind—actions or emotions—to retreat to his calm, quiet place, he said, oh, so calmly…oh, so quietly, "What I'm trying to do is exactly what I said I was trying to do, which is help some people get their apartments fixed up. And hopefully stay out of the news in the process." He paused, which was a mistake; he could feel the walls of his quiet place creaking under the pressure of the emotions they were trying to hold at bay. "I didn't ask you to pick me out of that group. Why did you do that, by the way?" And he could hear the tension in his voice, now. "What, exactly, were *you* trying to do?"

The question left behind a ringing silence, like the crash of cymbals in a stunning finale. As Phoenix listened to its dying echoes she was conscious of an overwhelming sense of frustration, even failure. It was the same way she felt when the perfect word, the perfect lyric, the perfect golden note eluded her...which made no sense at all.

What was it she'd expected...hoped for? With a few exceptions, she was used to either intimidating men or exciting them. She was used to seeing lust, awe, even fear in a man's eyes. She didn't know what to do with this man, this doctor who seemed neither intimidated nor excited, who gazed at her with his shaman's eyes and spoke to her without any nervousness at all. Like Patrick, she thought. Except that, unlike Patrick, with this man she had no doubt in her mind that the emotions were there. She knew it...*felt* it, like a tremor beneath her breastbone...like a knot in her stomach.

With their eyes locked and all senses focused with laserlike intensity on each other, it was a moment or two before either Phoenix or Ethan noticed the waiter. When he announced himself with a discreet cough, they sprang back from each other, straightening, Ethan thought, like two tied-down saplings when the ropes binding them are sliced through with an axe. They sat in a twanging silence while their plates were set before them, murmured identical automatic thank yous and barely noticed when the waiter asked if there was anything else they required and, unanswered, went away.

"What's the matter?" Ethan ventured, picking up his fork. Phoenix was simply staring at her plate.

"Spaghetti and marinara sauce. You ordered spaghetti and marinara sauce?"

"Yeah? So did you," said Ethan, mystified. She was muttering under her breath, now, shaking her head.

And suddenly she was laughing, silently but he could hear real amusement in it. "I can't believe you. You're having lunch with *Phoenix*. You have a beard. And you order spaghetti with red sauce. Now, that's confidence."

Ethan was smiling too as he stabbed his fork into the pile of spaghetti on his plate, though he still wasn't sure what the joke was. He did know it felt good to have her pleased with him again. Surprisingly good. Unbelievably good.

He watched, bemused, as Phoenix attacked her own plate with a gusto more in character with the rock star she was than the businesswoman she pretended to be. *Phoenix. This is Phoenix.* He wondered why he kept having to remind himself of that fact. And when the reality of it would set in.

"Were we quarreling just now?" She asked it casually, not looking up from her plate.

Ethan chewed and swallowed before he answered. "Nah—we don't know each other well enough to quarrel." But deep inside he felt a quiver of something.... Awareness? Anticipation? Excitement?

She nodded. "That's what I thought."

They ate in silence for a few minutes. Phoenix wondered whether the doc was just concentrating hard on getting spaghetti from plate to mouth without embarrassing mishaps, or if maybe he was thinking about what might be happening between them. And whether she was thinking about it, too. Which she was. She was thinking this Doc Brown, the president's son, was going to be more of a challenge than she'd expected. One she was actually looking forward to. She was enjoying herself more, in fact, felt more excited, more *alive* than she had since she'd come back to this miserable town.

She put down her fork and picked up her water glass. She

sipped, and still holding the glass, motioned with her head toward a nearby table. "The guy in the dark blue suit. I just figured it out—the phone call, the stalling tactics in the garage—he belongs to you, doesn't he?"

She felt a shiver of pleasure when the doc turned ever so slightly pink. Though the color may have been attributable to his sudden fit of coughing.

"Belongs to me? Not hardly." He drank some water to bring himself under control again. "His name is Tom, by the way—Tom Applegate. He's one of two guys I do my best not to inconvenience. The other one is Carl Friedenburg—I'll introduce you to them when I get a chance. If they lose track of me they have to answer to my dad—or my stepmom, which is much worse—so I try to be a good boy."

He spoke lightly, but it vexed him, she could see—the loss of privacy. She knew how he felt, of course. It occurred to her that, as different as their lives were in so many ways, she and this particular doctor might have some things in common. She could use that, she decided. She would play on it, their commonality.

"I met them once, you know," she said, tackling the spaghetti again. "Your parents. The president and First Lady."

"Really?" He paused with fork halfway to his mouth. "At the White House?"

"Uh-uh—it was in Dallas. About…five years ago. A benefit concert—world hunger, I think. Maybe you remember it?" He shook his head; Phoenix shrugged. "The Parish Family were among the organizers. That's your mom, right?"

"Stepmom."

"Right. Anyway, they came—President and Mrs. Brown. There was a big reception afterward, so we all got to meet them. Nice people, I thought—especially Dixie." She lifted her lashes and smiled at him. "Your dad seems a bit starched…"

"He can be that way sometimes," Ethan said, smiling back. "Dixie keeps it from being terminal."

Phoenix laughed, a rusty little chortle. "Really? And how does she do that?"

"I haven't a clue," said Ethan with a one-shouldered shrug. "It's just a way she has, I guess. She's always been that way—she…brings out the music in people."

"Interesting…" Phoenix murmured.

"What?"

She shook her head. But she was thinking now about Ethan's father, President Everett Charlton Brown. And that, if Dixie Parish, of the world-famous folksinging Parish Family, had managed to find music beneath that Mount Rushmore facade…well. It was interesting, that's all.

"I met your sister, too," she said, twirling spaghetti on the tines of her fork. "And her husband—he's Indian, right? A sheriff, or something like that."

Ethan nodded, perhaps not a wise move, given the forkful of spaghetti he was about to deliver to his mouth. "Native American. Apache. Arizona. Oops…damn."

Phoenix casually reached across the table and wiped the tiny smear of marinara sauce from a bare patch of his chin with her thumb. But inside, her heartbeat stumbled; she felt a surge of something she told herself was triumph.

"One of the advantages of being a rock star is that nobody expects you to be politically correct," she purred, licking the sauce from her thumb. She could still feel *him* there, like the residual tingle of electric shock—the slightly sandpapery texture of his skin…the coarse-silk weave of his beard against the backs of her fingers.

"I thought he was fascinating," she murmured, as Ethan calmly wiped his beard with his napkin. She smiled down at her plate. Oh, the emotions were there, all right…the fire, the passion. She'd *felt* it. Getting to it—getting past that shaman's calm, that incredible self-control of his—this was going to be fun. "I wrote a song about him. Believe it or not. What a coincidence, huh?" She slanted a look at him through her lashes. "It's true, though. Your brother-in-law was the inspiration for 'Wild Man, Gentle Heart.' He has such a *fierce* look—like Ghenghis Khan about to wreak havoc on the villagers. And yet…he has this gentle way about him…."

Maybe, she thought, that's all it is, this fascination he holds for me. I just happen to be a sucker for a gentle man.

"My sister apparently thought so," Ethan said. He was so quiet now. Unnaturally quiet.

"What about you?" Yes, and it reminded her of something, that quietness, something she couldn't quite put her finger on.

"Bronco's a good man."

"No, I mean, where were you that night? I seem to have met your whole family. Except you. Imagine, Doc, if we'd met five years ago…"

He picked up his water glass and held it, almost like a shield between them, it seemed to her. "Five years ago I was a med student—overworked and stressed out in L.A. I doubt I'd have been much fun." Over the top of the glass his eyes watched her…dark, quiet, wary.

Yes, that was what he reminded her of. A stag, hiding in the underbrush, watching the hunter. He was on his guard now, fortified against her. Time to back off a little, she thought, enjoying the game. Give him some breathing room.

She laughed, her husky trademark chuckle. "No offense, Doc, but you're not exactly a barrel of laughs now."

And as she'd thought he would, he smiled. It was a wry and self-deprecating smile, and it banished the wariness from his eyes. As she'd thought it would. But what came in its stead was something she didn't want to see. Something bleak and sad…like dark pools reflecting back the face of tragedy.

"Sorry," he said softly, "I didn't think this was a particularly funny situation."

She caught her breath and looked away, and Ethan didn't know whether the lurch he felt in his chest was triumph, or regret. In the strange verbal fencing match they were engaged in, he knew he'd just scored a touché. He felt no sense of victory, and yet…he wasn't sorry for it, either.

"We have—" The sports watch on his wrist emitted a tiny electronic beep. "I have to get back to the clinic," he said with an exhalation, without glancing at his wrist. He was conscious of conflicting feelings, now—both relief and regret. "Can we—"

Phoenix nodded and signaled to the waiter with a platinum American Express credit card. Out of the corner of his eye Ethan saw Tom Applegate fold his napkin and push back his chair.

"What I was going to say," said Ethan, "was, can we get together again to talk about this?" He hadn't wanted the job, dammit. But since he'd been designated spokesman for the residents of The Gardens, he supposed the responsibility for protecting their interests was his, like it or not. He told himself that was his only reason for wanting to see this woman again. He told himself that beyond that they had nothing in common, that she would complicate his life in unimaginable ways. A woman like this could easily make a man lose his sense of direction, make him forget his principles, his purpose.

I need to get away from her, he thought. *I need to get my bearings.*

"Listen," he said, "you don't have to leave if you're not—"

"I'm done here." She kept her face averted as she scrawled a signature across the check the waiter had brought in its leather folder, as brisk and efficient as any executive or attorney concluding a power lunch. Try as he would without seeming too obvious about it, Ethan couldn't make out the signature or the name on the card. She snapped the folder shut and shoved the credit card carelessly into the pocket of her dove-gray suit and rose. "Shall we go?"

"Sure." Her face was somber, Ethan noted. So still and set...the way it had been just before she'd walked out of the conference room. He wondered if it was just her way, to run when confronted with something she didn't want to deal with.

He followed her out of the restaurant, pausing at the entrance, as he'd learned to do, to let Tom Applegate go ahead of him. He waited for Tom's nod, then pushed through the door and found Phoenix waiting for him on the sidewalk, watching the interaction between him and his bodyguard and smiling a little half smile.

"Tom," Ethan said, "I'd like you to meet Phoenix."

The Secret Service agent nodded, deadpan, and said, "Nice meeting you, ma'am," like the well brought-up Southerner he was. He allowed himself to glance only briefly at the world-famous rock star before his eyes moved on, looking all around, up and down the street, watching the sidewalk...watching everything. Everyone.

In a voice rich with amusement, Phoenix said, "Nice meeting you, too, Tom." Then she linked her arm through Ethan's and murmured out the side of her mouth as they moved together down the sidewalk, "Can't be easy keeping a low profile when you've got six and a half feet of bodyguard following you everywhere."

He gave a huff of laughter but didn't reply. He didn't— because her scent was inside his head and her heat was inside him, and all his nerves and senses were converging on the source of that heat like moths to a candle flame. He tried to remind himself that this was *Phoenix*. Phoenix—

world-class performer and master of disguise. *Nothing about this woman is real.* Trouble was, his body didn't believe it. Not for a minute. His body knew only that she was a woman, vibrant and alive and unbelievably beautiful.

"Do you need a ride back to your clinic?" she asked as they approached the dark maw of the parking garage. "I can have Patrick send a car—"

"That's okay, Tom's got it covered." Smiling a half smile of his own, Ethan nodded toward the Secret Service agent, who was muttering into his wrist. Moments later an anonymous dark sedan with tinted windows rolled silently up the garage's exit ramp and stopped beside them.

"Wow, just like Dick Tracy," Phoenix murmured. "I'm impressed."

"Your tax dollars at work," said Ethan dryly. Tom had opened the back door of the sedan and was waiting for him. The car's engine idled, pumping out visible waves of heat. "About that meeting…"

"Sure. How about tomorrow? Come by the studio. After you get off work…before—doesn't really matter, I'll be there, working. You can meet the band."

"The band…uh, ours." He felt steeped in heat, his brain fuzzy. He frowned. "Working, you said?"

"That's what I said." Her smile was tilted, her voice rusty and sardonic. "What did you think? All us rock stars spend our days just layin' around smokin' pot and doin' drugs and partyin', right? Like I told you, I'm pretty much just a working girl, I have schedules to keep, deadlines to meet, people depending on me."

Ethan looked at her for a long moment, seeing the perfect oval of her face sleekly framed in raven-black, and for some reason remembering the way she'd looked when he'd first seen her that morning, with all that hair rippling down her back and slapping against the back pockets of her jeans. He had a suddenly and visceral sense of what it would feel like…cool and silky against his skin. He heard himself say, "I guess there's a lot I don't know about you."

"That there is, Doc." In the murky light of the garage her eyes seemed shadowed, even sad. "A whole helluva lot."

You idiot, this is Phoenix!

Yes, but her eyes were a woman's eyes, and her mouth a woman's mouth, and his mind kept asking him why he didn't just lean over and kiss it. His mind already knew how it would taste…how it would grow moist and soft under his…and nothing else mattered much, did it?

But it did. Half-suffocated by her heat, with the sedan's well-tuned engine pulsing inside his head, he said in a voice he couldn't hear, "There's a lot I'd like to know about you." And then, "Starting with your name."

How long did she stare at him in that thumping, suffocating silence, and him feeling trapped, imprisoned, helpless as a fly in molasses? He didn't know, but when she finally spoke her words thrilled him beyond his imagining, lifted his heart higher than any words she'd ever uttered, stirred his soul more deeply than any song she'd ever sung.

"It's Joanna," she said. "Joanna Dunn."

And he stood and watched her walk away down the exit ramp, her high heels click-click-clicking on the concrete.

He was barely aware of Tom's hand on his elbow, a polite reminder. He scarcely remembered getting into the car, hearing the door slam behind him, shutting out the heat. He did know that he spoke to Carl Friedenburg as Tom got into the front seat beside him, but he had no idea what it was he'd said. And his only thought, as the sedan rolled out of the garage and joined the flow of traffic in the stifling street, like the words of a great new song playing over and over inside his head: *her name is Joanna. Joanna Dunn.*

As he'd expected, Ruthie, Father Frank and Mrs. Schmidt were waiting for him when he got back to the clinic, lounging around the reception counter in a way that reminded Ethan of the cats in his aunt Lucy's barn back in Iowa, the way they'd lie with bodies at ease, eyes alert, springing to life instantly at his entrance to come running, tails aloft, meowing and twining around his legs, begging.

"How did it go?"

"What did you find out?"

"What was she like?"

He laughed out loud at his vision of the barn cats, surprising them, but he didn't try to explain. "It went fine," he said. What did I find out? *I found out her name is Joanna…Joanna Dunn.* But for some reason he kept that to himself, like a hard-rock prospector hugging to his heart the single gold nugget he'd found.

"What's she like, Phoenix?" Ruthie asked again, her dark eyes shy.

Ethan drew in a breath and exhaled it in a rush. "Not like anybody you or I've ever met before," he said on bumps of dry laughter. Everyone nodded, then shook their heads; it was the answer they seemed to have expected. He paused, then added almost guiltily, "We went out for lunch."

Ruthie gave an excited gasp. "You had lunch with *Phoenix?*"

"Wow," said Mrs. Schmidt, "were you mobbed?"

Ethan coughed and ran a hand through his hair—a gesture he realized he'd inherited from his father, and made a mental note to stop. "I was recognized—she wasn't. Believe it or not. She has a way of…just sort of blending in. Practically becomes invisible when she wants to be."

"Wow," said Mrs. Schmidt again, shaking her head. Ruthie sighed and leaned her chin on her hand.

"Did you talk about The Gardens?" Father Frank asked in a low voice, glancing over his shoulder. The doctor filling

in for Ethan, Sid Grenville, was heading their way, scrib-
bling busily on a chart, while behind him an elderly black
man wearing a hat and suit jacket with his overalls ushered
his frail-looking wife toward the door.

"Didn't have much chance," Ethan said in the same tone.
"It was mostly just…getting acquainted."

But, when he thought back over his time with Phoenix it
began to seem to him more like some strange sort of verbal
fencing match than real conversation. In his memory he saw
them circling each other…feinting and parrying, advancing
and retreating. He remembered his one small touché. Undoubtedly she'd scored a few off him, too, but all in all he
figured the score had ended up about even. She had, after
all, given him her name. He couldn't underestimate the importance of that.

"Hey, you made it," Sid Grenville said as he joined
them. Dr. Grenville was a tall, balding man with wire-
rimmed glasses and kind eyes. Not much older than Ethan,
he had a wife and two kids and was struggling to pay back
his student loans. He couldn't afford to spend much time at
the clinic, since he'd only recently ventured out on his own
and was trying to get a family practice established in offices
near the downtown medical center. And since that was clear
over on the other side of the harbor, Ethan knew it was a
considerable inconvenience for Sid to fill in for him in the
middle of a day like this.

"Sorry I'm late," he said contritely.

The other doctor shrugged and smiled as he passed the
chart off to Mrs. Schmidt and stabbed his pen in the general
direction of his lab coat pocket. "No problem. How was
lunch?"

"Great," said Ethan. "What'd I miss?"

Dr. Grenville filled him in on the morning's cases and
possible follow-ups, then took his leave. The door had

barely swooshed shut behind him before Father Frank got right back to business. "So. Where do we go from here?"

"We have another meeting." Ethan just did remember not to run his hand through his hair. "Tomorrow. At her studio—which reminds me, Bibi, I guess you'd better call that business manager of hers and find out where that is." His mouth quirked sideways with his smile. "She says I can meet her band."

"Oh, wow," breathed Ruthie.

Her brother glanced at her and said soberly, "Well, I guess it's better than nothing. Sure do wish we could get her to come down here, though. She doesn't have any idea what kind of conditions those people are living in. I don't think we'd have any trouble getting her to do what we want, if she could just…see it. She needs to see it with her own eyes."

"Yeah," said Ethan, "so do I." His old friend gave him a startled look. "Well, what did you think?" Ethan shot back angrily. "You think *I* have any clue how those people live? She asked me, you know—what they wanted from her. I didn't even know what to tell her. Hey—I didn't exactly go into that meeting prepared to act as spokesman for a whole neighborhood, you know. I was completely unprepared and unqualified—" A small shushing noise from Mrs. Schmidt warned him just a heartbeat before he heard it— the careful and polite clearing of a throat.

Then a voice—rich and liquid, with traces of the South— a vaguely familiar voice. "Excuse me—are you the doctor?"

A few feet away a woman was standing—a young woman, buxom rather than plump, dressed in a faded T-shirt and too-tight shorts and balancing a chubby baby on one hip. Her dull black hair wasn't any particular style, just pulled back in clumps and fastened with various rubber bands and clips, in the manner of frazzled mothers with no time to spare for primping. Her skin was the color of coffee with cream, and her dark eyes—her best feature—were almond-shaped and set at an exotic tilt.

When he saw those eyes Ethan felt a jolt like a punch to the gut, even before he recognized the child standing beside her in baggy pants, an oversized shirt and a baseball cap turned backward. A small child with arms folded defiantly across his chest, an angry tilt to his chin and a wounded look in his proud amber eyes.

Chapter 5

Michael Parker. Ethan had forgotten all about the otitus and the follow-up visit he'd asked for. Now, he didn't know what to say in the face of those accusing eyes. Guilt was heavy in his chest, helplessness a burning in his belly.

"My sister said he was supposed to come back here in three days to get his ears checked. It's been three days, so I brought him." When Ethan didn't respond the woman added with a touch of impatience, "My name's Tamara? And this here is Michael. My sister is—was Louise Parker, she the one got—"

"Yes— Hello, Michael, how're you doing today? Those ears feeling any better?" His voice was too loud, too jovial. The amber eyes regarded him in sullen silence.

"I been seein' he takes his medicine," Tamara said. Her voice had that strange liquid quality that sounds like tears, so he was surprised, when he was finally able to take his eyes from the boy at her side and give his attention to her once more, to find her gaze steady and her face impassive. "My sister said it was important, so that's what I done."

He nodded at Ruthie, who normally would have seen the patient to an exam room and taken care of the preliminaries, to let her know he had this one under control.

"It's good you did that," he said as he touched Tamara's shoulder and gestured with the other hand that she and Michael were to come with him. The tired way she gave the baby a hitch as she fell into step beside him made him wonder if she'd walked all the way from The Gardens carrying the child on her hip like that. "Listen, if you'd like, I can get the nurse or Mrs. Schmidt to take the baby—"

"Oh, no, that's okay. She ain't heavy." But she shifted the burden again, this time to her other hip.

Ethan pulled back the exam room curtain and ushered the three inside. "Okay, Michael, you want to hop up here and let me take a look at those ears?" But when he held out his hands to offer the boy a lift up onto the table, he jerked angrily away.

"*Michael,* mind your manners," his aunt hissed, reminding Ethan poignantly of her sister.

"It's okay," he hastily assured her, and selecting a scope, squatted on his heels in front of the child. "I can look at him from here just as well. How 'bout it, buddy, you going to let me see what those bad bugs are doing in there?"

For his answer, Michael struck out with one wiry arm and sent the scope flying. It landed with a clatter and slithered across the tile floor.

His Aunt Tamara screeched, "*Michael!* What you doin'?"

The amber eyes regarded Ethan unflinchingly, searing their grief and anger into his soul.

"Hey," he said quietly, "I thought we were getting along better than that. I'm the one that's trying to make your ears feel better, remember? You want to tell me why you're mad at me?" But he knew. He could still feel those small fists pounding him, right over his heart.

"My momma's *dead*." Michael said the last word the Southern way, drawing it out, almost making it two syllables.

Ethan took a deep breath. "I know. I'm sorry."

Again the hard little fists thumped his chest, just once, the way they'd done that night, the night Louise Parker died. "You didn't *fix* her. You was s'posed to *fix* my momma up. An' you didn't, an' now she *dead*."

A hard knot of pain formed in Ethan's chest, just where the blow had landed. "I couldn't fix your momma, son, I'm sorry. I wanted to. I tried very hard to fix her, but...I couldn't."

He put his hands on the boy's thin shoulders, then slid them down to his arms. Michael squirmed, but this time didn't pull away. "Did you ever want to do something so bad, but you weren't big enough, or strong enough, and no matter how hard you tried, you just couldn't do it?"

Michael's gaze wavered. Then, unwillingly, he nodded. When he finally spoke, it was so softly Ethan had to lean close in order to hear. "Can't...reach the basket. Can't throw the ball high enough. Can't throw hoops like Michael Jordan." His lower lip quivered. The amber eyes shimmered for an instant like guttering candle flames, then spilled over.

Wordlessly, Ethan gathered the little boy into his arms. As he held the trembling body close he looked up and saw Tamara standing there, the round-eyed baby astride a canted hip and a tear rolling silently down her cheek. He watched her, still not speaking, his hands gently circling the knobs of the boy's shoulders, until she brushed the moisture roughly away with her fingers. This time when she spoke, oddly enough, now that there were tears, her voice didn't sound liquid anymore. Instead it was a whisper, dry as sand.

"I wanted to say thank you for what you done—what you tried to do for my sister. I know there wasn't nothin' you could do. They told us at the hospital. And...I wanted to thank you, too, for what you're doing for us—all of us—talkin' to that woman, getting her to fix up our building. Mr. Wilkins, he lives on the floor below me, he was there and he told me how you was the one gonna be talkin' to her, seein' we get done what needs to be done. I can't thank you enough, Dr. Brown. I just wish...'' Her voice trailed off and she looked away, brushing again at her cheek.

Ethan didn't know what to say to her; once again he felt frustrated, fraudulant, unworthy...and trapped. He cleared his throat as he rose to his feet, with Michael still clinging fast to his neck. Inside the fragile chest pressed against his he could feel the heart beating, quick tap-tap-taps that made him think of a bird, some small frightened animal.

Muttering something vague to fill the silence, he set the boy on the exam table and peeled the scrawny arms from around his neck. Clearly humiliated by his lapse into babyhood, Michael sat staring dumbly into a distant corner of the exam room while Ethan busied himself finding another scope, and a wad of tissues with which to mop up tears and a runny nose. For several interminable minutes, the only sound was the rustle of fabric, a muffled sniff.

Then Tamara spoke in her normal liquid voice, but pitched a little too loudly and too high. ''Dr. Brown, could I ask you a question?''

Still bent over Michael and intent on his examination, Ethan shot her a glance. ''Sure.''

''I heard this rumor? Somebody said you was the president's kid. That true?''

He straightened up slowly and looked at her, seeing the defensive cant of her head, the way her body was turned half away from him, as if to shield herself. Oh, Lord, he thought, what do I say? He knew if he denied it, it would cause this already grief-stricken woman considerable embarrassment. But there was nothing he dreaded so much as watching people's faces change when he said yes.

It was instinct—and an overwhelming wave of compassion—that made him speak to her first only with his eyes...silently imparting secrets, imploring trust. He breathed a small sigh and muttered, "Rumors..." as he bent once more toward his patient. Then quickly, before Tamara's face had time to register even a flicker of disappointment, he glanced back at her...and winked.

He heard the sharp sound of her indrawn breath and the beginnings of an excited, "Hot damn, so it's—" before he silenced her with a finger touched to his lips and a whispered, "Shh..." His reward was the warmth of her full-blown smile.

"Michael's doing fine," he said gruffly, giving the baseball cap a tug. "His ears look a lot better. Make sure he keeps taking the medicine, though. He needs to take it until it's all gone. And keep his ears dry—don't want any water in there."

Tamara was nodding, bobbing from one foot to the other in barely contained excitement. "I will—I been tryin' to do right by him. He's my sister's kid, I don't want him goin' to no foster home. But it's hard sometimes, you know? I got the baby, I can't take him places like his momma did. She used to take him like, to the park and stuff on weekends—you know, to watch the ball games?" Her exuberance died like a ball running out of bounce, and she finished wanly, "I think he been missin' his momma some."

Some... Ethan thought, then, of the black-haired woman with magical eyes, flirting with him around a thin cigar, fencing verbally across plates of spaghetti...toying with him, he now realized. He thought of how he'd wanted to kiss her, lust ripening like summer fruit in the heat of an idling engine...and a little worm of shame coiled and curled inside his belly. This boy's mother, the anchor of his existence, was dead. This child would never know the warmth of her love, feel her arms around him, ever again. How could Ethan have let himself forget that, even for a moment? She was a witch, that woman, a spellbinder by any name, be it Phoenix or Joanna Dunn.

He made a vow, then, that hereafter whenever he was with her he would be on his guard and no matter how she turned on the charisma, he'd think first and always of this child, Michael Parker, and his mother, Louise.

Something else came to him then, too: he realized that above all else, he wanted Joanna Dunn—Phoenix—to think of her, too.

If asked, Ethan would have denied having an impulsive bone in his body. How was it, then, that he heard himself offering to take a motherless boy to the park?

Tamara gave a little gasp. "You mean it? You'd do that?"

"Sure." Shaken himself, Ethan shrugged and tugged on Michael's cap. "How 'bout it, guy? You want to go to the park with me?" Michael swiped a hand across his nose and grudgingly nodded. "All right, then." He scooped the boy up before he could object and set his feet on the tile floor, then turned back to his aunt. "Is Saturday okay?"

Tamara nodded slowly, still looking stunned. Then, recovering her senses, asked quickly in a high, disbelieving voice, "You sure you wanna do this?"

Ethan didn't dare answer that. To be honest, his only experience with children was a pediatrics rotation during his internship, and he was scared to death by the idea. Instead he said staunchly, "How about if I pick him up, say, about ten o'clock Saturday morning?"

"You wanna come down to *my* place? The Gardens?" In addition to disbelief, Tamara's face now registered panic.

"Sure," said Ethan with what he hoped was a reassuring smile.

"Uh-huh, okay, I guess that be all right...." She was still muttering dazedly as Ethan escorted them out of the exam room. The last thing he heard as they parted company was a whispered, "Oh, *man,* I don't believe this. The president's kid comin' to *my* house."

"Hey, Michael, I'll see you on Saturday, okay?"

Michael didn't reply or look back.

When Ethan rejoined Father Frank and Mrs. Schmidt at the reception desk—Ruthie was in another exam room seeing to a patient—Mrs. Schmidt's eyebrows were already raised. "Since when do you work Saturdays?"

"I don't," said Ethan, scowling at the chart in his hands. "I'm, ah…hmm. I'm picking Michael up. Thought I'd take him to the park…you know. Play catch, or something."

"Ah-hah." Mrs. Schmidt gave him a droll look and turned back to her books.

Grinning, Father Frank gripped Ethan's arm briefly by way of a farewell. "Hey, that's great."

"*What?*" Ethan demanded; he knew that look well.

The priest paused and looked back at him, no longer smiling. "You said you had no clue how those people live? Looks to me like you're on your way to finding out now."

"Entrances are hard, hard, hard…
Full of butterflies and—"

With a hiss of frustration, Phoenix broke off in midphrase and twirled half around on her stool.

"You ain't concentratin', girl," Doveman scolded, vamping softly, fingers tickling idly across the keys. "Somethin' on your mind?"

She shook her head—in perplexity, not denial—and after a moment rose and walked to the windows. Part way there she lifted her hands to her hair, still in its businesswoman's knot after her lunch with Dr. Ethan Brown, and with one deft twist and a shake of her head, set it free to tumble warm and heavy down her back.

"Your meeting today with those people—how'd that go?" Doveman's casual tone fooled nobody.

Phoenix snorted. "Well, I know one thing. They don't want my money. They want my blood."

Beyond the window the city was a jeweled tapestry laid out beneath a milky canopy—a night sky turned upside-down. *I wonder where he goes at night,* she thought with sudden irrelevance. *Does he have a warm lady waiting for him? Someone to hold him when the sirens wail...to laugh with him in a tumbled bed....*

"Can't really blame 'em," said Doveman. The music stopped and he turned on the bench to look at her. "So, where do you go from here?"

"I don't much like being outnumbered a dozen to one," Phoenix said dryly. She whirled away from the windows and paced back toward the piano, stopped halfway there and flopped down on the couch instead. "So, I picked a spokes-man. From now on we do this one on one."

Doveman cackled. "Lemme guess...a guy, right? Young...good-lookin'..."

She smiled, but for some reason didn't feel at all amused. "Well," she murmured, "he is that."

"But?" And there was something...an *alertness* in the piano man's voice. "Somethin' you ain't tellin' me."

"He's a doctor—his name's Ethan Brown." She paused, watching his face. It took him less time than it had her—all of four beats.

"What—you don't mean—you're not tellin' me, *the* Ethan Brown? President Rhett Brown Junior?"

Phoenix nodded, smiling, feeling better about it herself, now, enjoying his reaction. "Nothing *junior* about him, though. Seems like the real deal—his own man, I mean. Different from his father as night from day."

Shaking his head, Doveman muttered, "You don't say...Rhett Brown's boy..." And then, pointing a bent brown finger at her, "You met the president and the First Lady, didn't you? At that hunger gig down in Texas. You meet the boy then, too?"

"Uh-uh—he says he was in school out in California. Met his sister, though."

Doveman snorted. "Must be pretty young, if he was still in school five years ago."

"He said med school—I think that's later." Phoenix frowned. She didn't like to think about how young he was.

"Well—he's a doctor now, you say. Can't be too young if he's a doctor," said Doveman, as if he'd heard her thought. "So—" he rubbed a hand over his frosting of beard stubble, making a sandpapery sound "—what you plannin' on doin' with this young good-lookin' doctor? Plannin' on havin' things your own way with him, I expect?" Phoenix smiled and didn't answer. The piano man leaned his hands on his knees and leveled a look at her. "Girl, I wouldn't get too cocky, if I was you. If that boy's anything like his daddy, he might not be so easy to get around."

"Well," said Phoenix carelessly, "I invited him here tomorrow, so you'll get a chance to see for yourself. Then you can tell me what you think." She sat up abruptly. "What are you doing?"

Still bent almost double, Doveman paused in the painful process of getting up from the piano bench to give her a look. "I'm callin' it a night, that's what I'm doing. You ain't in the mood, that's for sure. Girl, all you got on your mind right now is that young Dr. Brown, and how you're gonna get him into your bed and wrapped around your little finger—among other things. I'll be talkin' to you again when you get y'head on straight."

Phoenix said nothing, but from under her lashes watched him make his slow, stiff way to the iron and chain-link cage that connected the loft to the studio below.

Into my bed? Sure, why not?

She'd thought about it—so what? The passion was there—she'd *felt* it, like some powerful force rumbling deep below the surface. All she had to do was tap it. She felt a shiver of excitement, now, remembering the rasp of his skin against her fingers...the heat and vitality radiating from his body in waves as she'd stood next to him there in the garage. The strange force she'd felt then, like a powerful magnet, or a vortex, pulling her closer, pulling her...

"Doveman—" He stopped just inside the cage and turned to look at her, one hand on the lever, waiting. She drew a breath and said it. "I told him my name."

There was a pause, then... "You don't say," the piano man said. Phoenix heard his Camels-and-bourbon chuckle as the cage creaked slowly out of sight.

Ethan stood in the shadowy main hall of the old warehouse, converted at who-knows-what-cost into a state-of-the-art studio, watching Phoenix and her band rehearse. He wasn't sure what he'd expected—nothing magical, certainly, nothing like the adrenaline rush of a live concert performance with all the attendant hype and the contagious excitement of thousands of screaming fans. He felt rather like an explorer hiding in the jungle watching some mysterious pagan rite—utterly fascinated, maybe a little scared. Guilty as hell. He hadn't expected to enjoy himself so much.

Just watching her—that was the source of a good part of the enjoyment, and most of the guilt. He told himself he wasn't supposed to be susceptible to the woman that way, that he was on his guard now, that he knew better. It was like telling himself he wouldn't burn when the flames touched him.

Watching her perform was like watching some incredible spectacle of nature, like an erupting volcano or a lightning storm, or a once-in-a-lifetime sunset. The breath catches, the heart beats faster, and it becomes impossible to look away. In the intervals, talking quietly with the band, she was simply poetry in white leather pants and a silver beaded tank, with her hair knotted loosely halfway down her back, swinging to and fro and now and then catching the light reflected off the silver beads in tiny flashes of blue fire. Her voice drifted to him in uneven ripples, sometimes a husky murmur that made him think of intimacies shared in tumbled sheets, sometimes a scratchy cackle that made the juices rise in the back of his throat as if in response to the smell of bacon frying on a Sunday morning. Then she'd begin to sing, and his heart would quicken and his skin prickle with goose bumps.

The number they were rehearsing was one Ethan hadn't heard before—which added considerably to his excitement, the incredible idea of being among the very first on the planet to hear a new Phoenix song. This one was classic Phoenix, performed with her trademark driving beat and throat-tearing passion—like all of her best stuff, a little bit sad—about entrances and exits, saying hello and saying goodbye. He would like to have heard the whole song, but he wasn't to have that chance; she seemed dissatisfied with it and kept stopping and going back over the same phrase, trying new chords, variations in tempo. Her frustration was tangible; Ethan felt it like an unscratchable itch between his own shoulder blades.

He wasn't sure how long he watched before one of the members of the band noticed him standing there in the shadows and said something to Phoenix. She called an immediate halt to the rehearsal and motioned him over, striding out to meet him and greeting him like a lover, with an arm around his waist and a kiss on the mouth. A quick, proprietary kiss—he barely had time to register her warmth and her scent, the cushiony press of her breasts against his chest, the satin brush of her lips. To register a hot, bright stab of anger: *What is this? What's this for?*

But, of course, he knew. The anger passed as quickly as it had come, and was replaced with amusement. It was obvious to him that the purpose of the kiss had been to brand him—stake her claim and state her intentions—publically. A risky move, considering how little she knew him—or, maybe not. Perhaps to someone of her massive self-confidence it didn't seem like a risk at all.

"Hello, Doc," she purred, "I see you found us."

"Wasn't that hard," Ethan said. "I had somebody call your business manager for directions."

"Well, I'm glad you made it." A smile curled the corners of her mouth, for some reason reminding him of the way she'd looked yesterday in Kaufman's office with that little cigar between her lips. She bobbed her head, looking behind him. "Where's that tall, dark and handsome bodyguard of yours today?"

"Tom's off duty. Carl's out in the car."

"Ah." Her eyes sparked at him from beneath half-lowered lashes. "Well, come meet the band. Hey, guys, say hello to my friend Ethan. He's a doctor."

"Hey, Doc."

"Ethan…"

"Hey, how's it goin'?"

The conventional greetings tumbled from their lips as she called them off, like a roll call of rock music greats: Ed Cooley on drums; Dan Rowe, bass guitar; Bobby Stubblefield, lead guitar and backup vocals; Max Plotkin, guitar and vocals; and on keyboards, legendary piano man, Rupert Dove.

The formalities taken care of, Phoenix stood back and watched him. Dr. Ethan Brown. She hadn't had much chance to do that yesterday, she realized; she'd been too busy playing with him. He hadn't seemed all that real to her then, just a pawn in her own little game.

Now, strangely, he seemed to her the only person in the room who was real. Next to him the others—the members of her band, even Doveman, people she'd known for years—seemed like characters in a play, actors in costume, even cardboard cutouts, static and two-dimensional, while he moved among them in vital and full-fleshed 3-D.

Watching him, she was conscious of an unfamiliar and nameless dissatisfaction—oh, she was too proud to call it longing, or admit that it shook her to her core. Deep in the sequestered recesses of her heart, just for an instant, a light had shown, as if somewhere someone had opened a door— just a crack, no more. And it was she who slammed it shut, trembling inside.

Ah, but he *is* a darlin' man, she thought. Too damned beautiful for words. Retreating into the familiar realm of the senses, she gathered the image of him and his smile and chocolate eyes into her mind, curling into it like a cat in a nest of sunshine. Yes, she wanted him, no doubt about it. Her body wanted to know the secrets of his body…all of its pleasure spots and imperfections. Her mind wanted to know everything there was to know about him—whether he wore briefs or boxers, whether he slept in the raw, whether he woke up grouchy or sunny. Those answers she'd have soon enough—the question was not *if* but *when* she'd seduce him…how soon she'd have him in her bed.

Seduce. Such an old-fashioned word for a modern concept—the notion that a woman could call the shots, control the pace and decide the outcome of her relationships. Phoenix, of course, would have it no other way. But why, then, did she have this nagging dissatisfaction, this sense that something wasn't right? It was the same thing with that damned song. She should have had it all down, the control was in her hands, and *still* it didn't feel right. There was something missing, some obscure harmony, the perfect tempo… Ah, hell. Sooner or later she'd find it.

This business with the Doc, though…something was missing there, too. She had a vague sense of things she wanted to know, but since she'd never wanted to know those things before, she didn't even know the right questions to ask. She knew that she wanted Dr. Ethan Brown, and that she'd have him—of that she had no doubt at all. When it came to men, Phoenix always got what she wanted. What made her uneasy was the possibility that this time, maybe having wouldn't be enough. That getting this man into bed on *her* terms might not be what she wanted after all. That maybe…

No. It made no sense to her at all.

"All right, guys, let's call it a day." She hooked the doc's arm with hers and gave it a little squeeze as she made a "wrapping" motion with her free hand. Her heartbeat had quickened; she wondered if he could feel it. "Doc and I have some business to discuss. Everybody back here tomorrow morning, okay?"

There was a nice but unexpected solidity to him, she realized as she allowed herself to lean, just lightly, against him—unexpected, perhaps, because there seemed to be no excess flesh on him anywhere. But his shoulders were broad, his bones long and strong—including the ones in his face. For all his beauty, there was nothing even remotely soft or pretty about him. He would be handsome, she thought, even when he was old.

Never before in all her memory had she ever pictured a potential lover—or herself—that way. *Old.* And that thought surprised—even frightened—her.

During the cage's slow journey upward, noting the way his quiet eyes took in everything—curious but not awed—Phoenix tried out various seduction scenarios in her mind. And dismissed them all out of hand—first because her instincts told her with a certainty that they weren't going to work with this man, but more so because even the thought of trying one of her usual scenarios out on Dr. Ethan Brown filled her with an urge to burst out laughing. She would feel—and look—ridiculous, she thought, like a grown woman playing child's games. Sliding her eyes sideways to study him under cover of her lashes, she thanked God for at least giving her the intuition to know that *this* man did not play—perhaps would not even understand—games.

But, if that was true, she realized, then she was sailing in uncharted waters. None of the rules and guidelines she was accustomed to living by would apply. For the first time since childhood, Phoenix felt unsure of herself.

The cage clanked to a halt. She unlatched the chain-link gate and stepped out onto the loft, then held it for her guest. He followed without hurry, not warily, but looking around with an undisguised interest she found refreshing. But then, everything he did was like that, wasn't it? Different, somehow. And it occurred to her that there was only a fine line between refreshing and disconcerting.

"Would you care for something to drink?" she asked as she crossed the carpeted floor to the kitchen, which was separated from the rest of the loft only by a curving, granite-topped counter. How useful are these little conventions, she thought as she opened the refrigerator. The grease that eases us through awkward places... "I have...bottled water, diet soda or beer. Oh—and bourbon."

"Beer sounds good." He'd stopped at the counter, she saw, not crowding her, conceding her the kitchen...as her personal space? she wondered. *Or a woman's place?* Oh, yes, he was just possibly old-fashioned enough to think so.

She hid her smile in the cool emptiness of the refrigerator. "Bottle or glass?"

"Bottle's fine."

She selected a bottle of imported beer for him and one

for herself and set them on the countertop. The imported brand required an opener, and by the time she'd located one and successfully popped off the tops, her guest had left his post at the counter to go politely exploring. She followed him to where he stood beside the baby grand, gazing at and not *quite* touching the keys.

"You play?" She held out a moisture-beaded bottle.

His eyes lifted and bumped hers, and the force in them took her by surprise. Her breath caught audibly, the sound thankfully lost in rustles and clinks and a murmured "Thanks..." as he took the bottle from her hand. She had an idea, then, of touching her bottle to his—a tiny toast...a subtle enough promise, suggestive of either comradship or intimacy—but somehow with this man even that small gesture seemed contrived...silly. Instead, she lifted her own bottle to her lips and drank, shielding herself from his gaze with her lashes.

"Not piano," Ethan said, answering the question he barely remembered being asked. "Just a little guitar."

He drank some ice-cold beer that scorched his throat. In that one brief glimpse he'd had of her eyes before she'd dropped the familiar curtain across them, there'd been a sense of something eager and innocent, like a little girl offering a handful of just-picked wildflowers. His response to it had been instant and unnerving—a tightening in his throat, a stinging behind his eyelids. And in its aftermath, a pounding in his blood.

"Really?" Her voice was husky and rich with interest. "Where'd you learn to play? Ever do any singing? Play with a band?"

Laughing, he waved her enthusiasm down—shamelessly flattered even though he was well aware her intent was only to disarm him. "Lord, no—to your last question. To the second, only for my own enjoyment—or chagrin. No, wait—I take that back. I sang a solo once. It was 'The

Cheese Stands Alone'—you know, in 'Farmer In The Dell'? For Parents' Back-To-School Night. I was in first grade.'' He took another sip of beer, shaking his head even now at the exquisite discomfort of the memory. "I'm definitely not a performer."

"But," she said softly, "I think you *like* to sing. And, you play the guitar. Who taught you? Did you take lessons?"

He shook his head. "Dixie taught me—my stepmom."

"Oh—of course."

"Not necessarily, actually. Believe it or not, my dad plays, too. And sings—or at least, he used to, when he was young. It was a family thing. He and his brother sang with my grandmother—for church and weddings and funerals, mostly. From what I've been told, they were pretty good. My dad stopped singing, though, when his mother—my grandmother—died. She was killed in an automobile accident, along with my grandfather, before I was born..." He stopped suddenly, frowning at his beer bottle, wondering what had possessed him to make such a speech. It wasn't at all like him. "So," he said in determined conclusion, "that's it—my musical history in a nutshell. What about you?"

She stared at him over the top of her bottle, her gaze guileless—and utterly false. "Beg your pardon?"

"What started you—" he nodded in the general direction of the piano "—on the way to being...Phoenix?"

"Doc, I was born singing," she said. And she turned from him in sudden and complete withdrawal.

Chapter 6

As often as possible, when he was in med school and during his internship, Ethan had sought refuge from the craziness of Los Angeles and the stresses of the hospital by driving up the coast. For someone raised in the heartland, the ocean was a source of endless mystery and fascination, and he'd found that the cold, damp wind and astrigent sea smell helped clear his head. At the same time, the terrifying vastness of it seemed to lend a certain perspective to the tragedy and suffering he witnessed on a daily basis, that might otherwise have become too great a burden to bear.

He'd found pleasure in discovering secret places, stretches of coast as yet unspoiled by developers, where only the footprints of an occasional jogger or horseback rider marred the narrow ribbons of sand that separated the cliffs from the pounding surf and herons came to feed among the rocks at low tide. In the tide pools, he'd found the sea's small miracles—tiny fish and hermit crabs, and sea anemones that looked like flowers but shrank into all but invisible mud balls when he touched them with a curious finger.

Phoenix's withdrawal reminded him of that—the shrinking, the sudden transformation from beauty into dull brown nothingness. He felt the same sharp sense of disappointment and, at the same time, fascination.

What had he expected? That she would magically reveal to him things about herself that had been withheld from the rest of the world?

There was, he'd discovered, a great deal about Phoenix the world didn't know. He'd asked Mrs. Schmidt to find out what she could via the Internet through her computer-smart friend at city hall, but so far all that had netted him was information he could have read off the jacket of any one of her CDs. Phoenix's existence, it seemed, had begun with the Academy Awards telecast when she'd performed Rupert Dove's Oscar-nominated song, ''Love Child,'' from the movie of the same name when she was just fifteen. That song had eventually won her and its composer two Grammys apiece and made Phoenix a household word, but nobody seemed to know anything about her background. There was no mention anywhere of birthplace or family.

Even this place…this loft, Ethan thought, turning from the piano and the shuttered eyes to wander in casual curiosity. Expensively furnished, comfortable enough, even elegant in a Spartan sort of way, but utterly without personality. There were no books or magazines, no photographs or knickknacks, not even a single article of clothing carelessly dropped on a chair. He realized that he was probably somewhat of a slob himself—domestically, at least—after years of bachelor-student living, on a schedule that by necessity put housekeeping far down on the list of priorities, but even so, he found this lack of clutter…lonely.

''You lived here long?'' he asked, and was faintly surprised when her husky laugh came from close behind him. After the suddenness and totality of her withdrawal, he hadn't expected either the laughter or the nearness.

''Because it looks like nobody does?'' She moved up beside him, her eyes silvery with amusement. ''I don't live here, actually. This is just temporary, just until the album's in the can. And the tour…'' She left it hanging, her eyes going to the bank of windows that made up one whole side of the loft almost as if they'd been pulled there against her will.

He thought about asking her where she *did* live, but the memory of that shrinking withdrawal kept the question locked inside his mind. Though he did let her see it in his eyes, knowing she was probably expecting him to ask, and held her gaze long enough to give her the chance to answer if she wanted to.

When she didn't, he turned away from her once more, picking up the thread she'd left dangling. ''The tour—I've heard the rumor. Is it true that the reason you're starting this tour here, in this city, is because it's your hometown?''

He waited for her to come beside him again. When she slid a look sideways at him, shook her head and murmured, ''Rumors…'' he recognized his own tactic and almost laughed out loud.

Instead, he shook his head, saying nothing.

''You're doing it again,'' Phoenix said, taking a sip of beer.

''Doing what?''

''Laughing at me.''

He shrugged, not looking at her, watching the city turn from pink to purple and the lights wink on like stars in the dusk. ''Like I said before, it's not you I'm laughing at.''

''You're laughing at yourself.''

''That's right.''

''You want to tell me why?'' Her smile was sardonic. ''No offense, Doc, but like I said, you're not that funny.''

He smiled down at his beer bottle. The huskiness in her

voice...the growing dusk...her nearness—oh, he knew it wasn't the beer that was making his head swim.

"What you said...the way you said it—" and there was a burr in his voice he didn't recognize "—I've said that, you know—done the exact same thing, when people ask for information I don't want to give."

She was turned toward him; he could feel her eyes. "I just don't give out personal information, Doc. Sorry."

"But you did," he said softly. He turned now, to face her. The city seemed like an eavesdropper looking over his shoulder. "You told me your name." Again he waited for the shuddering rejection of her withdrawal.

Instead, her eyes shimmered at him in the twilight. The silence shimmered, too, felt in the skin like the subaudible hum of electricity. His heartbeat leaped into his consciousness, like the sudden awareness of a ticking clock.

"That wasn't for public consumption." Her lips seemed barely to move; her voice was a whisper, like windblown sand.

He answered as softly, "I never thought it was."

"You'd best just forget you ever heard that name."

"Why? It's a beautiful name...Joanna Dunn."

Joanna... Seeing the word form on his lips, hearing it whispered in his voice...something came into her heart, something warm and tiny, and incredibly fragile. Panic-stricken, desperately afraid of losing or destroying it somehow, she closed herself like protecting hands around it, hiding it from view.

Did he even know, she wondered, that he was leaning so close to her...that there were only a few scant inches between his lips and hers? Did he know how fast, how hard her heart was beating? Was his heart pounding, too? If he touched her now...if he touched any part of her, it would be like a thousand tiny points of light pricking her skin. Her skin would shiver and her breasts grow tight, and the melting warmth inside her would pour into her legs, and they would tremble and weaken....

Fear seized her. She made a small, wordless sound and whirled away from him, while somewhere in the back of her mind the Phoenix she thought she knew was jumping up and screeching *What are you doing? Are you crazy? He was about to kiss you—isn't that what you wanted?*

And the newcomer inside her, the stranger curled protectively around a newborn emotion that hadn't yet been given a name, replied, *Yes, oh, yes. But not like this.*

Ah, of course. The familiar Phoenix nodded in relief. *Because it wouldn't be on my terms. Because I'm not in control of my emotions.*

The newcomer merely smiled.

Shaken, she strode to the couch and sat, slipping off her sandles and pulling her bare feet under her. Sitting cross-legged like that—the lotus position, wasn't it? Wasn't yoga supposed to help with serenity?—she felt her confidence coming back. She took a swig of beer and said airily, "Hey, have a seat, Doc. You want to talk about those apartment buildings I own, or not?"

She watched him as he came and sat in one of the chairs across the coffee table from her, watching for signs that he'd been affected in any way by what had almost happened between them. But he seemed completely at ease, his eyes as calm and wise as always. *Shaman's eyes.*

"Yes, of course I do," he said quietly. "That's what I came for."

She felt a bright, hot flare of anger. "Are you sure?" she purred wickedly, and was delighted to see something flicker at last in those imperturbable eyes. "Come on, admit it— you came mostly out of curiosity. You wanted to see for yourself—'Phoenix in her natural habitat.'"

He studied her for a moment, eyes slightly narrowed.

Then he smiled. "I'm not going to deny it. Hell, what did you expect?"

"Hey—" she smiled back "—not that I mind. Goes with the territory!"

"Yeah, I guess." But the smile was gone, and the eyes were quiet again. Thoughtful.

"This doesn't have to be complicated, you know," Phoenix said, before she could begin to squirm under the weight of that scrutiny. "I do want to do the right thing. I'm not an ogre."

The beer bottle paused just shy of his lips. "I never thought you were."

"It's so simple, really. All you need to do is give Patrick—my business manager—a list. He'll see that it's taken care of."

Once again he took his time answering. She could hear the whisper of an exhalation as he leaned forward, the bottle of beer loosely clasped between his knees. "The thing is," he said quietly, "it really *isn't* that easy. I don't pretend to be an expert, but I think I'm fairly safe in saying what's wrong with those apartments isn't going to be fixed with some spackling and fresh paint."

"Then *what?*" She threw it at him almost desperately. "What is it you want from me?"

Perhaps because she asked it just that way—What do *you* want?—Ethan answered her truthfully. "I want you to come down there," he said, as intense as if at that very moment lives hung in the balance. "Look for yourself. Put on one of your disguises if you want to, but come with me." It was what *he* wanted; nobody had ever suggested such a thing to him, probably even Father Frank would think him out of his mind to dare expect *Phoenix* to personally tour a run-down tenement. The only thing he didn't understand was why he wanted it, and so badly.

She regarded him from across the bare expanse of coffee

table, sitting cross-legged and sharply upright, remote as a statue of Buddha. A statue with diamond eyes...

"That's not going to happen." Her voice was empty of emotion, smooth and dry as sunbaked clay. "I'll arrange to have Patrick send somebody down to evaluate the buildings. Based on that report, the decision will be made by the people I pay to handle my business affairs either to repair or demolish them." She lifted her hands and shoulders together as if to say, *That's it—end of story.*

She had more ways of withdrawing, Ethan thought, than any human being he'd ever met. Shrinking, hardening, freezing, distancing...even jokes and games...they were all the ways she had of protecting herself, of keeping other people from getting too close. He understood that, he supposed, given who she was. What he didn't understand was his own profound disappointment.

Keeping his movements deliberate and slow, he rose, walked to the counter and placed his empty beer bottle on the polished granite. There was no reason for him to stay longer. He'd gotten what he came for. He'd come to discuss repairing the buildings she owned in The Gardens, and he'd done that. He'd been informed of her plan of action, which he could now report back to Father Frank, who would in turn inform the tenants committee. He'd done very well, actually—and it was a shock to him to realize that fact, so deep and personal was his sense of failure.

He's leaving, Phoenix thought, and was bewildered by regret so sharp it was almost pain. Seized by a panic that was totally alien to her, she unfolded her legs and rose from the couch in one strong, fluid motion, waving her bottle like a flag. "Have another?" And to her own ears her voice sounded too high and just off-key.

"Thanks, but I'd better be going." His voice was off, too—his voice, his smile—everything seemed wrong.

"Stay and have dinner with me." She hadn't meant it to

sound like an order, dammit. But she wouldn't beg. *Phoenix does not beg.* She strolled toward him, making the movement of her body graceful, fluid, subtly inviting.

He watched her come, smiling in a way that for some reason made her throat ache. "It's tempting, but..." His eyes revealed a sadness she didn't understand. "It's been a long day."

"Well—" she drew herself together and halted, her arms folding across her body in a way that felt defensive and unfamiliar to her "—why don't you give me a call or come by tomorrow? Maybe I'll have some information for you by then."

He shook his head, narrowing his eyes in that way he had, as if the light had suddenly become too bright. "Can't tomorrow—my EMS ride-along night."

Anger flared inside her like a Fourth of July star burst. "Fine," she said silkily, looking away from him...dismissing him, "make it the next day, then. Or whenever." He was of no consequence to her. She didn't give a flying fig what he did or did not do.

He nodded and picked up his bottle, lifting it to her in a little salute. "Thanks for the beer." He set it down again and turned and left her standing there.

Phoenix stood absolutely motionless until she could no longer hear even the squeaking and creaking of the elevator. Then she lifted her bottle to her lips and drank the last of her beer. It burned like acid going down. Burned so, it brought the tears to her eyes.

Even after he noticed the young Doc Brown had gone on his way, Doveman stayed at the piano in the studio. Working. Playin' around. Waiting.

It was maybe fifteen, twenty minutes before he heard that old elevator creak and groan its way up...then back down again. "That good-lookin' doctor left mighty early," he said a few minutes later to the silent presence in the shadows. "I take that to mean things are not going well." He cackled, secure in knowing he was the only person alive could get away with talking to Phoenix like that.

Ignoring the jab, she came to the piano and slid herself onto the bench beside him. "Hey, Doveman, what you doing here so late?" She sounded tired.

"Oh, you know... 'Hard Sayin' Goodbye.' I been tryin' out some new harmonies...thought maybe a minor key..." He played a few bars for her.

She listened a bit, then jerked her shoulders impatiently, like a child. "You ever think," she said suddenly, "maybe it's the whole premise of the song that's wrong? I mean, 'Hello is easy'? *Sez who?*"

Doveman played a minor chord and left it hanging. "Hello *is* easy, girl. You and the doc, you done said hello already, and it was so easy you didn't even know you was doin' it." He played a few more chords, switching back and forth between major and minor. "It's what comes after— what happens between hello and goodbye—that matters. Hard, easy, good, bad—makes all the difference in the world."

She watched him for a while, not saying anything or singing, or humming along like she'd generally do, just watching his bent old fingers travel over the keys. When she finally spoke it was in a voice so low he had to stop playing to hear it.

"Doveman? He scares me."

Doveman shrugged. "Stay away from him, then."

She didn't reply, and after a while he added, "But you aren't going to do that, are you?"

He was laughing softly when she left him, his old heart light with hope and a whispered "Hallelujah" on his lips. The girl-child he loved like his own was hurtin', and he didn't think it odd at all that this should make him feel so glad. It was, after all, what he'd been praying for, oh, Lord, for so many years.

The lights were burning late that night in the master bedroom suite at 1600 Pennsylvania Avenue, Washington, D.C.

"If you'd call more often," the president of the United States was saying, "maybe you wouldn't give your stepmother and me a heart attack." He broke the connection, cradled the telephone and settled back into a bank of pillows, while the First Lady came to snuggle against him.

"What's goin' on, darlin'?" Dixie asked in the Texas drawl she mostly saved for him alone these days.

Rhett ran a hand through his hair—a habit he'd tried hard to kick and seldom indulged in anymore, except in private family moments like this. "Not sure," he said, frowning. Figuring out his son never had been easy for him; times like this it seemed well nigh impossible. "You know Ethan. He doesn't say a whole lot. It's hard to know what in the world is going on with him."

"He called," Dixie pointed out. "There must be something. Something big."

Rhett nodded, still feeling bemused. "He wants me to pull some strings—see if I can get some information for him."

"Wow. Must be something *really* big. If that boy is even willin' to acknowledge he's related to the most powerful man on the planet, much less take advantage of that fact..." Dixie was laughing when Rhett leaned over and kissed the top of her head.

"Hush, woman. Wait'll I tell you what he wants me to find out."

"Do tell."

"It's about a woman."

"Oh, my Lord. A *woman*." Dixie's eyes were wide. "You're kiddin' me."

Rhett was solemnly shaking his head. "God's truth. He wants me to find out everything I can about...are you ready? Phoenix."

"*Phoenix?* You mean the singer?"

"That's the one. Remind me to ask Mrs. Oxford tomorrow, will you? She'll know how to go about it."

"I'll take care of it, if you want me to," Dixie offered— as he'd hoped she would. Well, it was more or less her bailiwick, after all.

Rhett put out his arm and Dixie came into its curve with the sweet ease of long habit. "Didn't we meet her?" he asked as he reached with the other arm to turn off the lights.

"Yeah, we did. In Dallas, remember? Mama and Daddy's 'Feed The World' benefit. I thought she was..." she searched for the word "...dynamic."

"Hmm. Not at all Ethan's type, I wouldn't think."

"Hmm...well," Dixie murmured, "I know a whole lotta people wouldn't't've thought I was your type, either." She giggled, and he felt a surge of familiar delight as his mouth found hers.

Ethan had *chosen* to go back to the studio on Thursday. He told himself that. He told himself he had no reason not to, his evening was free, and, he thought, he might even get some more information to pass on to Frank and his committee. He told himself it was simply the sensible thing to do. That it was also the adult thing to do; staying away just because Phoenix had all but ordered him to come was the kind of childish game-playing he abhorred.

He told himself those things over and over again, repeating them in his mind like a difficult formula he wanted to commit to memory. He said them also like a mantra, trying to block out the other reason—probably the main reason, possibly the only *real* reason—for being there. Because. *He wanted to.*

He'd wanted to see her again. She was in his mind, and he couldn't get her out. She'd invaded his solitude like the noisy neighbors who'd lived downstairs during his student days, playing music at all hours of the day and night, never loud enough to warrant a complaint, just loud enough so that it was always there, eating away at his concentration, robbing him of the sleep he'd needed like an addict needs his drug. She tried to invade during his working hours, too, and the effort it took to hold her at bay left him feeling drained, every bit as exhausted as he'd been back in those nightmare med school days.

Her face hovered like a specter on the edges of his consciousness; her eyes mocked him, haunted him with memories of the little girl he'd been allowed to glimpse for one brief moment in their depths. Her voice, her husky laughter…they played unendingly in his head, like one of those annoying bits of song.

He'd thought—he'd hoped—that by taking some sort of definitive action he'd at last be able to put her out of his mind. So he'd called his dad. *My father—the president of the United States.* He, Ethan Brown, had called on the leader of the free world to get information for him about a rock star. It made him cringe to even think about it. What had he been thinking?

But…it had been late at night and he'd been desperate for sleep. Afterward, relieved, he'd finally drifted off with her words *I don't give out personal information* echoing in his mind, only to wake up with her scent lingering in his memory, as vividly as if she'd just risen from his bed, as if she'd just that moment stepped beyond his line of sight. So vividly, he'd almost expected to find the imprint of her head on the pillow next to his, and the sheets beside him still warm from her body, to hear her voice, singing in his shower.

Phoenix in his bed? What *was* he thinking?

Oh, she wanted him in *her* bed, of that he had no doubt. And how, he couldn't have said, but he somehow knew that the two did not amount to the same thing. Not the same thing at all.

So. He'd come back to her studio tonight of his own free will, because it was the grown-up, sensible, logical thing to do. And because he'd wanted to see her again. *Needed* to see her, if only to remind himself of all the reasons why he'd be a fool to choose to do so again.

Now, standing in the darkened recording studio watching Phoenix work, Ethan could only wonder what kind of fool he'd been to think he'd ever had a choice at all.

She didn't know he was there, yet. She was alone in the soundproof booth, and what he could see of her, from the waist up, was dressed in a tiger-print halter top that left her entire back bare, with her hair twisted and looped into a coil on the back of her head to keep it out of the way of the headphones. She seemed to him like some rare and exotic specimen in a museum case, a creature so fragile it must be protected even from the air, so delicate it might not survive the slightest touch.

He felt a sudden and extraordinary sadness, seeing her like this, isolated in her tiny glass island of light. Somewhere, he knew, a technician manipulated banks of controls, experimented with sound levels, adjusted the mix—terms he'd heard somewhere but didn't really understand. Knowing that didn't change the impression he had, of utter and complete *aloneness*. With her eyes tightly closed and headphones clamped over her ears, she was in her own private world…a place where, he realized with a deep sense of sorrow, he—and perhaps no one—could ever follow.

"She should be wrappin' it up soon." Ethan gave a start at the sound of a voice so close by, prompting a cackle of laughter and a raspy, "Didn't mean to make you jump."

He nodded at the man who'd come silently to stand beside

him—a black man with close-cropped gray hair and a frosting of white beard stubble, sinewy flesh hung on a frame that had once been for a larger man but was now in the process of shrinking. Something about the way those yellowed old eyes studied him told Ethan there was no need to explain.

"Just me, old Doveman." He offered his hand and Ethan took it; it felt papery but strong.

"Hi, I'm Ethan Brown."

"I know who you are." The piano man sounded amused. He jerked his head toward the recording booth. "She's been at it all afternoon long. That song been giving her fits. Just won't come the way she wants it." He shook his head in a resigned sort of way. "Well…she's a perfectionist, always has been. All the great ones are. And she's definitely one of the great ones."

Ethan didn't bother with a reply; the comment needed none. What he was thinking was that the statement had a certain irony, coming from Rupert Dove, a man who'd qualify as one of the greats in his own right.

It also occurred to him that standing here beside him was the one person who'd been with Phoenix since her beginnings, and of all the people in the world, just possibly the one who knew her best.

Impulsively, he asked, "How long have you known her?"

The piano man laughed softly. "Long enough."

"Since before she was Phoenix?" Ethan paused, conscious of the risk he was taking. "Did you know her when she was Joanna Dunn?"

Doveman turned his head and gave him a sharp look. "Be careful, boy. There's three people in this world knows about that."

"I wondered." Ethan let out a rush of breath as the significance of that sank in. "Why me?" he said in an angry whisper. "Why did she tell me, do you know?"

Doveman shrugged. "Who knows why any woman does what she does?"

"Especially *this* woman," said Ethan with a wry smile. He paused, and after a moment added in magnificent understatement, "She's a hard person to get to know."

The piano man acknowledged that with a cackle of rusty laughter, and then was silent, his gaze fixed on the lonely figure in the lighted booth. After a while he spoke in the slow, thoughtful way old people sometimes do, taking up just where they'd left it. "Hard on the outside maybe. But...that woman in there—" he nodded toward the booth while he turned his eyes to Ethan "—there's somethin' you got to know. Oh, she's done a lot of livin', that I know. A whole lot of livin.' But what you got to understand is, her heart's still a virgin. You know how you handle a virgin, don't you, boy? You take it slow...you go gentle. And you got to expect some resistance."

Chapter 7

Doc and Doveman—they'd been talking about her, Phoenix could tell. They had that "male bonding" look—and how men managed it was a mystery to her—a look that was at the same time superior and guilty as hell.

In a way, she was glad to have an excuse to be annoyed. An excuse to ignore the leap of—Oh, God, what *was* it— joy? Excitement? Whatever this terrible thing was that made her stomach drop and her heart lurch headlong into a new tempo when she stepped out of the booth and saw the two of them standing together. How long had they been there in the shadows? she wondered. Watching her.

A shiver that was not all displeasure raced along her skin, rousing senses and awakening nerve endings. Muscles and tendons coaxed her body, almost against her will, into a new and more sensual alignment.

"Hey, Doc," she said as she joined them. And she hid both the annoyance and excitement behind lowered lashes and a purr so blatantly sexy it could never be taken seriously. "So, you decided to come back and see me."

Oh, but that little half smile of his…how could she stay mad when he looked at her like that? Suddenly feeling like a high school kid hoping this cute boy was about to ask her to the dance, she slapped on brusqueness to cover her vulnerability in much the same way she might put on a baseball cap to hide her hair. "Too bad—I don't have any information for you—Patrick hasn't gotten back to me yet."

The doc merely shrugged, no more affected by her curtness than by her come-on. "So, I guess I came for nothing, then."

Panic and pride fought within her, anger hovering on the sidelines: *What's he going to do, walk out on me again? Well, God help him if he does. Nobody walks out on Phoenix twice. Nobody.*

Panic won, though there was no sign of it in her voice when she purred, "Oh, I don't think so, Doc."

And after that there was silence. Phoenix realized all at once that they were alone, she and the doc, alone in the empty studio. At some point Doveman had faded into the shadows and left them there, and she hadn't even noticed. She wondered if the doc had. In the stillness she could hear her own heart beating, feel his solid presence less than an arm's length away. She felt a sudden and intense desire to reach out and touch him, to lay her hand on his chest, to feel the beating of *his* heart. She wondered if—oh, she wanted it to be—his heart was beating as hard and fast as hers.

She didn't touch him. Instead she heard a scratchy voice say softly, "Where do we go from here, Doc?"

Even in the dim light she knew he'd narrowed his eyes in that way he had of doing when something had hit home. She knew, too, that his voice would be even quieter than usual when he answered. It was—she almost had to strain to hear it. "I'm not sure I know what you mean."

She turned to stroll without intent across the empty rehearsal hall, and he kept pace with her. Her stomach felt like a lump of lead and her heart as though it was in her throat, so she took special care to make her voice airy, her tone light. "The last time you were here, I asked you to stay and have dinner with me. You turned me down, Doc." She gave a low chuckle; he'd never know how it felt to her—like rocks tumbling in her chest. "That doesn't happen to me too often. I guess I'd like to know why you did it."

She could feel him there so close beside her, feel the heat of his body, his solid quietness. How strange, then, that when he spoke he seemed so far away, as if his voice had reached her from another dimension. "I guess I didn't see any point in staying."

"Any *point?*" She halted, and a beat later so did he. "For God's sake, Doc, I *like* you." Her voice was gravelly with irony. "Is that so strange? Call me crazy, but the other day I thought there was a chance you might like me, too."

He nodded. "I might." His face was turned toward her, but she couldn't see his expression. "To tell you the truth, I don't know whether I would or not. I don't know you well enough."

She laughed, a helpless little hiss of exasperation. "I thought that was the point in having dinner—to get to know each other. What is this, Catch-22?" She was trembling inside; never had she felt herself so far out on a slender, shaky limb.

His head was bowed, his arms folded across his body—the very picture of a kindly doctor intently listening while a patient tells him where it hurts. Again, in silhouette she saw him nod. "I guess it would be, except that, like I said the other day, I don't think you really want me—or anyone else—to know you. You seem to try hard to make sure nobody can."

Anger flared, and this time, because it felt so much better

than that terrible trembling vulnerability, she didn't try to hide it. "Why, because I don't give out—"

"—personal information," he finished with her, then nodded. "I'm no expert, but I imagine it's pretty hard to get to know a person without it."

"You asked about the *past*," Phoenix said furiously. "The past has nothing to do with who I am. Hey—you want to know about me? Ask me anything. *Now*. Go ahead—I'll tell you anything you want to know. Ask me, What do I like to do in my spare time? What's my favorite comfort food? Do sad movies make me cry? Answers—take long walks and dance in the rain, root beer floats, and never— but when little kids sing it just destroys me. Want more? Come on—*ask me, damn you!*"

For a second or two her oath hung there in its own vibrating echo. Then there was a quickly indrawn breath, and the doc's quiet voice. "All right, then, I'll ask you one. Tell me this. Who are you, really? Are you Phoenix, or Joanna Dunn?"

Then it was she who caught a breath, as a familiar little draught of fear blew threw her. *Who am I?* She saw herself standing at the windows looking out upon the city that had haunted her nightmares for as long as she could remember...heard Doveman's voice saying, "Maybe...you should just be yourself. Joanna Dunn." And with a deep sadness she didn't understand, heard herself answer, "Doveman, I haven't been that person for so long, I don't know who she is anymore."

She found that she was rubbing her upper arms, and that her skin was rough with goose bumps. Leaving the doc standing there, she walked slowly toward the bandstand, dimly backlit from this angle, the bulky shapes of sound equipment and speakers, instruments and mikes looking mysterious and abandoned, like some electronic age Stonehenge.

"Tell me, Doc," she said without turning, "what if I wasn't…'a rock-and-roll legend'? What if I was just some little ol' girl named Joanna Dunn, and you…"

"If I weren't…the First Son?" He said it without amusement, his voice harsh with unexpected emotion, and unexpectedly near.

She whirled to face him. "Yeah. Suppose you were just some guy named Brown—Bill, say, or Jim. Or…Leroy. What would you do? Right this minute—what would you do?"

The stage lights painted shadows across his face, then drew new ones as he smiled. "Bad *Bad* Leroy Brown? Me?"

"Hey—" she gave her head a defiant little toss, coaxing her self-confidence out from wherever it had been hiding "—where I live 'bad' is good. Answer my question, Leroy."

He moved closer, two slow, rocking steps. "First of all, I'm having trouble seeing you as just 'some little old' anybody."

She found that she was smiling, too, and bewilderingly at the same time felt an urge to cry. "*Joanna*, then." She felt as if the word had been ripped from her throat. *Oh, and damn you, Doc, for making me have to do this!* "So, what would you do? If it was just us…"

What would I do? Ethan knew what he *wanted* to do. What probably any red-blooded male would have wanted to do under the same circumstances. And from the way she was smiling at him, he was pretty sure she knew exactly what that was. So it was probably not so much presence of mind as good old-fashioned macho pride that made him instead say, "What would I do? Okay…right now, I guess…I'd probably be trying to get up the nerve to ask you out."

She gave a husky little chortle. "Nerve?"

"I'm known to be somewhat shy."

"Uh-huh." Her voice was rich with amusement. "Let's assume, for the sake of discussion, you did get up the nerve to ask. And I said yes. So, where would you take me?"

Oh, Lord. *Where would one take a Phoenix on a date?* Then he reminded himself, No—not Phoenix, just…Joanna.

"Well," he said, watching her, "after I showered for half an hour and about drowned myself in aftershave and cologne—"

"Uh—"

"What's the matter?"

"I'm not crazy about men's cologne."

"Scratch the cologne, then…"

"And I rather like your beard."

"Okay, scratch the aftershave, too—just lots of soap, mouthwash and deodorant, I guess. Man—you're hard on a guy's self-confidence, you know that?"

"So I've been told," she murmured. There was a pause while she pulled the fantasy back into place, like the slipping pieces of a complicated costume. "Okay, so assuming your grooming passes muster, then what?"

"Then, since my finances—" and he cleared his throat delicately "—are a little tight—"

"You're cheap, you mean."

"—I guess I'd pick you up and take you somewhere for Chinese food—"

"Chinese!" He heard surprised approval in her voice.

"Yeah," said Ethan, "because it's cheap, and because I'm pretty good with chopsticks, and I'm trying to impress you."

Her laughter was a delighted hiccup that invited him to join in. And there was something wickedly tempting about it, too, rather like being invited to go skinny-dipping, or sneaking a smoke—or a kiss—behind the school gym during recess. He felt prickles of response roll across his skin like a wave of static electricity, raising awareness like the fine hairs on his arms and the back of his neck.

"I'm already impressed," she murmured. "And then?"

"Then…as I said, money's tight, so I guess we'd go for a walk along the riverfront, and we'd come to a place where there's a live band playing, and the music is spilling out into the street, and we'd stop for a while and listen. And maybe…you'd let me take your hand."

"*Let* you? If you didn't, I'd think there was something wrong with you. That maybe you didn't like me, or else you're—"

"Shy," said Ethan, smiling. "I told you that, remember?"

"Shy…right…" she murmured, and with flawless timing, reached up and with one invisible movement released whatever it was that had been holding her hair up and out of the way of the headphones. He watched, fascinated, as the blue-black mass uncoiled itself and slithered down her bare back like a living thing, and was unprepared when a wave of desire hit him like a sucker punch, leaving him feeling dazed and slightly weak in the knees.

"And then?"

He blinked away grogginess and cleared his throat. "Then…" But, oh, Lord, what was this thickness in his speech, like someone struggling out from under anesthetic? Or someone under the influence of a powerful drug? *A drug? Oh, yeah…a drug named Phoenix.* "That would depend," he said carefully.

"On what?"

"On…how things are going. How we both feel. If it feels right, maybe we go back to my place—"

"*Your* place?"

"*My* place," he said firmly, "and we put on some music, and we talk, maybe dance a little. And if we get hungry, we feed each other leftover Chinese food straight out of the take-home boxes…''

''Because you're good with chopsticks, and you want to impress me.''

''Right…''

''And then?'' But he could barely hear her whisper over the thumping of his heart.

He paused and then replied with gravel in his voice, ''We get to know each other.''

She didn't reply at once, and in the silence, looking at her, it struck him suddenly that she wasn't playing a game any longer, that for reasons he couldn't begin to imagine, she was vulnerable to him. Maybe even afraid. *We get to know each other,* he'd said to her. Was it those words that had put that look in her eyes? A look of fear and longing…

Go on, ask me! She'd hurled it at him too quickly, brash and full of bravado, he realized now, like a cornered child with her back against the wall. He wondered if she knew how much she'd revealed about herself with those off-the-top-of-her-head answers. *Dance in the rain…root beer floats… small children singing…* They were the answers a very young girl might give, he thought, remembering that glimpse he'd once caught in her eyes of eagerness, innocence and yearning. A lonely little girl standing on the edge of the playground, watching the other kids' games.

The vision vanished a moment later, though. There was nothing remotely childlike about her laughter, or the husky burr in her voice when she said, ''Okay, then. Let's do it.''

He looked at her, hating to destroy the moment, knowing his words would snuff the sweet little flame of liking that had kindled between them so unexpectedly, there in her darkened studio. The game had been fun, for him a sidetrip into fantasy that was all the more exciting because it was so completely against his nature. But Ethan was a doctor;

he was also the son of the president of the United States. He couldn't afford to believe in fantasy.

In the end he said nothing, but only smiled and shook his head.

"Come on, Leroy." She hooked her arm through his. "You asked me out on a date, I'm accepting. You said you'd pick me up, you're here, I'm ready, so…pick away. I have my heart set on dim sum."

"Joanna…"

"Yes, Leroy?"

He was fighting laughter. She was batting her eyelashes at him so outrageously, and he didn't know whether to grab her and pull her into his arms or just grab her and shake her. He was fairly sure, though, which of those things he'd wind up doing if he were insane enough to put his hands on her. So he said mildly instead, "Aren't you forgetting something? Like…a six-and-a-half-foot bodyguard?"

"*Ethan Brown* has a bodyguard," she reminded him. "Leroy doesn't."

"Leroy also doesn't have a car. Do you—uh, does Joanna?"

"Ah." She was silent for perhaps two beats. Then she held up one finger and murmured, "Don't go 'way," and before he could stop her she was running across the studio, vanishing into the shadows.

He watched her, as always fascinated by the way she moved, like some wild creature… *Tiger, tiger*… Yes, a tiger, he thought, disappearing in tall grass. He'd be crazy to go after her. She'd eat a man alive.

But, was he also crazy to *like* her? He'd been determined not to, had come here armed against the possibility, had steadfastly dismissed any attraction he felt for her as the remnants of teenaged fantasies. What, then, had changed? Watching her just now, in spite of the sexy rock star clothes, the buzz beneath his breastbone had felt less like the adrenaline rush of lust and more like the sweet warmth of…*liking?*

But that seemed too pale a word, somehow.

What was happening, he realized, was that when he looked at her now he wasn't seeing a rock-and-roll superstar named Phoenix. What he felt when he looked at her was nothing like the adolescent panting after a sex symbol he remembered—with some embarrassment still—from his high school days. What it was was desire, pure and simple— grown-up desire, of one man for one particular woman. Somehow, in just a few minutes, with her little game of make-believe she'd managed to transform herself into a woman—a girl, really, for she'd also seemed to become magically younger—named Joanna Dunn. And had drawn him into the game with her and made him believe in it.

He wondered whether it had been so easy for her to make him believe because of her incredible magnetism, the same charisma that had held concert audiences in thrall the world over…or because he just wanted so much to believe. He'd do well, he told himself, to remember that this woman was above all things a performer—even for an audience of one.

"Here you go." She was back, slightly out of breath but more from excitement, he thought, than exertion. He could see it shining in her eyes as she held up something small and metal, something that jingled when she shook it, picked up a bit of light from somewhere and winked it back at him like a conspirator in her mischief. "Wheels." He caught the keys she tossed to him one-handed. "I borrowed them from Stewart, the sound man." Her voice was rich with self-congratulation. "It's Japanese—a 'sport-utility vehicle,' sort of brownish, he said—that should be anonymous enough, don't you think? Stewart says everybody's driving them now." She hooked her arm through his in the way that was becoming familiar to him and gave it a squeeze. She was smug, altogether pleased with herself, as she added, "Come on, Leroy—you drive."

What could he say to that? How did a man say no to Phoenix? Though the truth was, he had no wish at all to say no. He was enjoying the game too much, even knowing full well that it *was* exactly that—a game. Even though he hadn't forgotten for a minute what it was that had brought him there. Just for good measure he said it silently, like a mantra, *Michael Parker, and his momma, Louise.*

"Where is this brownish Japanese SUV?" he inquired as he allowed her to tow him along.

"All the guys park out back, where the loading bays are. This building used to be a warehouse, did you know that?"

"Never woulda guessed," said Ethan. But he was smiling, and she laughed with him, a rich little chortle that warmed his insides like a slug of straight whiskey.

He was thinking, with a shameful absense of regret, about Secret Service Agent Carl Friedenburg, sitting in an anonymous sedan with tinted windows parked in a Handicapped zone just outside the building's street entrance. He knew he should find a way to let his protection know there'd been a change in plans, as he'd done the last time Phoenix hijacked him. He also knew he wasn't going to. Childish, perhaps. Foolish, undoubtedly. *But...just this once.*

Early in his father's first term, chafing under the restrictions placed upon him by his family's explosion into the limelight and resentful of the loss of his cherished privacy, Ethan had taken pleasure in finding ways to outwit the United States Secret Service and its agents charged with the responsibility for protecting his life. It was Dixie who had finally set him straight. On one of his rare visits to his family's new and temporary home, she'd sat him down in the dauntingly elegant upstairs sitting room and told him the story of how his sister, Lauren, had been kidnapped on the eve of his father's nomination by a militia organization bent on destroying the election process. Bent on, in effect, usurping the two-centuries-old peaceful transfer of power as set forth in the Constitution. In other words, a coup.

He'd understood for the first time then, what it would mean to the country—what it would mean to his father—if he or Lauren were to be taken hostage. Understood that it would render Rhett Brown incapable of fulfilling the obligations of his office every bit as surely as a bullet to the brain. He'd done his best, ever since, to cooperate in seeing that such a thing never happened.

He wasn't sure how he was going to justify this, when it came time to face the music. He didn't want to think about that right now, to tell the truth. For now he wasn't First Son Ethan Brown, anyway, just some guy named Leroy Brown, out for the evening with a girl named Joanna Dunn.

"There—that must be it." Pointing, she gave his arm an excited little squeeze as they hurried down the concrete steps that led from the loading docks to the parking lot. "Here— you have to press the button on that little key chain thingy. It'll squeak if it's the right one."

Ethan pressed the button. A brown sport-utility vehicle parked with its nose against the dock not only chirped a response, but obligingly unlocked its doors and turned on its interior lights as well. Leroy and Joanna grinned delightedly at each other.

While Leroy was still wondering whether or not he should open the door for her, Joanna ran around to the passenger side of the SUV and hopped in. Leroy opened the driver's side door and slid behind the wheel. He felt like a kid, holding back nervous laughter while the nerves in his belly jumped and twitched with a glorious excitement.

It took him a minute to find where the key went, but he finally got it inserted. "Well," he said, "here goes."

She gave a low chuckle. "You sure you know how to drive?"

"I did once." He was trying to think how long it had been since he'd driven himself anywhere. Roughly seven years, he imagined. He fastened his seat belt, then turned the key. He felt unbelievably pleased when the engine fired. Throwing Joanna a triumphant look, he ran his window down and shifted into reverse. "Buckle up," he said confidently.

The night was warm and muggy, the way it can be on the east coast in June. Humidity not yet thick enough to be called fog made halos around the streetlights, and the air felt soft on the skin. While Leroy backed the SUV out of its parking space, Joanna ran her window down all the way and propped her elbow on the sill. They went bumping off across the potholed parking lot and into a deserted street, and the wind reached in through the open windows and grabbed playfully at her hair. Instead of rolling up the window, she caught her hair back with her hand and, eyes closed, lifted her face to the wind.

Glancing at her, Ethan felt a clutching at his throat and a burning in his eyes, the way it did sometimes, once in a great, great while, when something overwhelmingly beautiful caught him by surprise. He drew a careful breath and looked away again. *I wonder what she's thinking....*

I'm having fun, Joanna thought. It was so much easier than she'd expected, being Joanna Dunn. Why had she been so frightened by the prospect?

I haven't been that person for so long, I don't even know who she is.... She'd said that to Doveman, and it was true. But if she didn't know who Joanna was, then she could be anything she wanted her to be, couldn't she? The thought made her feel almost giddy—carefree and young and slightly naughty, like a child playing hooky from school.

The car had stopped moving. Opening her eyes, she saw that they'd come to an intersection policed by a flashing red light. Instead of moving on again, for some reason her "date" was sitting motionless, frowning at the windshield in front of him.

"What's happening?" she asked, her heart quickening. Was he having second thoughts already? Oh, but she didn't want the game to be over! She didn't want the evening to end.

Still frowning, he glanced her way but past her, looking up the street, then down the other way. "I'm not sure. Which way's the river?"

She burst out laughing, half with relief. "I don't believe it—a guy who asks directions!"

He waited a moment, then prompted with a touch of impatience, "Well?"

She raised both hands and shoulders in an exaggerated I don't know. "You've been here twice, which way did you come?"

"I don't know, I wasn't driving. When you aren't driving you don't pay attention." He was obviously vexed by his ignorance—typical male. Oh, she liked this Leroy Brown. He was so much easier to understand than Ethan.

She nodded and murmured, "I suppose that's true."

He glanced at her. "How long has it been since *you* drove yourself anywhere?"

She didn't have to think about it. "That would be…never."

"*Never?* You mean you don't—"

"Nope—never learned to drive. Don't know how." She stared defiantly into the intensity of his gaze, refusing to yield to the unspoken pressure to explain.

She could have told him that on her sixteenth birthday, the milestone that would have made her eligible for a driver's license in California, the state she'd been living in at the time, Phoenix had performed before a sell-out crowd at The Forum, and that under the circumstances, learning how to drive a car had seemed pretty irrelevant.

But that had been Phoenix. Tonight she was Joanna, and didn't want to think about Phoenix at all.

"What the hell, Leroy," she cried, "let's take a chance. Hey, we have a fifty-fifty shot at being right." Clamping one hand over her eyes, she stuck her other arm out the open window and pointed. "*That* way!"

"That way it is," Ethan said, and felt himself begin to smile as he pulled forward and made a hard right. Her laughter was impossible to resist.

He wasn't really all that lost. Once he located the river he knew he could find his way back to his own neighborhood, and from there to the shopping center where there was a nice little Chinese restaurant both he and the Secret Service knew well.

"Water dead ahead!" she crowed. "Am I a good navigator, or *what?*"

"Best I ever had," said Ethan. But he knew exactly where he was, now, and the knowledge was a heaviness inside him. Guilt sat in his chest like a lump of clay.

They were coming to the traffic light at the intersection with the busy boulevard that ran along the riverfront. If he turned left there, they would come very shortly to the shopping center and the restaurant; from there it was a few blocks up the hill to his apartment on the second floor—the Secret Service occupied the first—of a modest row house in a moderately run-down middle-class neighborhood. But if he turned right…in an equally short time they would come to Church Street. Another right, then a few more blocks and they would be at the clinic. And beyond that, just a stone's throw away from St. Jude's Church, lay the boundaries of the urban jungle known as The Gardens.

It would be so easy. Phoenix wouldn't even know where he was taking her until it was too late, and even if she did, what could she do? She couldn't drive herself, and only a woman bent on suicide—or a raving lunatic—would dare venture out alone on those streets at night.

He'd wanted to get her down there to The Gardens to see the buildings she owned with her own eyes, and this was his chance. He might never have another one like it.

Not only his chance, he reminded himself. It was his duty.

Chapter 8

So easy.

The silence in the car felt viscous. Ethan moved in the silence as if through heavy mud, or in the kind of nightmare where the arms and legs felt like lead and the heart pounded and lungs burned with futile efforts to make them do his bidding. In that same silence he watched his hand swim through the unforgiving substance that had taken the place of air and grasp the turn indicator lever.

He watched the arrow slowly blink: *left...left...left...left.*

"You know where you're going?" Her voice sounded hollow to him, as if it came from a great distance.

Grimly, he nodded. The light changed, and he pulled out into the intersection. "I promised you Chinese," he said as he made the turn. "The only place I know of is right down here a ways. It's not far from where I live, so I eat there quite a bit."

"Ah," she said. But he thought she sounded wary, and he could feel her eyes on him, as if she sensed...something.

Had heard something in his voice. Glancing at her, he saw that the fun and laughter had gone from her eyes, and where it had been now there was uncertainty, suspicion, even fear.

He tasted regret, a sharp bitterness on the back of his tongue. The game was slipping away. He'd lost Leroy, and didn't know how to get him back. And if he lost Leroy, what would become of Joanna? Would he lose her, too? Forever? The thought filled him with an aching sense of loss. He suddenly knew with profound certainty that he didn't want to lose Joanna.

"The food's not bad," he said, speaking rapidly, fending off despair. "But the best thing about the place is that it's family owned and operated—very old-world. I've been going in there for about six months now, and I don't know if they've recognized me or not, but if they have, they're too polite to say anything."

She said nothing for a heartbeat, then gave a sudden sharp cry and clamped one hand to the top of her head.

Ethan threw her a look, his own heart thumping. "What?"

"My hat—I forgot it. I don't have anything—not even my glasses. And in these clothes— Oh…" She broke off, swearing under her breath. Ethan could see her struggling against the shoulder belt, tugging at her hair, trying to rake some order into it with her fingers.

"Hey," he said, forcing laughter, "don't worry about it. Like I told you, even if they do recognize you, they're not going to make a fuss. They're way too polite for that. Besides—" a break in traffic came and he made a fast left turn into the shopping center parking lot "—who's gonna pay any attention to us? We're just Leroy and Joanna, remember?" He glanced over at her and caught a wild, bright look in her eyes—a look that as a doctor he knew very well, had seen way too many times. Panic—pure panic.

He pulled into the first empty parking space he came to,

silently cursing himself. Because it had just come to him that she *was* "just Joanna," and that in a way, that was her problem.

As Joanna, she'd feel unprepared. Unprotected. Phoenix was comfortable with celebrity; she'd had a lifetime's worth of experience in handling herself in public, coping with adoring crowds and pushy fans. Joanna Dunn, on the other hand—whomever she was—very probably had no experience with any of those things.

As Phoenix she knew how to wear disguises, keep the walls up, keep her distance. As Joanna she was *vulnerable*.

He put the SUV in park and turned off the key. Freed from his seat belt, he turned to her, smiling. "Here," he murmured—or some such thing. He had no real awareness of the words he used. All he saw were her eyes, silvery in the dimness; all he heard was the distressed sound of her breathing; all he felt were the rounds of her shoulders fitting themselves sweetly into his palms. Her scent filled his nostrils, faint and heady as the first whiff of new grass in the springtime.

He saw her fleeting look of surprise when he indicated with the pressure of his fingers that she should turn, not toward him, but away. Then, with a slight *giving* in her shoulders and the accepting sigh of an exhalation, she bowed her head, let go of her hair and gave it into *his* keeping. He gathered it into his hands, concentrating on the warmth and weight and feel of it, mostly to keep himself from the paralyzing realization of what he was doing. The texture was unexpected—springy, not soft and silky as he'd imagined. But he shouldn't have expected softness, not with this woman. She was much too vibrant, too full of life and energy for softness.

"What do you want to do with it?" he asked.

"Hmm…I dunno…braid it, I guess…" There was a pause, and then, "Y'sure you know how?"

Ethan laughed, a chuckle low in his throat, and began deftly to divide her hair into three parts. Under the heavy mass of hair her neck was warm, humid...damp with sweat. The desire to put his mouth there became so powerful he couldn't breathe, and the lack of oxygen made him dizzy.

He had no way of knowing how many seconds passed before she murmured, "Hmm...guess you do know. Don't think they teach that in med school. What was it, a long-haired girlfriend?"

He laughed again, not because he thought anything was amusing, but because he so badly needed the loosening effect it had on him. His body was tight with wanting her, every muscle tense with self-control. Slowly, slowly, his hands slid the length of each hank of hair, weaving in and out, exchanging, laying one over the other... Gradually, he felt the muscles in his jaws unclench and his breathing flow again.

"When I was little..." he began slowly, his voice gruff because talking about himself had never been easy. "My sister, Lolly—Lauren—had a horse. And she was nuts about that horse. It seemed to me she spent *all* her time brushing, combing, feeding and riding that horse. I was more than a little jealous, I guess—up to that time it had been pretty much just the two of us. Anyway, I used to hang around the stables, whining for attention, begging for something to do. Lolly was pretty bossy, and she really didn't want anybody but her touching her precious horse, but once in a while she'd hand me a brush or something and let me help. Then, I guess she'd seen it in a magazine, or on television or something—I don't know where—but she got this idea she wanted to braid the horse's mane and tail. Well, she started out fine, all gung ho, but after a while..." he paused to smile at the memory. "Let's just say, that horse had a *lot* of hair. And there I was, the perfect sucker. She put me up on a stool and showed me how, and I mean I stood for *hours,* braiding that horse's mane. My arms ached, my back hurt, I *itched...* Anyway, that's how I learned to braid hair.

"You know, come to think of it—" he leaned back to get a better look "—your hair's just about the same color that horse's tail was."

She gave her rusty little guffaw. "A horse's ass— I'm flattered." And her voice was music to his ears. Because it was Joanna's voice again—husky, playfully wicked.

She held herself still, head cocked at a listening angle, listening with her whole body for any signals his might send her. The rhythm of his hands, the gentle tugging...there was something magical in it, she thought, like some mysterious eastern massage therapy, maybe. Except that, instead of sending her into a state of blissful relaxation, this massage seemed to have awakened every nerve in her body. Her scalp tingled; her breasts felt so tight they *hurt.* The skin on her naked back burned with awareness. Nerves in the sensitive ticklish part of her flinched in anticipation of his touch. I am tinder, she thought, waiting for the spark. All it would take is a touch. *One...touch.*

"All done." His voice so near sent a shiver careening between her shoulder blades. "Got anything to tie it with?"

He lifted the end of the braid and passed it over her shoulder. If he touches me, she thought... *All he'd have to do is lay a hand there now...brush the backs of his fingers down the side of my neck...stroke with one finger over the bumps of my spine...*

She would turn, then, and it would be so easy... He was so near, so enticingly near. She closed her eyes and inhaled deeply, and was overcome with a terrible sense of longing at the scent of him, like an alcoholic, she thought, savoring the smell of whiskey.

What would it be like to kiss him? She'd kissed so many men in her lifetime, why should she imagine kissing *this* man would be any different? And yet, she knew that it would be. Somehow, she *knew.* And perhaps it was because of that knowledge that the thought of kissing him filled her with a longing so intense it felt like pain. Longing…and fear, too. Fear that it might not ever happen. Fear that, for the first time in her life, with *this* particular man, it might not be within her power to make it happen.

She felt a surge of anger at that thought. She was *Phoenix.* Phoenix did not suffer rejection. Phoenix did not know self-doubt!

From somewhere a quiet voice responded: *No, but apparently Joanna does.*

But how can she? Phoenix argued. I can make her anything I want her to be.

And the answer came, amused: *Are you sure?*

"Look, Joanna—if you don't want to go in, I understand." He touched her arm and she jumped as if he'd burned her.

What's the matter with you? Phoenix furiously scolded herself. *Quit acting like a damned virgin!*

Then it struck her, with a clarity that made her gasp. That was it in a nutshell, wasn't it? In a very real sense, Joanna *was* a virgin. It might have been a long time since Phoenix had given herself to a man, but Joanna? Joanna never had. Hell, no wonder she had doubts!

Laughter rippled through her. This might turn out to be more fun than I expected, Phoenix thought, shivering with a new delight. All the excitement of the first time, and none of the pain…

Her laughter had a curious effect on Ethan. It wafted through the car like a cool fresh breeze, stirring, diluting and finally dissipating the sultry heat, the smell and taste and tension of sex. Oh, the desire was still there, raging hot and heavy in his belly, but it came now with an edge of disappointment, an awareness of a moment forever lost to him. The laughter was rich and full of confidence—a delightful and contagious sound. But there was nothing vulnerable about it. And as he watched the lights and shadows cast by passing cars chase each other across her naked back, he realized that he'd liked her vulnerability, liked it very much. More than that. It had touched him deeply, and he *missed* it. At the same time, as someone raised by strong, bossy and independent women, Ethan wondered what that said about *his* character, and felt vaguely ashamed.

"You don't have to come in if you don't want to," he said softly. His hand hovered near her shoulder, tingling with the pressure building in its muscles, nerves and tendons to *touch*. "I can go in and order take-out for both of us." Fascinated, he watched her loop the bottom third of her braid into a knot.

She turned her head to look at him. The thick rope of her hair caressed her cheek, hiding her smile while her eyes sparkled at him like a maiden flirting over the edge of a fan. "But," she purred in a voice rich with double meanings, "you don't know what I like."

Juices pooled at the back of his throat. "That's true."

"I'll go in with you, and we can order take-out for both of us. You said your place is near here?"

He motioned with his head. "Just up the hill."

"Sounds good to me." She reached for the door handle while her braid slithered over her shoulder and dropped like a weighted mantle down her back.

Shaking his head to clear it of the cobwebs induced by her nearness—and remembering just in time to remove the keys from the ignition—Ethan opened his door and got out. She came around the car to join him, her eyes silvery in the artificial light, shining with excitement, and came against him so naturally he didn't have time to be surprised. Her hip brushed his; her arm slid around his waist. His arm dropped across her shoulders as if it had been doing so all his life.

"Hey, Leroy."

"Hey, Joanna."

Laughter came like breath to them, blown back by a breeze of their own making as they crossed the parking lot, matching long, exuberant strides. Heads turned and eyes followed them, accompanied by smiles of envy, or perhaps simply vicarious enjoyment.

"Protective coloring," Joanna said in a whisper that quivered with laughter, leaning close to his ear. "A handsome young couple out on the town..."

"That's us," Ethan murmured as he held the China Palace's laquered red-and-gold door for her.

"Everybody looks, nobody sees..."

"Sounds like a song title."

She threw him a sharp, bright look but didn't reply.

Then for a while they were busy poring over the menu and arguing about each other's choices like a couple of long-standing. Joanna insisted on the Szechuan items labeled on the menu with little warning tongues of flame; Ethan replied loftily that he wasn't into pain with his food. Joanna scoffed at Ethan's preference for the sweet-'n'-sour and honeyed entreés, dismissing them as "kid stuff." Ethan had never tried dim sum; Joanna promised him he'd love it, but he wasn't convinced.

In the end they ordered way more food than the two of them could possibly eat, and while it was being prepared, they walked around the shopping center looking in store windows. Most of the smaller shops were closed at that hour on a week night, but a grocery store and pharmacy down at the far end of the shopping center was doing a booming business, and a shop selling frozen yogurt and ice cream cones was crowded and noisy with teenagers. They paused outside the ice-cream shop and looked at each other with raised eyebrows: *Shall we? What do you think?* Then, smiled, shook their heads and moved on.

People were all around them, coming and going between the parking lot and the stores, paying them no attention, intent on their own business—all sorts of people, all ages and genders, races and descriptions, many in family groups, carrying small children, pushing babies in strollers. Confident in her ''disguise,'' Joanna moved among them as if they didn't exist, and somehow Ethan felt himself included in the enchantment, wrapped up with her in her magic cloak of invisibility. A dangerous notion, he knew, and there would be hell to pay when the Service found out about this, but for tonight he was having a hard time caring.

''What?'' Joanna said, giving his arm a little squeeze, and he realized only then that he'd stopped walking.

He said nothing for a second or two, then looked down at her. ''Nothing, really. I was just thinking, it's been a long time since I've enjoyed myself this much.''

But if that's true, Phoenix thought, then why isn't he smiling? Why is there such sadness in his eyes?

Aloud, she said with a teasing laugh, ''Is that because you're out with me? Or because you've escaped without your bodyguards?''

His smile was off-center. ''Both. Don't you see, it's the combination of the two that's important.''

''Ah. Of course.''

They were standing in the shadowed doorway of a closed-up shop, arms linked, shoulders touching. It should have been an easy thing, Phoenix thought, to stretch up just a little bit and kiss him. But for some reason it seemed an impossibility. His eyes still held that sadness as he watched the flow of people to and from the parking lot. For the moment he'd gone somewhere far away from her, and the distance between them was too wide to bridge.

Jealous, she fought to bring him back. ''It's not so terrible, you know—being famous. I manage to actually enjoy life most of the time.''

He gave her a quick smile, the kind an indulgent parent might give an adorable but demanding child. "Yes, but it's different for you. You chose that life. I didn't."

They were walking slowly now, back the way they'd come, no longer pretending to be Leroy and Joanna. No longer laughing. No longer touching.

After a while Phoenix said softly, "What do you miss, Doc? About your old life—before you—"

"Became First Son?" He raked a hand through his hair—a gesture that seemed to embarrass him, because he then jammed both hands between his arms and sides and drew a sharp breath. "Oh, man. So many things. Little things. Everyday things. You know?"

But she shook her head; she couldn't remember anything different.

It was a while before he spoke again, and then it was in the same slow, self-deprecating way he'd told her about braiding the horse's mane. "My first year at UCLA, I was pretty lost. Living in the dorm, homesick like you wouldn't believe. I used to tool around campus on my bicycle, go down to Westwood, walk around the Village and mingle with the tourists. Second year was better. I had friends, I was learning my way around L.A. Even got brave enough to drive the freeways, which opened up all kinds of possibilities. On breaks we used to drive up to the mountains to go skiing, or we'd go to the beach, or maybe the desert. Third year was even better. We'd go to these little hole-in-the-wall clubs to listen to bands nobody'd ever heard of, or for the heck of it, maybe drive down to Venice Beach and wander among the weirdos. Los Angeles was like this great zoo of humanity, and it was all mine, to study or just…enjoy. And then…"

"Then," Phoenix said with a little ripple of sympathetic laughter, "Papa Brown went to the White House." But what she could see of his answering smile had no amusement in it.

"It started that summer, actually, right before the national convention. Before I even knew what was happening, these large, totally humorless men had taken charge of my life. I was taken to Dallas, where the convention was being held, to be with my dad and Dixie—I wasn't asked, you understand, just more or less collected, like a stray piece of luggage. Later I found out it was because my sister, Lauren, had been kidnapped by some sort of militia organization trying to blackmail my dad into pulling out of the race, but at the time I was resentful as hell."

"I can understand that," Phoenix murmured.

He glanced at her as if he doubted it. "Anyway, the next couple of years were pretty grim. There'd been a lot of threats—I guess there always are, but it was worse because of Dad's stand on gun control. So the Service was *very* tense. There was no more mingling with crowds, no more foolish excursions into dangerous but fascinating parts of the city—which I'm sure made my parents much happier. The bike went to some kids' charity. Since then—for the last seven years—if I want to go anywhere, I'm driven there in a car with tinted windows. My roommates are Secret Service agents—great people, and I do trust them with my life, but—for some reason they are physically incapable of smiling."

The last was delivered with a smile of his own—wry, but real. He'd seemed determined to lighten his mood and tone with that cataloging of his grievances, Phoenix noticed, as if he felt ashamed for complaining. Something stirred within her, a strange unrest she did not, for a moment, recognize as anger because it was on someone else's behalf rather than her own. What was this? *Empathy?* Highly unlikely; Phoenix had not gotten where she was by getting bogged down in other people's troubles.

She was silent, distracted, her mind awhirl as she waited for Ethan to open the restaurant's gaudy red-and-gold door for her. It didn't occur to her then that perhaps the unfamiliar feelings of empathy were Joanna's.

Later, back in the brown SUV, steeped in the warm peanuty smells wafting from the two large bags packed full of white cardboard cartons tucked in around her feet, the confused, disoriented feeling persisted. Like getting off of a merry-go-round and finding yourself on the opposite side from where you got on. Suddenly the world seemed different.

"Tell me something," she said, when Ethan had the car started and everything seemed to be buckled in, lighted up and ready to go. "What did you want…before all this happened, before you got famous? What kind of life did you see yourself having?" The words felt scratchy and unfamiliar in her throat; it wasn't the kind of question Phoenix would normally think to ask of anyone.

"What kind of life did I see myself having?" He repeated it with a surprised chuckle. Then he took his time answering, and when he did speak, there were no traces of the laughter. "I saw myself opening up my medical practice in a little town straight out of Norman Rockwell, some little town that really needed a doctor, most likely somewhere in Iowa. I'd have a wife and some kids and a modest house, and I'd spend my life helping people feel better."

"And now?" And why was there an ache in her throat, and a lump the size of Kansas? She looked over at him and saw him shrug as he put the car in gear.

"That hasn't changed." He glanced at her, his eyes quiet and dark. *Shaman's eyes.* "A wife and kids…helping people. What else is there?"

What else is there? The question screamed like a Klaxon in her mind, trying desperately to drown the timid little voice she didn't want to hear. The voice she hated, never

ever wanted to acknowledge. The voice that could not possibly exist inside *her.* Not Phoenix.

But it did exist, and she heard it anyway—the voice of the little girl no one thought to invite to the party. *What about me? What about me?*

Fear—and hatred—of her own vulnerability made her cruel. Where do you fit in his sweet little scenario? she mocked herself? The answer is, stupid—*you don't.* No part for you in that play, no way José. A wife? Kiddies? *Phoenix?* Who are you kidding?

She was astonished when the voice argued, with surprising tenacity for one so timid: *Why not? Others have done it—Cher, Madonna, Streisand—why not Phoenix?*

The brown sport-utility vehicle rolled through quiet streets lined with old trees and old row houses made of brick and trimmed with curlicues of wrought iron. Behind iron window guards, yellow light cast welcoming beacons in the darkness. People sat on cement steps, talking or making out in the warm, humid night. Somewhere a dog barked…then another. A moment later she heard it, too—the distant wail of a siren. And in spite of the heat, she shivered.

Why not Phoenix? The answer came as it always did, in the faintest of whispers. She shrank back against the seat and tried to block it out, but of course she could hear it anyway—the uncompromising judgment, merciless…final: *unworthy. Unworthy.*

Ethan noticed Phoenix becoming more and more withdrawn as they drove through the quiet streets, coming closer and closer to his place, and he thought again of sea anemones. It crossed his mind that perhaps she suspected he was taking her somewhere *else,* some place she didn't want to go, and that she was preparing herself, armoring herself against an anticipated assault on her emotions. But only briefly. He was too busy shoring up his own defenses in readiness for the reckoning that surely lay ahead of him.

The necessity for doing such a thing made him resentful; knowing he was completely in the wrong made him self-righteous. Full awareness of all that, understanding the workings of his own psyche, made him tense and cross. He argued with himself. True, he was a grown man, he had no business being so inconsiderate and selfish. But—he was a grown man, and if he wanted to spend an evening in pleasant intimacy with a beautiful woman in the privacy of his own home, he had a right to do so, didn't he? Of course he did. *But…*

Street parking was hard to come by in Ethan's neighborhood, since most of the row houses lacked either garages or driveways. For security purposes, however, the Service had designated and the city had so marked the area in front of Ethan's building as a strictly enforced tow-away No Parking zone. He pulled the SUV into the empty space, stopped and turned off the motor.

"This is it," he said. "I live on the second floor. Tom and Carl occupy the first. Third floor's empty."

He got out of the car and went around to help Phoenix with the food. He had the door open and was leaning over to reach for a bag when a big brown hand closed on the window frame. A deep voice snapped in a quiet Southern accent, "Watch your head."

Phoenix's eyes met Ethan's, then slid past him and upward. "Aye aye, sir," she murmured cheekily, husky with laughter.

As Ethan moved back to make room for her to get out of the car, he glanced at the Secret Service agent. He wasn't expecting to see amusement in Tom Applegate's impassive face, and he wasn't disappointed. "Ah…about the car—" he began.

"Carl called." Casting a quick look in all directions, the agent slammed the SUV's door, then, without actually touching them, managed to herd both Ethan and Phoenix across the sidewalk and up the steps. "He's out looking for you now."

"Ah. Look, I'm sorry," Ethan said, and meant it even though his voice probably didn't sound like it. Once everyone was safe inside the vestibule, he turned to the agent and added in an undertone, "Please tell me you didn't call my dad."

Dead serious, Applegate replied, "No, sir, not yet. I was gonna give you another fifteen minutes." Behind him, Phoenix smothered laughter with her hand.

"The car belongs to her sound man," Ethan said. "Somebody'll have to see it gets back to him. And uh…she'll be needing a ride home…eventually." He coughed, annoyed with himself for the twinges of embarrassment. "She, uh…doesn't drive."

"Sir, let us worry about the logistics." Applegate was securing the front door.

"Yeah. Okay. Sure." Gathering up the shreds of his pride, Ethan touched Phoenix's elbow and they started up the stairs. After a few steps, he paused and looked back at the Secret Service agent, who was now muttering to his wrist. "Listen, shall I—"

"Just knock on my door when you're ready."

"Uh-huh. Well…hey, listen, would you care for some Chinese? We've got plenty."

"No thank you, I've already eaten. You have a good evening, sir."

Good evening? As they continued on up the stairs, Phoenix looked over at him and mouthed the word. Her eyes were shimmering with laughter…and maybe something else.

"I believe he thinks we're settling in for the night," Ethan said dryly. He was beyond being humiliated by this sort of thing.

"Hmm," she murmured, "I can see why this would drive you crazy."

"Well, I look at it this way—it's only for another year and a half."

"A year and a half? What happens then?"

They'd reached the second-floor landing. Ethan shifted the sack he was carrying and paused with his hand on his apartment doorknob. "My father will no longer be president," he said softly. "Nobody kidnaps the children of ex-presidents." He turned the knob and pushed open the door, reaching for the light switch. He turned on the light, then stood back to let his "date" go ahead of him.

"Well, here we are," he said—or some such thing. He really didn't know *what* he said just then, because as he followed Phoenix, rock-and-roll legend, into his apartment his heart was sinking into a slough of dismay.

Chapter 9

"It's a bit of a mess," Ethan said with grand understatement, lunging forward to snatch at the several pairs of
sweats draped over the couch, and the socks, running shoes
and three days worth of newspapers on the floor beside it.
"I, uh…didn't know when I left here this afternoon that I
was…having company."

He heaved the gathered armload through the nearest doorway and pulled the door firmly shut upon the disasters lurking within. Then, in a heated and breathless state he could
not recall having experienced since adolescence, he turned
back to Phoenix.

The world-renowned legend of rock and roll was wandering through the clutter in his living room, gazing with
undisguised curiosity—even fascination—at the overflowing
bookshelves, the tower of CDs that had recently fallen over,
strewing plastic cases like toppled dominoes across the floor
beside the stereo…his old acoustic guitar propped against
the wall. The untidy piles of medical journals that covered

every flat surface—except for the top of the television and stereo system, which were unavailable due to the jumble of framed photographs already there—snapshots, mostly, except for Lauren's professional wedding portrait. They were all there, his whole family: his dad and Dixie—a snapshot of the two of them laughing together, taken while his dad was still governor of Iowa. A photo of Lauren and John and their two boys on horses, with the Arizona scenery spread out behind them. A series of several beautifully composed pictures of Aunt Lucy and Uncle Mike Lanagan and their daughter, Ethan's cousin Rose Ellen, taken on their Iowa farm by their son, Eric, who was on his way to becoming a photojournalist. One stunningly beautiful portrait done in black-and-white—also by Eric—of Great-great-aunt Gwen, who'd died peacefully the year before at the age of one hundred and five. There were others—Uncle Wood and Aunt Chris, their daughter, Kaitlin. Even a snapshot of Ethan's mother, Elaine, with her husband, taken during a vacation somewhere in the South Seas.

Watching Phoenix as she studied the photographs one by one, Ethan was struck suddenly by a memory of her loft...its elegance, its emptiness...its loneliness. He felt his sense of dismay and embarrassment leave him, like sand running out of a sack.

Relaxed, now, quiet inside, he walked to the couch and placed the bags of Chinese food on the cushions while he cleared the coffee table of medical journals, books, newspapers and the remnants of this morning's breakfast.

"I thought we'd eat out here, if that's okay," he said, setting out white cartons, paper napkins and paper-wrapped chopsticks. "The kitchen's pretty small." He did not add, "And very messy," which he figured by this time she'd know was a given.

Phoenix nodded, but went on looking at the arrangement of photographs. Then, in an impulsive, uncharacteristically awkward motion, she picked one up and tilted it to show him. "This your mother?" Her voice was gruff, almost harsh.

Ethan straightened, looked and said, "Yup." He walked toward her, breathing suspended, moving carefully and slowly, the way he might have approached an unexpectedly tame fawn in the woods.

She watched him come, her eyes never leaving his face. When he was within touching distance she turned back to the snapshot in her hands. "You look like her."

"Well, I have her coloring, anyway. Both my sister and I got the blond hair."

She said nothing for a while, though he sensed she wanted to; he could almost see the unasked questions hovering on the tip of her tongue. Then, abruptly, she put the snapshot back on the stereo. "Big family," she remarked, lightly touching several of the photos as if setting them to rights.

"I guess." Though it had never seemed so to him. Still with that feeling that he was about to attempt to pet a wild creature, he murmured, "What about you?"

"No family." She said it lightly, blowing it away like dandelion fluff in a summer wind. She pivoted and moved away from him, a moment later pouncing on his guitar with a pleased cry, as if she'd only just discovered it.

"You *did* tell me you play." She settled herself on the arm of the couch with her ankle propped on her knee, cradling his guitar across her lap. Her fingers moved on the strings, playing seemingly random chords as she looked up at him. "You said Dixie taught you, right?"

"Right." It occurred to him as he looked at her that he ought to be feeling wonderment of some sort—this was *Phoenix*, sitting in *his* living room, playing *his* guitar. Instead, he felt an indefinable tenderness that was intertwined somehow with sorrow, and a frustrating sense that he was close…*so close* to understanding something of profound importance about this woman named Joanna Dunn.

She smiled to herself as she played; her eyes, shielded from him by the heavy fall of her lashes, were only an elusive twinkle, like stars glimpsed through a canopy of trees. No longer just random wanderings, the melody she was playing was familiar to him—a lullaby, if he wasn't mistaken, something about a mockingbird. An odd and unexpected song for Phoenix to choose, he thought. Out of all the songs in the world, an old folk lullaby.

He hummed along, then sang a few bars very softly, and felt the quiver of a powerful but nameless emotion deep inside his chest when after a moment she joined him.

"Did your mother sing that to you when you were small?" he asked when the words he could remember ran out. Reaching…reaching with a gentle and reassuring hand toward the fawn in the forest.

Still softly playing, she said without looking up, "I don't remember my mother."

"No photographs?"

She shook her head. There was silence…the fawn trembled. A lump formed in Ethan's throat. Then, with a final *thump* of her hand on the chords to still their vibrations, she set the guitar aside…and the fawn scampered away into leafy shadows. "Nope," she said lightly, "not a one."

She slipped off the arm of the couch onto the cushions and reached for a carton. "Mmm…this must be the kung pow chicken."

"Who *did* you learn that song from?" he persisted as he sat on the couch beside her, careful to match her casual tone. Still searching hopefully in the shadows for the vanished fawn, unwilling yet to concede the moment lost.

She shrugged. "Who knows?" She handed him one of the sets of chopsticks and tore the paper wrapping off hers. "Could have been anywhere—once I hear a song I usually don't forget it.'' She bit her lip, concentrating on breaking the chopsticks apart.

Mission accomplished. Her eyes flashed silver, the first time she'd looked directly at him since she'd held his mother's picture in her hands. ''What about you? Dixie, I suppose.''

''Probably.'' Suddenly short on breath, he snapped apart his chopsticks and dug into the nearest carton.

Watching him, eyes gleaming, she speared something that trailed long strands of vegetables and lifted it to her mouth. Her lips parted...her tongue came out to snare the stragglers...the bite disappeared. She chewed with her eyes closed, making soft pleasure sounds...

''How old were you when your folks split?''

''Beg pardon?'' Ethan mumbled through a mouthful of something he absolutely could not taste.

Her eyes were studying him, glowing with the intensity of her curiosity and a purpose he couldn't begin to understand. The question had caught him by surprise in more ways than one. For one thing, he was only just adjusting to the loss of his fawn; he hadn't expected her to turn back into a tiger. And then, at that moment his parents in *any* context were the farthest thing from his mind.

Asking her to repeat the question at least gave him time to find his way out of the sensual quagmire he'd wandered into. He was moderately pleased when he was able to swallow without choking and say calmly, ''My mother left when I was five.''

''Did you miss her?''

It should have been a silly question. What five-year-old child wouldn't miss his mother? But she asked it with child-like curiosity mingled with an element of wistfulness, so that it seemed to him unbearably touching...almost heartbreaking. As if a blind child had asked him what it was like to see.

"I did," he said quietly. "Terribly, at first. I was only five, after all. After Dixie came to take care of us, things were much better. Eventually I hardly missed my mother at all, except after a visit, or talking to her on the phone. That would sort of bring it all back. But…the visits and the calls came farther and farther apart."

"I take it you don't see much of her?"

"I saw her fairly often when I was in California, since that's where she and her husband live. Other than that…no. She calls me on my birthday. Christmas. Things like that." He paused, chopsticks poised. "What?" Through some sort of shimmering veil, he could see her watching him the way a cat watches a particularly interesting species of mouse. *"What?"*

Still she said nothing. Roughly two seconds into the silence it occurred to Ethan that the shimmering veil he was having trouble seeing through was tears. And that they were present because someone had apparently ignited a blowtorch inside his sinus cavities. His body temperature, he estimated, must be somewhere near boiling.

"Holy cow," he wheezed, staring incredulously into the carton he was holding. "What *is* this stuff?"

"Oh, dear me," Phoenix said in a tiny and tightly controlled voice, "I think you might have gotten hold of some of my Szechuan by mistake." She barely made it through the sentence before dissolving into gales of helpless laughter.

Ethan stared at her through his tears in utter disbelief. His head was on fire, his eyes and nose were running like faucets, he could barely draw breath, and she was *laughing?*

"Water," he croaked, and lurching to his feet, staggered off to the kitchen.

She found him there a few minutes later, hunched over a sink piled full of haphazardly rinsed dishes, refilling a coffee mug with water straight from the tap. She went up behind him and put her hands on his waist.

"Hey, Doc, come here...let me." Her voice felt low in her throat and still warm with the laughter. She felt warm all through her insides, in fact. As if she'd downed a straight shot of whiskey.

He drew back from the sink to give her a look of dark reproach. From the beard on his chin to the roots of his hair, his normally golden tanned skin had a distinctly ruddy cast. For some reason when she looked at him the warmth inside her seemed to gather itself into a hot ball, right in the middle of her chest.

She steered him firmly toward the kitchen table until his backside come against its edge. He leaned on it, folded his arms across his chest, closed his eyes and gave a sigh of surrender. When Phoenix heard that sound, the ball of heat in her chest melted...pooled in the lowest part of her body.

She moved closer to him. When the cold water touched his face he started and caught her wrist, his eyes crossing slightly as he focused on the wet towel in her hand. She saw a flash of dismay in their nut-brown depths before he closed them again. "You've been in my bathroom," he said in a thickened murmur, and gave another small sigh. "I suppose you know, this means you have to marry me. I have *no* secrets from you now."

Laughter tumbled again through her chest, and she caught her lower lip between her teeth to hold it back. Doc's defenses must really have been laid low, she thought, for him to say such a thing. She felt sure it wasn't the sort of joking around that came naturally to him.

"I'm sorry," she said in an unreliable voice, left ragged by the recent excesses of mirth. "I...truly am." A residual bubble of laughter burst from her in spite of her best efforts to stifle it.

"Oh, yeah," Ethan said dryly, "I can see that."

"No—really. I am. I was going to say something when you first picked up that carton, but then you started eating, and you didn't say anything, so I thought...you...liked it..." Her voice had grown softer with each word until finally it just sort of...faded away.

Slowly, she raised the damp towel to his face. When she touched his forehead with it, just above one eyebrow, he closed his eyes. And that was her undoing. Such a small thing. Such an enormous thing—an expression of total trust. What it did to her was so unexpected, so sudden, she could neither prepare herself nor defend against it. Wanting struck her like a rogue wave, nearly knocking her off her feet. The laughter and the warmth inside her were washed clean away, leaving her cold and shivering with a need to be held, to be wrapped in his arms and pressed close to his warm, solid body.

"Like it?" he murmured, eyes closed. "I couldn't even taste it, not at first. Next thing I know, I've got tears streaming down my face."

"It does sort of sneak up on you...." Shaken, she drew the towel across his eyebrow, then pressed it, oh, so gently against his eyelid. She heard the soft rush of his breath, released in careful measures through his nose. The tender, shadowed skin beneath his eye flinched, and she felt an overpowering desire to kiss him there.

But...in another moment her hands would tremble, and she couldn't have him know how fragile she was, how undone by his nearness. So, to keep them from betraying her, she set them in motion once more, laying one lightly on his shoulder to steady herself while the other drew the towel downward over his cheek to where the boundaries of his beard began. Framed in neatly trimmed honey-brown, his lips seemed utterly defenseless, and tempting as forbidden fruit.

So focused was she on his mouth, so steeped in the imagined feel and warmth and taste of it, that she didn't even know at first when his hands intercepted hers. Lost in a fog of uncertainty, not knowing which way to go, afraid to take even the smallest step lest she stumble over a terrifying precipice from which she knew there would be no return, she stood helplessly while he removed the towel from her hand.

Slowly, warming her cold hand in both of his, he drew her fingers to his lips.

Fascinated, she watched her fingertips press the satiny cushion of his lips, while tears inexplicably gathered in the back of her throat and she braced herself in utter panic, certain she wasn't going to be able to hold them off. Then…she felt his breath flow like heated oil over her fingertips, seep between them…into her palm. A glorious warmth spread over her hand and all through her, poured deep inside her—the sweetest and most intense pleasure she had ever known. The fog lifted; lightness filled her. She caught her breath and smiled.

"I meant to seduce you, you know," she whispered.

He opened his eyes, looked deep into hers and gravely replied, "I know."

A laugh spiked through her chest and emerged in a sharp little cry, more like a whimper. Had she been so obvious? She must have been—it surely couldn't have been his ego that had led him to such a certainty. She'd never met a man with less ego.

She didn't know what to say. Didn't want to say *anything,* afraid even one more word would alter the course they seemed set on, like a pebble beneath the wheel of a runaway wagon. But it was impossible to be silent. "This isn't the way I planned it," she murmured, frowning.

Again he replied, "I know." And this time, it was he who smiled.

Still holding her hand in both of his, he turned it and

pressed his mouth against her palm. His eyes narrowed slightly in that way he had, but didn't close, instead clinging to hers in silent question. Her heart gave a painful leap. She was afraid, so afraid, that he wouldn't find the answers he wanted, afraid that if her eyes were indeed the windows to her soul, he would look inside and might not like what he found there. That he would *stop*. And she desperately did not want him to stop.

Almost without her conscious will, her fingers unfurled against his cheek. When they met the warm and slightly sandy texture of his smooth-shaven skin her whole arm tingled. Desire was a crushing weight inside her; her legs trembled with it.

Though she was never conscious of having given it permission, she felt her body sway toward his...bow into his embrace, powerless as a willow in the wind. His hands were like breath on her skin...his breath a caressing touch. His lips pressed melting warmth into the hollow of her throat...his hands brushed shivers across her back. Her hands found their way to the warm, strong column of his neck like fledglings coming home to roost.

Wanting came to her now, not as a weight but like a song, like the inspiration that sometimes brought her out of a sound sleep late in the night with the words already clear in her mind and the music true and right on her tongue. Wanting, and certainty... Bursting with awe, trembling with the terrifying wonder of it, she closed her eyes and leaned into him, silently pleading. Praying. *Let this be. Just... please...let this...be.*

His lips began to move in short sweet paces along the side of her neck, his beard the barest whisper on her skin. She shivered, nerve endings prickling as if a thousand Fourth of July sparklers had exploded at once inside her. A soft moan came from her throat, a sound she'd never heard herself make before. His gentleness was exquisite torture...both delicious and intolerable. She was torn between sensual ecstacy, wanting to roll and wallow in it like a cat in a puddle of sunshine, and a passion so urgent and intense she felt almost angry—and much more tiger than pussycat. She wanted to rake at his clothes and hurl herself against him, feel his weight bearing her down, crushing the breath from her; she wanted to encircle his body with her legs and feel his heat and strength deep inside her.

Her moan became a growl. She rocked against him, passion making her movements jerky and graceless as her hands clutched first at his shoulders, then pushed upward, fingers driving through the dense thicket of his hair. She turned her head, not to give him access to her neck, now, but to deny it, instead frantically seeking...no, *demanding*. Her heart gave another leap, this one of joy. Her body sang, her whole being danced when she felt his chest harden against her breasts, when his muscles tightened beneath her belly and thighs. When his hands swept down to grasp her buttocks and his mouth came, at last, to cover hers.

Seduce? This man? How foolish she felt now to ever have imagined that she could—like reaching with supreme confidence to pet a kitten and instead finding herself holding on for dear life to a tiger's tail. She felt scared to death, exhilarated, out of control, and with no idea in the world how to let go. For Phoenix—the Phoenix she knew—it should have been a terrifying, completely intolerable place to be, and it was. Oh, it was. And at the same time, she never wanted to leave. She ricocheted between helpless wanting and total panic, her heart knocking in syncopated rhythms. *So much feeling.* Too much. She wasn't used to it. Had spent a lifetime insulating herself against it...hiding from it behind various disguises. Her responses felt raw and trembly, like parts of the body that haven't been used in a long, long time.

As if he understood that—the physician always—he withdrew from the kiss gently, holding her against him for a few moments longer and pressing short fervent kisses into her hair, almost as if in apology. She drew back from him, some sort of light remark balanced on her lips. And as the thunder of her own heartbeat receded, she heard it, too, and understood the reason for the apology. The telephone was ringing.

"I'd better take this," he murmured, his eyes calmly searching hers. "It rings in downstairs. There's only a few people they put through up here."

She nodded and shifted to one side, a hand going casually to the tabletop to help steady her. She wondered if he'd noticed she was trembling. *Of course he had.* She hoped not.

His hands slipped from her waist to her arms…rubbed lightly over her goose bumps, igniting fresh shivers. He kissed her once more, softly, on the lips, then left her. She watched him walk out of the kitchen without a trace of a wobble in his step, but it was several minutes before she trusted her own legs enough to follow.

In the living room, Ethan located the cordless phone amongst the clutter of food containers on the coffee table and cleared his throat in an experimental sort of way before he punched the on button. "This is Dr. Brown."

"Hey, Ethan—honey…"

A smile spread across his face as he answered in the Texas style, "Hey, Dixie, how're you?"

"Didn't mean to call so late—I just never can remember which nights you're home. Anyway, I won't keep you long, and I know you can't talk—Tom said you had company…?" He heard the eager curiosity in his stepmother's voice, though he knew she respected his privacy too much to ask outright.

"That's right," he said in a neutral voice, watching Phoenix as she came toward him, not with her patented Phoenix stride, but tentatively, as if she wasn't certain of her welcome or her place.

It came to him suddenly that it must be *he* who had robbed her of her customary self-confidence and presence, and he knew a shameful moment of pure masculine elation at the thought that he could have that kind of power over such a woman. But that feeling was followed quickly by a sense of sorrow and loss that surprised him. Because he suddenly knew that, whatever it was he was trying to accomplish with this woman, whatever it was he wanted from her, changing her in any fundamental way was not part of it.

"I thought you'd want to know what we found out—about that information you wanted?"

"Yeah, right."

"Well, I have to tell you, so far there isn't much. There isn't any history on Phoenix at all prior to when she was about fourteen. We have a date of birth, but no place, no family, no nothing."

"What about the other one?" Ethan's eyes were following Phoenix's movements as she poked in a desultory way among the cartons of Chinese food, selected a sweet and sour shrimp—one of *his* selections—and put it in her mouth.

"Joanna Dunn? I'm still workin' on that." He heard the sigh of exhaled breath. "It would help a lot if you could narrow it down some, sugar. This is a great big ol' country."

"How about here?" he said without inflection. Phoenix had wandered over to the stereo and was squatting beside the toppled stack of CDs, slowly putting them to rights, stopping to read a label now and then.

"Here…? Oh—you mean where *you*… Well, sure. Okay, that'll help. Give me a couple days—I've got some things on my calendar, and I have to tell you, I am *not* lookin' forward to entertainin' the Japanese prime minister and his wife. They make me go through these trainin' sessions to make sure I get all the protocol right, but it never seems to help, I'm still bowin' when I'm supposed to be smilin', know what I mean?''

"Dixie, you'll do fine," Ethan said, laughing. They both knew there wasn't a soul on the planet who didn't love the First Lady, in spite of—perhaps because of—her breezy Texas ways.

"Well, let's hope so. Anyway, I'll get back to you if I find out anything, okay?''

"Thanks, Dixie. Very much." He paused. "Is...Dad there?''

"'Fraid not—he's downstairs goin' over his 'remarks' for the prime minister." There was regret in his stepmother's voice.

"Well, tell him I said hello. And that everything's fine."

"I sure will." There was a pause, and then, "You'd tell us if it wasn't, right?''

"Of course," he murmured, and wondered if it was true. He could tell by his stepmother's exhalation that she wondered, too.

"Well, okay, sugar, I'll say bye-bye then. You have fun, and take care now.''

"I will, Dixie."

"Love you."

"Love you, too."

Phoenix didn't look up when he placed the phone back on the coffee table. She'd put a CD on the stereo, the volume turned so low he couldn't tell which one it was until he walked over to stand behind her, close enough to touch her but not doing so.

"The Parish Family—good choice," he murmured, faintly surprised. His eyes had begun to follow the path of the braid he'd woven into her hair...thick and loose between her shoulder blades...tapering to the knot she'd tied, bumping now against the place a bra strap would cross if she'd been wearing one…the loose end curling slightly as it brushed the strip of tiger print material at her waist. He thought how close he'd been just a few minutes ago to loosing that knot…unraveling his own handiwork and filling his hands with the vibrant mass…his nostrils with the scent of it. He still could. The knowledge made his stomach churn.

She threw him a look, a sardonic little smile, over her shoulder. "Dinner interruptus?"

His laughter felt uncomfortable and no doubt sounded as false as he felt. "There seems to be plenty of food. Would you care to join me?"

She shook her head and looked away, the corners of her mouth pinching with the strain of maintaining the smile. "I seem to have lost my appetite." *Along with the moment,* she thought. Because she'd seen by the quietness in his eyes that they weren't going to be picking up where they'd left off in the kitchen. Obviously, the doc had come to his senses, and she was damned if *she'd* be the one to bring it up. Desire was one thing; pride was another. Phoenix did not beg.

She snatched at a breath as she moved away from him, like a diver coming up for air. "It's getting late. Maybe we'd better see if Mr. Tall Dark and Dangerous down there has worked out those logistics yet."

"Sure." She watched him retrieve the cordless phone from the coffee table mess and press a single button. He mumbled into the phone for a few moments, then punched the button and put the phone back among the cartons. He looked at her and said in a neutral voice, "Any time you're ready."

She lifted her hands and shoulders together—an elaborate "couldn't care less" gesture. "I'm ready."

Propelled by some sort of flight instinct, she crossed the room in a few effortless strides. Even so, they got to the door at the same time and she barely managed to snatch her hand away in time to avoid making contact with his when he reached to open it for her. Frozen, heart knocking, she said in a muffled voice, "You don't have to come."

"Yeah," he said, quietly wry, "I do. Tom won't leave me here unguarded."

She glanced at him...then looked a longer moment, and saw what she'd somehow missed before. Behind the quietness...acknowledgment, and deep regret. She felt something warm and soften inside her, and the jittery coldness of wounded pride give way to a trembling, yearning *ache*. Slowly she reached out and touched two fingers to his lips. Her fingers warmed instantly, as if they remembered....

"Bye Bye Leroy Brown," she whispered.

His lips curved under her fingertips; his breath blew soft sweet memories of his taste and warmth against her skin. "Bye bye, Joanna..."

She gave a little hiccup of laughter. "At the stroke of midnight the scullery maid turns back into a princess..."

"...And the bad boy into First Son."

"Cinderella in reverse." How was it that she could still laugh, when the trembling ache had become a shudder of longing? "Now it's back to the real world...."

Once again he'd taken her hand in both of his, enfolding it as though it were a precious treasure he wanted to protect. For a moment, just a moment, while his lips hovered between a word and a kiss, she allowed herself to think...to hope... But then he slowly lowered her hand. "I had a good time tonight."

"Yeah, me, too." And oh, how proud she was that her voice was light and no more scratchy than normal.

Why, tell me, why...is it so hard to say goodbye?

The lyric blew through her mind like a train whistle in the night, and she felt her entire being shudder with the suddenness of understanding, as if rocked by the gust of the train's passing. *Doveman, you were right—goodbye is hard, and it's what comes between hello and goodbye that matters.*

And this, she was all at once determined, would *not* be goodbye. If Phoenix had anything to say about it—and she sure as hell did—there was going to be a whole lot more "between" to come before she and Dr. Ethan Brown said goodbye.

"By the way," she purred as he was reaching across to open the door for her, "if you still want that report on those apartment buildings..." He paused; she heard a soft but unmistakable catch in his breathing, and felt a nice little glow of triumph at the thought that she might actually have made him forget his precious agenda, for even a little while. "I should have it by tomorrow, if you want to stop by."

"Can't tomorrow." He gave a smile and shrug of apology as he turned the knob and pushed the door open. "My ride-along night."

"Oh—right." She went ahead of him onto the landing, quelling small twinges of annoyance. Phoenix was not accustomed to having to bend her schedule around someone else's. "Saturday, then."

"Uh...can't Saturday, either." He closed the door with a tug and a click, then paused with his hand still on the doorknob. She turned to look at him and caught the shadow of evasion in his eyes. "I have plans...sorry."

"Ah. I see." Both her nice little glow and the annoyance abruptly faded and were replaced by a cold green greasy lump she had no trouble recognizing as jealousy. *Phoenix—jealous?* The thought was appalling.

Even more so was her mortification when his eyes softened with understanding. And his smile...oh, how she resented his confidence, especially since she seemed to have so little of it herself, lately.

"Nothing like that. I promised...someone...I'd take him

to the park on Saturday. I really can't cancel on him. Sunday, maybe?''

What could she say to that? The regret in his eyes was real. "Maybe," she said lightly, turning toward the stairs. And then, trying hard to sound amused, "The park...sounds like *so* much fun. Especially for your bodyguards. Where is it? Somewhere around here?" The beginnings of an idea were forming in her mind.

The doc looked startled, then frowned. "What? No—over near the clinic, I think." He gave her a crooked smile. "To tell you the truth, I forgot to ask—how many parks can there be?''

"Right..." Phoenix purred.

They went down the stairs together, side by side but carefully not touching, both very much aware that ever-vigilant Secret Service Agent Tom Applegate was waiting for them at the bottom.

They rode home in the back seat of the SUV, mostly in silence, with Tom driving. And when they left each other, what they both said was *not* goodbye, but simply, "Good night.''

Piano music greeted Phoenix as she made her way through the darkened studio, the notes floating down from above as if they were a gift come straight from Heaven. Partly she thought that because to her the person making the music had indeed been a gift, whether from God or Fate or some other power she had no way of knowing; and partly because the music itself was so lovely, she thought it might very well have been divinely inspired. Listening to it made her swell inside with an unutterable sadness.

And so, of course, she was smiling as she stepped out of the cage.

"Hey, Doveman—you're up late." She crossed to the piano and gave his bony shoulders a squeeze as she dropped a quick kiss onto the bare spot on top of his head. "You shouldn't have waited for me. I'm a big girl."

The old piano man chuckled as he shifted on the bench to make room for her the way he always did. "Now, you know ol' Doveman don't close his eyes 'til he knows his chick is back safe and sound in her nest."

Phoenix was silent for a moment, rocking her body slightly to the rhythm of the music. Then she said softly, "You were right—it needed the minor key."

Doveman nodded, watching his fingers work their magic. "Ain't nothing harder or sadder than sayin' goodbye. And it don't matter how many times you do it, it don't get any easier. I think maybe it's even harder when you get old...."

Old... Doveman is old.

Fear came unexpectedly, clutched at her stomach and turned her body cold. Doveman. He'd been both mother and father to her for most of her life. She couldn't imagine how she would ever do without him. Panic-stricken, she wanted to throw her arms around him and hold on to him so tightly that nothing—not even Death—would dare to take him from her. At the very least, she wanted to put her arm across his shoulders, kiss his white-stubbled cheek. Tell him she loved him.

So, of course, she got up from the piano bench and walked away from him. She went toward the windows, silently rubbing her arms.

Behind her she heard Doveman say softly, "Well, I'll be goin' on to bed now."

She nodded without turning. "'Night... And thanks...for waiting."

His chuckle was lost in the clanking and groaning of the cage as it sank slowly from view.

Oh, but it's so hard...hard...hard to say goodbye.

Phoenix stood alone looking out on the spangled city, with the song playing in her mind, at last complete, lyrics a perfect blend with the music…absolutely right. She should have felt a sense of elation. Instead she just felt frightened and lonely.

How could she ever say goodbye to Doveman? When the time came, would she somehow find the strength? The courage? She'd never had to do so hard a thing before.

She hadn't said goodbye to her mother. She'd never had the chance.

Beyond the window the city lights wavered and blurred. Tears spilled over and ran warm down her cheeks. ''Doveman,'' she whispered, though she knew he'd long since gone, ''I can't remember my momma's face.''

Chapter 10

Children's voices drifted upward into the heat-hazy sky along with a golden cloud of dust.

"Hey, battah-battah-battah..."

"Throw it here, throw it here!"

"Throw it—No, throw it to first, throw it to first!"

"Go, go, GO!"

"Way to go, man, way to go."

"Oh, man..."

"That's okay, we'll get the next one... Hey, battah-battah..."

"What about it?" Ethan said. "Want to stay and watch awhile?"

Beside him, Michael shook his head and restlessly joggled the basketball he carried in his arms. His face wore a look of disdain.

"You know," Ethan pointed out, "Michael Jordan played baseball, too."

Michael threw him a startled look but recovered in time

to say with a sniff and a carefully offhand shrug, "Yeah, but he stunk at it." Still, he lifted one arm and pointed. "Basketball court's over thataway."

"Right..." Ethan sighed inwardly. He'd figured he could probably hold his own when it came to baseball, but basketball...that was another story.

As they crossed the grassy verge that separated the baseball diamonds from the jogging path, inspiration struck. "Hey, Tom," he called to the tall black man who happened to be coming along the path just then, "you ever play any basketball?"

The Secret Service agent was wearing jogging shorts, a loose-fitting tank that neatly hid his weapon, a towel around his neck and a shine of honest-to-God sweat. He paused to wipe some of the sweat from his face with one end of the towel before he said without any discernible signs of amusement, "You're kiddin' me, right?"

White, liberal, awash in chagrin, Ethan stammered, "Well, uh...I mean, I just thought—"

"I'm six foot seven and black—what do you think?" Tom Applegate looked down at Michael, who was gazing up at him in utter awe, and *winked*. "North Carolina Tar Heels—NCAA champs my senior year."

Not one to allow himself to be intimidated for very long, Michael put a hand on his hip and stuck out his jaw, aiming it upward in the general direction of the Secret Service agent's altitude. "Hey—you know Michael Jordan?"

Ethan shrugged Tom an apology; forget those Tar Heels, man—this was the only test that mattered. He didn't know who was more surprised—him or Michael—when Tom nodded and said, "Sure I know Michael. Played basketball with him, too. We went to high school together."

Michael's mouth was hanging open. He didn't have to close it to say, "Uh-*uh!*"

He looked for verification to Ethan, who again shrugged

his shoulders. "Hey—if Tom says so, it must be true. Secret Service agents never lie."

Michael slanted Tom a suspicious look with one eye closed. "What's a... S-Secret Service agent? Is that like some kind of cop?"

"Sort of." Tom plucked the basketball from Michael's arms. "So, you want to go shoot some hoops, or not?"

He gave Ethan a look, and as they began to move along the jogging path together, Michael sandwiched between them, muttered under his breath, "Sir...straight ahead, about...ten o'clock? Just to the left of that tree..."

His heart rate mysteriously accelerating, Ethan followed the agent's directions. A woman was standing there, casually watching them from the shade of some pin oak trees, one shoulder leaning against a lichen-encrusted trunk. She was tall and willowy, and wore a long white skirt of some kind of gauzy material that started low on her hips, with a white stretchy top that left her shoulders and most of her middle bare. A white cowboy hat worn straight on her head shadowed her face and completely hid her hair.

Ethan looked back at Tom, eyebrows raised in question. Tom lifted a hand and spoke briefly to his wristwatch, then nodded. "Go ahead—Carl's got you covered."

Ethan muttered, "Thanks," gave Michael's shoulder a squeeze and added, "Catch up with you in a few minutes." then angled off the path, jogging across the grass toward the trees. The smell of crushed grass drifted up from his feet, filling his senses and adding itself to the list of things he knew he would ever afterward associate with Phoenix.

Still twenty feet or so away from her, for reasons he didn't entirely understand he paused, bent down and plucked a dandelion from the grass. He straightened and stood looking at her, holding the stem of the fragile white puffball in his fingers.

He didn't know what to make of her—or of himself, and

the way he felt, seeing her. He thought of all he knew about her—and how little. He knew that, however unintentionally, he'd made her want him, that last night's kiss had been as real for her as for him. But real for *whom?* Whom had he kissed last night, Joanna, or Phoenix? The way he understood it, Phoenix wasn't even a real person, she was a *persona,* an invention, a collection of personalities that could be changed at will to fit the demands of a fickle record-buying public. A man would have to be insane to allow himself to fall for one of them, when she might be gone tomorrow…like a dandelion in a puff of wind.

And as for Joanna…he had no idea in the world who she was, much less how to find her again.

She smiled when he started forward again, but crookedly. "I wondered when you were going to notice me."

He smiled back, the same way, and nodded, taking in her costume. "Another nice disguise."

She hitched one shoulder as she pushed away from the tree. "I prefer to think of it as protective coloring."

"Whatever it is, it didn't fool Tom for a minute—he's the one who spotted you."

"Yeah, well, that's his job." She held out her hand when she saw the dandelion. "Is that for me?"

He offered it to her with a curious reluctance, his heartbeat tapping in quick time at the base of his throat. "If you want it," he said. She took it from him, holding it as he had been, with the delicate stem between two fingers and thumb. He expected that she would immediately lift it to her lips and blow it to pieces.

She did raise it to her face, but instead of blowing the fluff away, cupped her other hand around it as if to protect it from stray breezes while she studied it. Her features were grave and still. Then her lashes lifted and her eyes came back to Ethan, and he was caught off-guard by the sadness in them. "It's so perfect, isn't it? By tomorrow it will be gone, you know."

He nodded, a lump coming into his throat. "That's true." What was she telling him? A warning? That whatever this was between them would be gone tomorrow, too? That, he already knew.

"I guess…some things you just have to enjoy while you have them," she said on a lightening breath.

They began walking by mutual unspoken consent, it seemed, through the trees, paralleling the jogging path, Phoenix still holding the dandelion with a hand cupped protectively around it.

"I wasn't stalking you, you know," she said after a moment, flashing him a smile. "I was just…curious."

"To see if I was *really* going to the park…or who I was going with?" Ethan said, teasing her.

She dismissed that with a little spurt of laughter. *As if…* She aimed a smile at her sandaled feet as though she found it entertaining to watch them play peekaboo with the hem of her skirt. "No, actually, I wanted to see what 'regular' people do on a Saturday in the park."

"Well," Ethan said, looking around as they walked, "as you can see, that covers a pretty wide range."

Her gaze followed the same path his had taken, touching on groping lovers, picnicking families, joggers, bicyclists, in-line skaters, a toddler chasing squirrels, a young man throwing a Frisbee to a dog wearing a bandanna around his neck, and a group of out-of-shape men with their shirts off courting heart attacks with a game of touch football in the muggy heat.

She nodded toward a family setting out food on a table nearby. "I actually thought about that—bringing a picnic."

Ethan grinned broadly at the thought of Phoenix toting a picnic basket. *Little Red Ridinghood? Look out, Wolf!* "You **did?**"

She nodded. "Yup. Then I remembered I don't own a picnic basket. Or anything to put in one, for that matter. Kind of put a damper on the whole idea." Her smile turned wry. She gave a shrug that seemed defensive, somehow, and looked away. "So—I just came. Without even so much as a bottle of water. Which reminds me—I'm thirsty. You don't suppose…"

"There's probably a drinking fountain around here somewhere." A thought struck him. "By the way, how *did* you come? Did somebody bring you? How did you know which park?"

She gave him a look that managed to be both direct and secretive. "I took a cab," she said evenly. "And, I told the driver to take me to the park that's closest to South Church Street—that's where your clinic is, right? Must be, because here I am. And here you are…" She was silent for a moment, once again watching her feet flash rhythmically in and out of view. Then she threw him another look, an altogether different one. Uncertain…almost shy. "You don't mind, do you? That I came? Because if it's not okay, just say so. I'll go." Her voice was gruff but her gaze was unflinching, and it came to Ethan that in a way she was opening herself to him, offering her vulnerability like a gift.

Unbelievably touched, he thought of the dandelion she still held cupped in her hands, and for the first time it occurred to him that perhaps it wasn't what was between *them* she was symbolically protecting, but only her own fragile self.

"Of course it's okay. I'm glad you came," he said softly. And reached over and took her hand.

The dandelion, suddenly robbed of its buffer, caught a capricious breeze and exploded in a tiny blizzard of fluff. Phoenix gave a stricken cry and halted, her free hand making an involuntary movement toward the drifting feathers, as if trying to catch them, to bring them all back somehow, if only she could...

Ethan caught her hand and, holding it tightly together with its mate, turned her toward him. "It's all right," he said in a fierce and unfamiliar voice, words that hurt his throat, "I'll get you another."

"Hey—nothing lasts forever." She said it lightly, but in the shadows beneath the brim of her hat, the skin around her eyes had a damp and fragile look.

He didn't know what to say to that. He wanted to deny it, argue the point, but didn't see how he could. The fact was, nothing *did* last forever. So he just looked at her. And then, because her lips looked so soft...so tender and sweet...he leaned over, tilted his head to avoid the hat brim, and gently kissed her.

He heard—no, *felt*—the small intake of breath...as if, he thought, he'd caught her by surprise; the slightest trembling, as if she were a maiden unaccustomed to being kissed. And he suddenly remembered what her piano man, Rupert Dove, had told him.

"What you got to understand about Phoenix is, her heart's still a virgin..."

He thought about that, and about the dandelion, while he held her hands enfolded and tucked between his chest and hers, and lightly brushed her warm, soft lips with his. He drew back to find that her eyes were bright and sharp with panic.

"I don't know what to do about you, Doc," she said fiercely. She pulled her hands from his and moved away, and he let her go, not following until there was an arm's length distance between them.

"You got to go slow...and expect some resistance."

After a moment she laughed, her famous chortle. "I can't get you out of my mind—why do you suppose that is?"

It was a rhetorical question, and he didn't reply—though

he could have told her he was having the same sort of problem himself. But he suspected she already knew that.

After a few more silent steps, she went on in a musing tone. "I told you last night that I'd meant to seduce you—" she gave a little gulp of laughter "—God, what a self-conscious little word that is—but you knew what I meant. You said you did." She glanced at him. He nodded gravely and she looked away again. "I thought it would be so easy—out of arrogance, at first, maybe, but later because…I *felt* something…" She left it dangling, while her finger made a jerky waggling motion between his chest and hers.

"It *should* have been easy." She halted and turned to him, her voice tense, hushed…angry. "It would be…so easy…for us to be together, Doc. Rock-and-roll legend and First Son, or Leroy and Joanna—take your pick—we're both consenting adults, without prior commitments—Lord knows, we've got the chemistry. Dammit, why can't we just…*be* together? Why does this have to be…why does it feel so *hard?*"

Ethan cleared his throat; he'd never had a conversation like this before, which was perhaps why his voice felt rusty. "Maybe," he ventured finally, "because we both know it's not that simple."

"I *know* that," she snapped, brittle and dissatisfied. "What I don't understand is *why.*"

He took a deep breath and caught himself just before he drove his hand through his hair—his father's favorite gesture when emotionally frustrated. Dear God, was he becoming so much like his dad—*starched,* Phoenix had called him!—uptight and unable to express his feelings? Valiantly, he tried.

"I can't speak for both of us, but for me, I guess it's because…just *being* together—for the sex—isn't enough." And even while the words were coming out of his mouth, he knew how priggish they sounded.

So he wasn't at all surprised when she smiled at him and murmured teasingly, "Oh, come on...you've never been with someone 'just for the sex'? Not ever?"

He felt his skin warming, but he smiled back. "Well...okay. I guess maybe there were times..." He shook his head and the smile faded. "But not...this time."

"Why is that?" she whispered, looking into his eyes.

He shook his head. The easy answer, *I don't know*...hovered on his tongue, but he knew she wanted more, and in a strange sort of way he felt he owed it to her. He drew another hard breath and began slowly, navigating through treacherous shoals of feelings he hadn't even sorted out for himself yet.

"I think...it's because I want more from you than that."

"That's what scares me, Doc," she said in a breaking voice, which she instantly halted, and calmed with a breath. And another. Whispering again, she went on. "What I'm afraid of is, maybe you want something from me that I can't give you."

He shook his head hard, denying it. "I don't see why. I'm not that demanding."

"Then what *is* it you want from me? Tell me!"

"What do I want from you? Nothing so hard, Joanna, believe me. All I want is—" *Your heart? Your soul?* But he couldn't say it. It *was* too much to ask, and way too soon to ask it. He had no right whatsoever to ask it.

She laughed, then, but without amusement, and gave him a long, appraising look that for some reason left him feeling vaguely ashamed. Then she turned and started walking again, with her arms folded now across her bare middle. "You know, Doc," she said in her rusty Phoenix voice, "I think you disapprove of me."

"*Disapprove* of you?" He repeated it in shocked denial. "I do not."

"Yeah, you do." And he could see the edges of her sad,

ironic smile. "I think you'd like it if you could peel off my Phoenix clothes—my disguises, you keep calling them—and see if there's somebody else under here—somebody you might like better." She glanced at him. "You called me Joanna just now."

Still shocked, and beginning to feel a little abused, Ethan said testily, "It's your name."

She made a disgusted sound and a throwaway gesture. "I haven't been that person for so long, I don't even remember what it feels like. Don't you understand? She's gone, Doc— Joanna's *gone*. And you know what? Good riddance. She was a loser—*not* a good person." She gave a high, sharp laugh. "Trust me—if you're hoping to find somebody inside here you think you might like better than me, you're out of luck. What you see is pretty much as good as I get."

She ran lightly from him then, before he could even begin to think what to say in reply. He knew a moment's heart-stopping dismay, something like what he imagined she might have felt when the wind had taken her dandelion. Then he saw the drinking fountain, and he understood that she was running *to,* not away.

He followed but stood back a ways, watching her step delicately between puddles in the bare patch of sandy ground around the block of stone-crusted concrete that formed the base of the fountain. Entranced, he watched her search out the mechanism that would turn the water on…experiment cautiously with the trajectory of the stream, looking as fearful and fascinated as a child with a mysterious new toy. His heart jolted into his throat when she bent toward the fountain, then halted suddenly, straightened up and carefully took off her cowboy hat. With the hat cradled against one hip she leaned down and touched her lips to the arching stream, and Ethan felt a powerful urge of his own to swallow…

Was this what it would be like, having her always in his

life? he wondered. With even the smallest, most ordinary acts seeming touched with magic, as if he was seeing them for the very first time?

Like a long-abandoned piece of machinery creaking to life, he stepped forward to hold the faucet on for her while she stroked cool water onto her cheeks, throat and chest like lotion. He gazed entranced at the glossy black coil of her hair as she smoothed back the sweat-damp tendrils clinging to her forehead, and thought about her nape, and how sweet and vulnerable it looked. Then she straightened and raised both arms, turning slightly toward him as she settled the cowboy hat into place over the mass of her hair, and his gaze dropped to her lithe and supple torso—how could it not?

"Good God," he said before he could stop himself, "is that a navel ring?"

She laughed, the coughing sound a surly tiger might make, then said dryly, "Yeah, Doc, that's what it is." She waited while he brought his guilty gaze back to her face before she shrugged. "See what I mean? You're shocked."

"I'm not *shocked.*" He shouldn't have been. As a doctor he'd personally encountered pierced body parts he'd have been embarrassed to tell her about. "Just…I hadn't noticed it before, that's all."

"But you disapprove." And how was it she could sound both amused and sad?

"No, I don't," he said, feeling twitchy and annoyed, suddenly, and very misunderstood. Because the truth was, what he found shocking about the navel ring was the fact that he *didn't* disapprove. He felt that he should, that ordinarily he would. But for some reason the fact that it was *her* navel ring made it not only acceptable, but somehow just one more delightful facet of the incredible and fascinating person she was. It frustrated him that he couldn't tell her that, and it only added to his frustration when a moment later she voiced his deepest feelings almost exactly in her own words.

"It just goes with who I am," she said in her soft-scratchy voice as they walked on again, not touching. "It's Phoenix. It's me. That's all." He could feel her turn her head toward him, but felt too exposed just then to face the sadness and irony in her eyes.

He was glad he hadn't when a moment later she added, "You know, Doc, funny thing is, I don't feel that way about you. I happen to like you a lot—just the way you are."

He'd never felt less likeable in his life. He felt, in fact, like nothing so much as a contrary child, a mass of confusion and contradictions, inadvertently hurting that which he only meant to hold.

He closed his eyes, needing to be away from her just then, needing to go to his quiet place and try to rediscover himself there—or failing that, at least to find his path again. Somewhere, he knew, there were important things he was supposed to do that he'd lost sight of, priorities he'd set for himself that he'd somehow forgotten. Somewhere along the line he'd wandered off the path on a quest of his own, this search for the ellusive and alluring being named Joanna, who for all he knew might exist only in his own mind. He sensed that he was very close to becoming hopelessly lost, and that he desperately needed some sort of compass to bring him back to where he belonged.

It was at just that moment, like an answer to an unspoken prayer, that he heard a childish voice calling, "Hey, Doc! Doc—where you been? Hey, come on, man."

He opened his eyes and found Phoenix watching him, blue eyes bright and quizzical in the shadows beneath the brim of the cowboy hat. Beyond her, behind the lattice of a chain-link fence, he could see the basketball court's cracked pavement reflecting heat in sluggish waves. And Michael, standing at the fence, the fingers of one small hand woven through the chain link, impatiently shaking it while holding the basketball precariously balanced on one scrawny hip. A short distance away, Tom Applegate waited under the basket, patiently mopping sweat.

"Better go," Phoenix said with a small jerk of her head. She glanced upward and added wryly, "You might want to hurry...."

He noticed only then how dark the day had gotten. The air lay on his skin like a hot, wet blanket, and somewhere in the distance thunder rumbled. He felt as surly as the weather, his thoughts humid and unsettled, confusion and frustration tumbling rampant through his insides. He stood and looked at her, part of him craving the peace and quiet only distancing himself from her could bring, part longing to plunge headlong into the emotional tumult, to hold on to her and never let go.

"Go," she repeated in a grating voice, forcing herself to smile. She waited until he had nodded and turned away before she sagged against the chain-link fence, shaken... shaking inside.

His eyes aren't a shaman's eyes now. The thought gave her a sharp and angry sense of triumph, but no satisfaction. Those emotions she'd been so smugly sure of, those passions she'd sensed churning below the surface of his quietness—all that and more she'd seen just now in those dark and turbulent eyes. But those feelings were in no way hers to control. Foolish, foolish Phoenix, she thought, to ever have imagined they might be.

Control *his* emotions? How, when she couldn't even manage her own? Avidly, she watched the trio on the basketball court—which, due to the combination of the heat index, a threatening storm and the sports season, they enjoyed unchallenged—tall, imposing black man in running clothes, cute skinny black kid in clothes several sizes too big, and Dr. Ethan Brown, the president's kid, blond, conservative and wholesome as shredded wheat in light blue jeans and a pale yellow polo shirt. It was obvious the doc wasn't much of an athlete; in spite of his size and naturally beautiful physique, he had none of Tom Applegate's feline grace. And yet of the three out on that court it was he who drew her gaze like filings to a magnet. *His* moves she followed, standing on the sidelines, clinging with both hands to the chain-link fence like a shunned child, with the ache of yearning behind her smile. She heard a little boy's laughter, but it was the doc's face she saw, smiling and flushed with heat and exertion as he scooped up the boy with the ball hugged tight in his arms and lifted him high, high toward the basket. She heard the childish shriek of delight as the ball clanged through the iron hoop, but it was the doc's quiet "Way to go!" as he executed an endearingly awkward high five that made her breath catch and tears gather sizzling behind her eyes.

What do you want from me? She'd asked him that only minutes ago, hadn't she? Now she knew she should have asked herself the same question. *What do you want from this man, Joanna?*

She was suddenly terribly afraid that what she wanted was something she'd have no earthly idea what to do with once she got it. Afraid that if she got it, and if she tried to make it work, she might harm this gentle and beautiful man irreparably. Afraid that with her selfish wanting she *would* try—and hurt him—anyway.

A large raindrop splashed onto the back of her hand. She looked up, startled, as if such a thing were completely inexplicable and miraculous, and when she did, another drop landed on her cheek. She was wiping it away when the three came, laughing, through the gate.

Tom Applegate was talking to his watch. "Carl's gone to get the car. He'll meet us on this side of the park," he reported when he'd finished.

Ethan glanced at Michael, who was looking mulish and disappointed, then said to Tom, "Why don't you tell him to meet us over at—" he just did stop himself from saying "The Gardens," and with a quick, guilty glance at Phoenix made it "—Michael's place. We can walk back. That way we can stop on the way and get a hot dog—how's that sound, Michael?"

Michael shrugged and said, "That's cool," trying hard to be offhanded. But he couldn't keep the grin from slipping through his pose of determined indifference.

"How 'bout you?" Ethan said, turning to Phoenix. He wanted to lower his voice to a level of privacy, make a joking remark about "regular people," maybe say something cute about Leroy and Joanna. But those were things between them, and it felt wrong, suddenly, to share them with anyone, even someone as unobtrusive as the Secret Service, or as oblivious as a child. What he offered instead was a rather stiff and formal sounding, "Would you like to join us for lunch? We can take you home, if you want to, after we drop off Michael."

"That's cool," she said with a shrug, in deliberate imitation of the child. Except that she didn't smile, and her eyes, before she turned to walk beside him, had a curious silvery brightness, as if a hard rain was falling somewhere just behind them.

Around them raindrops fell only sporadically, making quarter-sized dark spots on the sidewalk. Thunder growled and wind blew in fitful gusts, stirring the pea-soup air like an indifferent chef—though one inclined to carelessly throw in dashes of ozone and hot asphalt now and then for spice.

Thinking the storm only meant to shake its fist and then pass them by, they ignored it, taking their time, walking slowly, Michael bouncing the basketball, the adults taking turns retrieving it when it got away from him. No one talked much—Tom, because it was both his nature and his job to keep his mouth shut and his eyes open, Ethan and Phoenix making the child the center of their attention the way adults do when they need an excuse not to talk to each other. And yet their awareness of each other held more electricity and tension than the storm. It arced between them, bridging the gap between glances that tried hard to avoid meeting; it hummed a background to short, breathless comments and rose to cresendo in the silences. Walking languidly along, Ethan felt a constant need to wipe away sweat, and more winded than when he'd been running in the heat on the basketball court.

They stopped to buy hot dogs from a street vendor who was getting ready to close up shop, and surly about being forced to delay. Then a little later on from another pushcart, ices—a concoction Ethan was sure only a child could find palatable, consisting of sugar water, slush and a dye guaranteed to turn lips and tongues a goulish shade of blue.

While Ethan was paying the vendor for the ices a gust of wind blew Phoenix's cowboy hat off, and only Tom Applegate's quick reflexes prevented it from flying into the street.

As he returned the hat to its owner, with a meaningful glance at the darkening sky the agent said quietly to Ethan, "Sir, I think we need to be getting on."

"Right." Ethan offered a cone of blue slush to Phoenix. She gave it—and him—a quizzical look but gamely took it.

Knowing it was unwise, he allowed his gaze to linger on her hand as it tentatively enfolded the gaudy paper cone. It came to him as an oddly painful little revelation that it didn't look like a rock star's hand—at least not one that went with backless tiger-striped tops and navel rings. The nails were unmanicured but kept short and very clean. It seemed small and somehow defenseless to him, like the hand of a meticulous child.

"Hey, where's mine?" Michael demanded, handing the

basketball off to Tom with a trusting no-look pass and grab-
bing at the cones Ethan still had in his hands.

"I know your mama taught you better," Ethan said
sternly, holding the cones out of reach. Michael's face fell.
He looked so deflated Ethan had to fight to hold on to his
frown. "What do you say?"

"Can I please have my ice?" Michael mumbled, address-
ing his shoes.

"Much better." Ethan handed over the cone and gave
Michael's baseball cap a forgiving tug. He offered the last
ice to Tom, who declined—with obvious relief. With no
other choice left to him, Ethan took a tentative taste. The
syrupy sweetness made him shudder.

"Sir," Tom said again, quietly urgent, "if I'm not mistaken, the sky's about to open up on us. Unless you want
to get wet, we'd best hurry."

"What are you, his mother?" Phoenix said, making Michael giggle.

But they started moving again, walking quickly now, with
Michael having to hop and skip to keep up. The wind scut-
tled trash along the gutter and pushed impatiently at their
backs, molding Phoenix's skirt to her legs and slapping the
edges against Ethan's pantlegs. Lightning flickered, and
raindrops fell with a spattering sound. Moments later thunder boomed a tympany solo.

"Hey!" Michael cried in tones of outrage.

Tom had time to say only, "Uh-oh, here it comes." And
then the sky did open up.

They ran, Ethan holding Michael by the hand, Phoenix
with her hat clasped against her chest, Tom vigilantly bringing up the rear, though he could easily have outpaced them
all.

Phoenix ran laughing and gasping, filled with a strange
sense of euphoria. They would be thoroughly soaked, there
was no way to avoid it; her hat would be ruined, there was

nothing she could do about it. And something about that inevitability, and her helplessness in the face of it, was unbelievably liberating. She could have no control over this. And thus she was utterly and completely *free*.

She was aware that her skirt was plastered to her legs, that her hair had come loose and was clinging in ribbons to her face, neck and back. Blindly she ran, through a veil of rain, following Ethan's lead, trusting him to know where he was going, leaping flooded gutters, her feet splashing gloriously on the inundated streets. *Dance in the rain...* She'd told him, hadn't she, that it was one of her favorite things? At the time, she'd thought she was making it up, but maybe...maybe somewhere inside her, someone—Joanna?—must have known that it was true.

She was conscious of a feeling almost of disappointment when Ethan turned hard to the right and led them up some cracked concrete steps. Still euphoric and half-blinded by the rain and her own streaming hair, she barely noticed the peeling paint on the door frame, the broken pane of glass in the front door, the crumbling mortar. It was only when they were inside the vestibule, laughing, gasping and stamping away water, and the door was closing behind them with a sticky sound, that the first alarms began to ring in her mind. She was like an animal sensing the trap—too late.

Somewhere beyond the accelerated thumping of her own heart she could hear Michael's voice and Ethan's, laughing and exclaiming over the drowned remains of their ices. She knew that Tom was starting up the stairs, and that Ethan and Michael were following. She knew that, unless she wanted to stay and wait for them where she was, she would have to climb those stairs, too.

Claustrophobia coiled its tentacles around her, suffocating her with the smells of poverty and decay. It was hot in the vestibule, and even hotter in the stairwell, a dense and muggy heat that increased with every tread she climbed. But in spite of that, she felt chilled. Cold clear through to her bones.

But Momma, I don't want to go by myself. There's somebody creepy on the stairs...he looks at me funny. Please, can't you come with me, Momma?

One level...then another. The smells of cooking, urine and mildew made her want to gag.

She caught up with Michael on the third-floor landing. At the far end of a dusky hallway she could see Tom checking into recesses and doorways, cautiously alert, while Ethan moved purposefully toward him, apparently making for a door halfway down the hall. For some reason, though, Michael was dawdling behind, lingering in front of a door closer to the landing. When Phoenix reached the top of the stairs he turned his head and lifted his eyes to hers, and gazed at her for a long, silent time.

He had strange eyes for a child, she thought—almost yellow, like a hawk's or a tiger's, and they seemed to shimmer in the dim gray light. And then somehow, without any idea how it had happened, she found that she was holding his hand.

"This is where I used to live," the little boy said in a soft, gruff voice. "Before my momma got killed. She was on the balcony and it fell down, and now she dead."

Phoenix felt her stomach clench as if she'd been punched there, and the air force its way through her lungs to erupt in a soft, wounded gasp. Cold swept her, stinging like an icy blast. A rushing sound filled her ears. Her world seemed to shrink, her field of vision to sharpen and narrow until it contained only Ethan, standing there in the hallway, hand raised to knock, face turned toward her, mouth forming a question, the moment frozen in time as if someone had hit the pause button on a VCR.

"You bastard," she said softly and distinctly. Then she turned and ran down the stairs and out into the rain.

Chapter 11

Ethan's swearing brought Tom Applegate in three swift strides, one hand already going to the weapon at the small of his back.

"What's goin' on?"

"I don't know." But he did know. He did. He swore some more, although after a glance at Michael he was careful to keep it under his breath. On the other side of the door he could hear someone fumbling with the locks. The urge to run after Phoenix twitched through his nerves and muscles; the need to stay where he was filled his voice with a tense and edgy desperation. "Go after her."

"Sir, you know I can't do that." The Secret Service agent's quiet voice was muffled; he had his back to Ethan, now, having automatically placed himself between his protectee and the empty stairwell.

The door in front of Ethan opened, forcing him to bite back arguments he knew were going to be futile anyway. Michael's aunt Tamara peered cautiously through the narrow gap, then hurriedly slipped the chain and flung the door wide.

"Lord, you soakin' wet!" With the fat, big-eyed baby astraddle one hip and her face haggard with maternal fatigue and worry, she rounded on Michael. "Look at you, child— you 'bout half drowned. Get yourself in here and get out of those wet clothes. You gonna catch your death—and you just gettin' over them earaches… My lord, what *is* that on your tongue, boy? You all *blue*." She glared accusingly at Ethan as she dragged Michael past her into the apartment.

Then, suddenly recalling who it was she was talking to, she clapped a contrite hand to her forehead. "Oh, man. I am so sorry, Dr. Brown, I didn't mean to yell. It's just, I been so worried with the storm and all, and you not being back. I feel responsible for him, know what I mean?" She gave the baby a hitch, self-consciousness creeping over her now that she was assured her charge was safe and sound. Doubtfully, she said, "You…wanna come in for a minute? Dry y'selves off? Can I get you a towel, or…" Her glance flicked from Ethan to Tom and back again with something akin to panic.

"No, thanks, that's nice of you, but we're kind of in a hurry," Ethan said, and as quickly as he spoke them, the words still seemed to take forever. He reached a hand toward Michael, stopping just short of touching his baseball cap. Striving for outward calm and good manners, he felt jittery and out of breath; his mind had gone somewhere else, following Phoenix through driving curtains of rain. "We had a good time, though, didn't we, Michael? Shot some hoops…"

"Yeah, an' I even made a slam dunk, just like Michael Jordan! Doc…helped me…"

Ethan's chest felt achy and tight, and he could feel his pulse tapping against his belt buckle. He smiled. "Yeah, you did.'' To Tamara he added, ''We had a hot dog and an ice, by the way—hope that was okay.''

''That's fine. Michael, did you say thank you? Tell Dr. Brown thank you, now.''

''Thank you,'' mumbled Michael.

''You're welcome. We'll do it again sometime, okay?'' Michael nodded. Ethan held out his hand for a slap, the way he was learning to do. Tamara added her thanks, breathless with relief.

As the door was closing, Ethan heard Michael say, ''You know what? That guy Tom? He's sort of a cop, and he even knows Michael—'' The locks clicked one by one into place, but by that time Ethan was halfway to the stairs.

In the muggy vestibule, Tom had to grab him by the arm and hold him to keep him from bursting through the door ahead of him. ''*Dammit,* sir,'' the Secret Service agent said, in an uncharacteristic lapse of protocol.

Standing in the middle of the sidewalk with rain streaming down his face and into his eyes, Ethan felt hope wash out of him—the hope, faint though it had been, that she'd be waiting for him somewhere out here, huddled on the steps like a half-drowned kitten, perhaps. Tiger kitten…

Tom touched his arm. The back door of a dark sedan parked at the curb was standing open. Ethan bent down and looked inside, and his very last hope—the hope that she might be inside—evaporated. He got in and Tom slammed the door after him, then climbed into the front passenger seat. At the wheel, Carl nodded a courteous greeting, and the sedan pulled smoothly away from the curb.

For the next hour they drove up and down the glistening streets, peering past thumping windshield wipers, staring through curtains of rain…then fitful showers…then sprinkles. The storm passed and the sun came out and steam rose from sidewalks, stoops and rooftops. But there was no sign at all of Phoenix.

* * *

It was cool and quiet in the church. The storm seemed far away. In spite of the darkness outside, the interior light was a gentle golden color that made the air seem warmer than it really was, and Phoenix let it settle over her like a blanket. She was thoroughly chilled but too numb and too exhausted, now, to shiver.

She sat alone in a pew near the front of the sanctuary, on the side aisle so she was less likely to be noticed, gazing at a statue of the Virgin Mary holding Baby Jesus, and at the cluster of little candles flickering around her feet. It wasn't the first time she'd been in a Catholic Church, though it had been a good many years. One of her foster families had been Catholic, and for a time she'd been dragged relentlessly to catechism and forced to confess her sins. And what a boring recitation she'd always thought that must have been, since it was before she'd acquired a very interesting assortment of major sins, and before she'd gotten cynical enough to make up some minor ones. And, of course, the Big One she'd never been able to bring herself to speak of out loud, then or since.

Funny, though, that she could still remember some of the words. *Hail Mary, full of grace...*

"Hello, may I help you?"

Slowly, she shifted her gaze from the Madonna's face to the man who had just slipped into the pew in front of her. He was wearing a short-sleeved black shirt with a priest's collar, but she recognized him as the dark man in bermuda shorts and T-shirt she'd spoken to outside the church, the day she'd come to explore her old neighborhood. She narrowed her eyes and looked quickly away, as if from a too-bright light. "Sorry," she mumbled. "I'll go..."

"No, no—stay as long as you like." The priest's voice was light and easy, and, she noticed now, just slightly accented. After a moment he chuckled. "I wasn't sure it was

you when you first came in. You look a little different than
you did when we met in your manager's office.''

Phoenix said nothing; her lips twitched into a half smile,
but she felt no amusement at all. The priest was silent, too,
but she could feel his eyes on her, and for some reason that
awareness made her throat ache and tears gather stinging in
her sinuses.

After a while he said softly, ''This isn't the first time
you've been here, though, is it? I think I talked to you the
other day, out front—what was it, about a week ago? I was
cutting the grass, and you asked me for directions.'' There
was a pause, and then he asked in an even quieter voice,
''Tell me…did you find what you were looking for?''

She shook her head. To her dismay, a tear slipped onto
her cold cheek, warming it only briefly before she brushed
it away. A vast, aching emptiness filled her, along with an
appalling urge to hurl herself into the arms of this man with
the kind eyes and quiet voice and burst into a child's noisy
sobs.

Denying it, she whispered angrily, ''Find what I was
looking for? I can't even find my*self*. I mean, I used to know
exactly who I was. I thought I did. I'm Phoenix, dammit.
Phoenix! Now, all of a sudden it's like I'm losing my grip.
Losing myself. I don't think I know who I am anymore.…''

Tears were hot rivers on her face. Humiliated, she tried
to hide them with her fingers, but found her chilled hands
imprisoned instead between two nice warm ones. That reminded her so much of the doc, and the way he'd held her
hands in his and kissed her fingertips.… The ache inside her
grew intolerable.

''Crying's nothing to be ashamed of.'' The priest's voice
was matter-of-fact.

She blinked him into focus and found his kind brown eyes
resting gently on her face. The eyes reminded her of the
doc's eyes.

It came to her all at once and as an absolute certainty that she could trust this man.

Then it came to her, but gradually, like a tiny seed sprouting through winter-frozen ground, that maybe…just maybe…she could trust Ethan Brown, too.

She sniffed rather desperately, and the priest relinquished her hands. He took a large cotton handkerchief from his pants pocket and handed it to her as he said cheerfully, "You know it's not an uncommon thing, to try to find oneself. Maybe you're looking at this all wrong…"

Phoenix blew her nose and said damply, "Oh, yeah, how?"

"Well, there's more than two letters' difference between losing and looking, you know. One's a negative, the other's a positive." He paused. "You shouldn't ever be afraid of looking."

"But what if—" her voice broke and she caught a quick breath "—I look for myself, and I don't like what I find? What if the person I find…if she's…not…" She searched for the words, but the priest didn't wait.

"Worth loving?" he supplied, and smiled. "If that's what you're worried about, forget it. I've got a flash for you—there's no such thing. Everybody deserves to be loved." He squeezed her shoulder gently as he left her.

Phoenix blew her nose on the soft handkerchief, then sat for a long time, gazing at the Mother and Child and the flickering candles. Strangely, she didn't feel cold anymore.

Too unsettled, his mind too restless to face his empty apartment, Ethan spent the rest of the afternoon at the clinic, trying to focus on his perennial backlog of paperwork. It was late—past ten—when he finally said good-night to Tom and climbed the stairs to his apartment, so it was somewhat startling to him to hear a knock on his front door just as he peeled off his shirt, preparatory to stepping into the shower.

He hurriedly shut off the water and went to answer it, heart thumping, knowing that without an advance phone call it could only be the Service. And, given the hour, something of major importance. Chilled, emotionally braced for the worst of possibilities, he opened the door.

It was Tom, impassive as always, his face giving nothing away. "Sorry to bother you, sir," he said as he handed Ethan a manila envelope. "This fax came for you this afternoon. I thought you'd want to see it right away."

Ethan opened the envelope and drew out several sheets of paper. The top one bore the White House letterhead. And below that, in his stepmother's blunt, distinctive scrawl: *Hi, Darlin'—Could this be your Joanna? Love, Dixie.*

What followed appeared to be several pages covered with copies of newspaper articles.

"Yeah…" His heart was racing in earnest now. Unable to tear his eyes from the papers, he mumbled his thanks.

"No problem. Good night, sir." The Secret Service man gently closed the door.

Ethan carried the envelope over to the couch and sat tensely on the edge of the cushions while he dumped its contents onto the coffee table. Headlines leaped at him, but he forced himself to arrange the articles methodically by date before beginning to read.

The first was dated March 7, twenty-five years earlier.

Mother, Two Children Die In Row House Apartment Fire

A mother and her two young children died when a fire apparently caused by faulty wiring swept through their third-floor apartment Thursday afternoon. Firefighters arriving on the scene found the upper floors of the substandard structure fully engulfed in flames. Despite heroic efforts, they were unable to reach the victims. A spokesman for the South Church Street Station, which

was the first company to respond to the fire, said res-
cuers found fire escapes rusted away and windows
painted shut. Investigators were still on the scene late
Thursday evening, but preliminary reports indicate that
substandard conditions in the row house apartment
building may have contributed to both the cause of the
blaze and the fatalities.

The victims, who have been identified as Rachel
Evans Dunn, 27, and her two children, Jonathan, 9, and
Christina, 3, were trapped in their apartment by the
flames and apparently died from smoke inhalation. A
third child, Joanna, 9, who neighbors said was a twin
to one of the victims, was not at home at the time of
the fire. She is the only surviving member of the family.

Four others, including a firefighter, were treated for
smoke inhalation and minor burns and released.

Ethan sat for a long time, staring at the pages spread across
the coffee table. He felt cold—cold clear through to his
bones—and there was a brassy taste at the back of his throat
that he couldn't get rid of no matter how many times he
swallowed.

Could this be your Joanna?

Frustratingly, he still didn't know that—not for certain.
The follow-up articles were mostly about the investigation
into the cause of the fire and the case against the landlord,
who was subsequently prosecuted for various code viola-
tions and involuntary manslaughter. The child Joanna was
mentioned again in all of the articles as background, and
always identified as her family's only survivor. But as to
what had become of her after that, there was nothing. Nothing at all.

My name is Joanna…Joanna Dunn.

Was it possible? Could this little girl, who had escaped a

terrible death along with her entire family only by a matter of luck—or the grace of God—have somehow become the rock-and-roll legend known to the entire world as Phoenix?

Phoenix. The truth came to Ethan in blinding, white-hot revelation. Heart pounding, he tore through his bookshelves until he found his dictionary, but even before he looked it up, he knew that he was right. *Phoenix…the legendary bird, Egyptian symbol of immortality…said to perish by flames every five hundred years, only to rise reborn from its own ashes….*

Ethan had no idea how long it was before he rose from the couch and walked into the bathroom, peeled off his clothes and climbed stiffly into the shower. He turned on the water as hot as he could stand it, but even though his skin turned lobster red, he could not make the cold deep inside him go away.

"So, what would have become of her?"

Ethan put the question to Father Frank the next afternoon. Sunday's masses were long since concluded, and he'd found his old friend relaxing in the rectory kitchen over iced tea and a plateful of Ruthie's homemade cookies. Still feeling sick inside, Ethan had declined the cookies. Instead he toyed restlessly with the film of moisture on his iced tea glass. "I assume the father was long gone. If she was her family's only survivor, where would she go?"

Father Frank picked up a cookie, put it down and leaned back in his chair, rubbing a regretful hand over his rounded belly. "Into foster care, probably."

"Is there any way to find out?"

The priest shook his head. "I doubt it. Those records are confidential. It would take a court order, and even then…I don't know."

"Six years…" Ethan said softly, watching himself make interlocking figure eights on the tabletop with the bottom of his glass. "That's what's missing. At nine she loses her family and vanishes into the black hole known as child services. Six years later, at fifteen, she explodes onto the world stage when she sings Rupert Dove's Oscar-nominated song at the Academy Awards." He smiled wryly at his hands. "I've seen tapes of that performance. Man, she almost caused a riot." He shook his head, then let out a slow, defeated breath. "What happened to her during those missing years, Franco? How will I ever know?"

"Is it so important for you to know?" His eyes were quiet and dark—priest's eyes. Ethan could almost hear the unspoken "My son..."

For that reason, he was careful with his answer. "I think it *is* important...but not for me." And he was surprised, as he heard himself say the words, to find that they were true. "I mean, I believe it's important that I know, so I can...let *her* know..." He stopped, frustrated. Stymied.

His old friend Frank, however, smiled in perfect understanding. "So you can let her know it's *okay*—whatever it is."

"*Right...*" Ethan sat back with a grateful sigh, then, with restored confidence amended, "That *she's* okay. And that I—" He caught himself just in time.

"That you...love her anyway?" Ethan made a faint sound, a denial, and Frank gently persisted, "You do, don't you?"

"I don't know." Ethan frowned at his hands. It had become hard to talk. There seemed to be some sort of strange vibration deep inside his chest that was interfering with his voice, his breathing, even his heartbeat. "I think..." he had to concentrate on unclenching his jaws "...I may be...starting to." He frowned even harder. "It's just been happening so *fast*."

Father Frank laughed and reached defiantly for a cookie after all. "I'm no expert, you understand, but I hear it does that way sometimes.'' He studied the cookie intently, then said, ''You want my advice?''

Ethan threw up his hands. ''Yeah, I want your advice. Why do you think I'm here? You're my best friend—and a *priest,* for God's sake.''

Father Frank's smile was beatific. ''Exactly...'' He popped the cookie into his mouth with an air of getting down to business. ''Okay, so here it is. Ta-dah... Ask the one who knows.''

Ethan snorted. ''Easy for you to say. She won't talk about it. In fact, after yesterday, she may never talk to me again.''

Still chewing, Father Frank shook his head. ''Mmm-um— not Phoenix. You want to know about those missing years? If it were me, I'd ask Rupert Dove.''

Phoenix stood behind her old piano man, watching him make notes on the sheet of music propped up in front of him. His head was cocked back so he could see through the glasses perched on the end of his nose. She focused on the oval patch of shiny walnut-brown skin on his crown. ''Doveman, can I ask you a question?''

He cackled thinly but didn't look around. ''Since when you ask my permission?''

Newly discovered nerves jumped and skittered in her belly. She had an overpowering desire to throw her arms around his neck and lay her cheek alongside his stubbly jaw the way she had when she was a child, and inhale his familiar and comforting scent of Old Spice, whiskey and cigarettes. To curb the urge, she folded her arms across her middle and went to lean against the piano box.

''No—this isn't about music. I want to know something—'' she took a breath ''—about...when you found me.''

Doveman stopped writing. He took off his glasses, drew a handkerchief from his pocket and began to wipe them with it. Not looking at her, he said slowly, "What you wantin' to know?"

"Why'd you do it?" She made her voice hard. "When I tried to hustle you, why didn't you just turn me over to the cops? Why'd you take me in?"

It seemed a long time before he answered…just sat there wiping methodically at his glasses with the handkerchief, as if he hadn't heard her. Then he looked up, and his eyes had that sad, filmy look that made her heart lurch and her chest turn cold and fearful with the thought, *Doveman's old*….

"Why didn't I turn you in? Child, it never once entered my mind to do that."

"But *why?* I was a street kid—a hustler. I *stole* from you."

"Well…maybe I never saw that street kid…that hustler. All I saw was a little lost bird, got blown out of her nest by a storm. Nothin' to do with a bird like that, you know, but take her in, give her shelter, make her feel safe an' warm…"

"But," Phoenix whispered, "how did you *know?*" Her throat felt raw, as if all the tears she hadn't shed back then were burning there now, saltwater on her wounded spirit. "For all you knew I could've just…ripped you off and split."

The piano man smiled. "Oh…I knew you wasn't gonna do that. Not once you found out ol' Doveman had something you needed more than a baby need's her momma's milk." Phoenix made a small, frustrated sound, but Doveman shook his head. He held up his hands with their fingers gnarled and bent, the palms pale and lined like fine old parchment. "I had these, baby-girl. They was the keys…"

"Keys?" She cried it out, frustrated…aching.

"That's right." Doveman touched his own chest, just over the spot where *she* hurt so. "These old hands was the keys that let loose all that music you had shut up inside here. That music was born in you, child. You came into this

world with that music in your soul. Just didn't know how
to let it out. You was a lost and angry child until ol' Doveman came along with these hands and showed you how.''

''Then why,'' she whispered, dashing away tears, ''do I
feel so lost now? I have you, I have the music....''

Doveman shook his head. He swiveled on the bench, his
eyes going past her and far, far away. ''Because things
change,'' he said in his soft, ruined voice. ''Everything has
its time. Everything has its season. Time comes when ol'
Doveman and the music aren't enough anymore. Time
comes when you be wantin' somebody to love. Somebody
to love *you,* maybe make some fat pretty babies with you.
That's the way it's meant to be...''

Phoenix caught and held her breath. *I want something
more from you.*

*What scares me is...maybe you want something from me
that I can't give you.*

She cried out, with the harshness of fear, ''What if I
can't?''

The piano man's gaze jerked back to her, eyebrows raised
as if in amazement. ''Can't what? Can't find anybody, or
can't love?''

''Both!''

''Well,'' he shot back, exasperated, ''I know for a certainty you ain't gonna be able to do either one 'less you
love y'self first!''

Phoenix gave a snort of hopeless laughter. ''*Love* myself?
How am I supposed to do that when I don't even know who
the hell I am?''

Doveman just shook his head and didn't say anything.
Unable to withstand his gaze any longer, she pushed away
from the piano and walked, as she so often did, to the windows. From there, with her back to him she said softly,
rubbing at the goose bumps on her arms, ''Yesterday a priest
told me I wasn't lost at all...just *looking.* As in, searching

for? Trying to find something, i.e., *me*." She gave another of those high, hurting laughs. "He might be right, but what I didn't tell him is that I have no clue at all where to look. None…"

Feeling so desolate, it came as a shock to her to hear the rusty wheeze of Doveman's laughter. She turned with the hurt of betrayal in her eyes and an angry reproach on her lips, to find him regarding her the way she imagined a doting father might look upon his slightly foolish child.

"Well, now," he said with an exaggerated lifting of his shoulders, "I don't know about *you*, but the first thing *I* generally do when I want to find something is, I go back and look in the place I was when I lost it."

Stepping from the dark sedan while Tom Applegate held the door for him, Ethan looked up at the squatty redbrick building silhouetted against a fading sunset as if it were a holy place, a sacred shrine to which he'd come seeking answers…or at the very least a soothing balm to quiet his uneasy soul. The shadowed and dusty windows gave him little hope of, either.

"You don't have to come in, do you?" he said to Tom as he slammed the car door. "I don't think this is going to take long."

The Secret Service agent regarded him for a long, tense moment, no doubt assessing his duties and weighing the likelihood that Ethan might give him the slip out the back way again. Apparently concluding the risk was minimal and his protectee's intentions pure, at least this time, he gave in, but on a soft exhalation of long-suffering. "All right, sir. I'll wait here."

The front door was locked. Ethan pushed on a button unobtrusively located to the left of the door and heard a bell's strident shriek echo and resound behind the solid brick walls. He waited, fidgeting, and had just turned to go back down the steps, thinking he'd try the loading dock entrance, when the door clanked open behind him.

"Hey, Doc, how y'doing?" Rupert Dove greeted him in his cracked voice. "Saw you on the monitor...sorry I couldn't get here any quicker. These ol' legs don't go like they used to." He cackled, then turned somber, though his eyes still held a certain brightness. "What can I do for you, Doc? Sorry to tell you, but if you're wantin' Phoenix, she ain't here."

Ethan smiled, even as he wondered what those sharp old eyes would make of it. There was, he thought, something almost birdlike about their intensity. "That's okay," he said, "it's you I came to see."

"Me!" The old man reared back as he said it, but Ethan had the feeling he wasn't really all that surprised. "Well now. You'd best come in, then. Come on in, son."

He closed the heavy door, than led Ethan past other doors, also closed, past the empty recording studio and control room, into the rehearsal hall. As before, the huge room was dimly lit, the only illumination coming from the bandstand, music stands and sound equipment softly backlit like the chancel of a church. Ethan would have been glad to stop there, glad to have this conversation in the camouflaging darkness, but Rupert Dove led him on, straight through the hall.

"May's well be comfortable," he said as he waved Ethan onto the elevator ahead of him. Following, he clanked the cage gate shut and threw Ethan an unapologetic grin. "Got my smokes hid upstairs."

In the loft, Rupert Dove waved his guest to the couch with a careless gesture and made a beeline for the baby grand. He fished a half-empty pack of Camels and a book of matches from its innards and lit up, carefully putting the extinguished match in his pocket before he turned back to Ethan, coughing smoke. "What can I get for you, son?"

The old piano man waited while Ethan shook his head, then settled himself on the piano bench. Ethan felt sure it must be his customary place; he looked so natural there—like part of the instrument itself. Rupert Dove took another deep drag from his cigarette, coughed alarmingly as he tapped ash into the palm of his hand, then looked narrow-eyed at Ethan. "Well then—what can I *do* for you?"

Ethan leaned sharply forward and frowned at his hands, fingers laced together between his knees. His heart was racing; he hadn't imagined this would be so hard.

"I expect," the old man prompted gently, "you're wantin' to ask me about *her.* 'Bout Phoenix."

"Not Phoenix," Ethan said, looking up and straight into the old man's eyes. "Joanna." Before the piano man could say anything, Ethan pulled the folded paper with the copy of the newspaper article on it from his shirt pocket, unfolded it carefully, then stood and stepped across the space between them. He handed it to Rupert Dove, then sat down again and waited while the old man took a pair of glasses from his pocket and put them on. Breathing in careful measures, Ethan watched the slow movement of his lips as he read.

"Oh, my, my…" Rupert Dove said softly when he'd finished.

"Is that her?" The question came more harshly than he'd meant it, but he didn't apologize.

The piano man took off his glasses and carefully folded them and put them back in his pocket before he replied. His eyes no longer looked sharp, but were filmy, now, and sad. "I expect it probably is."

"But you don't *know?*"

"I never did know for certain what happened to her folks. She used to have bad dreams, you know, when I first found her. She'd be screamin' and talkin' in her sleep, talkin' wild, about some old tenement building and about fire, and, oh, terrible things. Then she'd wake up cryin' for her momma.

Sometimes she'd cry for them, too—the little ones. Called 'em John and Chrissy. But I never could get her to talk about it when she was awake, so I never did know for sure how it all happened. Or why she lived and all them didn't.'' He shook his head and lifted the cigarette to his lips.

"What happened to her afterward, do you know?" Ethan's voice was rough. "How did *you* meet her?"

"How'd I meet her?" The piano man laughed softly as he watched the fingers of one hand tap cigarette ash into the palm of the other. He shook his head. "Ah...man. She was a street kid—thirteen years old and a regular little hustler. I'd seen her around, you know, seen her watchin' the street musicians play for change. Saw the way her face'd just light up, like she was standin' on the steps of Heaven itself. Figured anybody loved music that much must have a pretty good portion of it in her soul, so...I took her in. Gave her a chance." He gave a shrug as if to say, "And the rest is history..."

Ethan felt cold to the bone, hollow and fragile as glass. "She was on the *street?*" he said in a cracking voice, feeling as if it was he who was cracking, coming apart inside. "Why wasn't she in a foster home? She was only nine...."

"I expect she was, at first. In a bunch of them, most likely. From things she told me way back then, I gathered she didn't take to it too well. Not all that surprising—she was bound to be pretty messed up in the head over what happened to her folks. And then...I think somebody messed with her...other ways. That's when she ran away, figured she'd take her chances in the streets."

"My God," Ethan whispered. "My God...how old was she, do you know? How long was she out there on her own? How in Heaven's name did she survive?"

"She'd have to tell you that," Rupert Dove said flatly. "Anyway she could, I expect." He rose and went to extinguish his cigarette under a stream of water in the kitchen sink. When he returned to his bench, he sat himself straight up with one long-fingered hand rounded on each knee and fixed Ethan with a look that was more hawk than dove. ''I'll tell you what I do know. Whatever she did out there, it was what she had to do to survive. It didn't touch her *here*.'' He tapped his chest with one bony finger. ''It's like I told you before—that girl has a virgin's heart. And a soul just as sweet and beautiful as a child's. She did what she had to do, and she ain't ashamed of that. That ain't the reason—'' He stopped and looked away, and Ethan quietly finished it for him.

''—she hates herself?''

''The reason she hates *Joanna*,'' Doveman corrected. ''And thinks everybody else is sure to hate her, too. I don't know why that is. Whatever it is, it's something only Joanna knows. And she ain't talkin'.'' He drew a deep breath and coughed long and hard, and Ethan felt the chill of sudden realization. He knew what, as a doctor he should have guessed long before this. But it didn't take a battery of tests to tell him Rupert Dove was dying.

He felt himself buffeted inside, rocked and pummeled as if he were facing into a strong and gusty wind. And, as during similar stormy times in the past, he cast about in his mind for a safe harbor, a peaceful place in which to shelter from the tumult of his emotions…his own quiet place. But for the first time in his life he found that the peace and restoration he wanted—*needed*—could not be found in quietness, in solitude. For the first time in his life it wasn't aloneness he wanted.

He wanted the company of another person. A very *specific* person. He wanted Joanna. Wanted to be with her, see her, talk to her. Touch her. Wanted her nearness with a sharp and frantic hunger that made him like an addict running on empty. There were so many things he wanted to say to her.

Important things. Things as important, it seemed to him, as life itself. His life, certainly.

"Where is she?" he asked Rupert Dove, in a voice he didn't recognize. "I need to talk to her."

The piano man lifted his hands. "Couldn't tell you, son. She told me she wanted to find Joanna, and didn't know where to look. I told her she ought to look in the place where she lost her, but only she knows where that might be..."

Where do I look for Joanna?

An image flashed suddenly into his mind, as if someone had turned a spotlight on a darkened stage. He saw a face at the end of a long, dark hallway...Joanna's face, gone suddenly pale as death, and silver eyes as wild and forsaken as rain. And lips forming an accusation he couldn't hear.

He lurched to his feet. Rupert Dove rose more slowly, but still in time to clutch at his arm as he turned. "You know where she is, boy?"

"I think I might," Ethan said. Remorse filled his throat with gravel; shame coiled like steel bands around his chest, making it hard to breathe. *You bastard.* That was what she'd said to him, there in that stuffy hallway. And what a bastard he'd been, right from the beginning...self-righteous and judgmental. He wondered if she would forgive him. He remembered, suddenly, the image of the fawn in the woods, and thought bleakly that it would serve him right if he'd lost her forever.

In a hard voice, sparing himself nothing, he told Rupert Dove about Saturday's outing, about meeting Phoenix in the park, and what happened afterward.

"I didn't plan it," he said, the taste of disgust on his tongue. "But when I realized I had a chance to get her into that building...I'd been trying to get her to come down there to the Gardens. I thought she didn't have any idea what it was like to live like that." He broke off, muttering softly, and thrust his hand angrily through his hair. "I didn't know, Doveman," he whispered.

The piano man's hawklike stare pierced through his despair. "You think she might've gone back there—to that building?"

"I think so...yeah."

"Then what are we standin' here for? Let's go find her."

As the cage groaned and clanked its way downward with unbearable slowness, Rupert Dove gave a soft, wheezing laugh. "Funny thing is, you know...*she* said the same thing to me, the day she found out she owned the building where that poor woman was killed."

Ethan caught a hurting breath. "What's that?"

"'Doveman, I didn't know....'"

Chapter 12

Phoenix had made it only as far as the second-floor landing. She sat on the top step with her arms clasped around her legs and her knees tucked up to her chin, eyes wide-open and staring into the lurking shadows. She was shivering uncontrollably, shivering with a fear she didn't understand, with a cold that had nothing to do with degrees on a thermometer, and a strange desolation that blanketed her whole being like a damp, musty fog.

Joanna, don't you dawdle, you get that milk and hurry right on back, now, you hear? I'm depending on you. Promise me, now.

I will, Momma. I'll come right back, I promise....

Smells drifted up from the floor below—the familiar smells of mildew, human waste and decay...and a cooking smell, acrid and pervasive. Somebody was burning dinner. Something made a rustling sound in the trash that had collected in the corners of the stairs. Shuddering, she drew her feet closer. Somewhere a baby began to cry.

Waves of revulsion washed through her, leaving her weak and hollow. She drew deep, strengthening breaths—and coughed. The burned cooking smell from downstairs was stronger.

Bracing one hand on a wall so coated with grime that the graffiti hardly stood out at all, she rose stiffly to her feet and lifted her eyes to stare upward into the shadowy stairwell. One more floor to go.

The third floor. That was where the boy, Michael, lived. Lived with his aunt, now that his mother was dead. She'd go there…knock on his door…and tell him what? That she was sorry? She didn't know. She hadn't thought that far. It was just that…she could feel his hand creeping into hers, like a baby animal snuggling close to its mother for comfort. She could see the sadness in his strange golden eyes as he looked up at her….

Momma, why do I always have to be the one to go? Why can't Jonathan?

Joanna, you know your brother's not as strong as you are. Doctor says he has to be careful not to get too tired…

I don't care! I get tired, too. I have to work all the time. I always have to watch Chrissy, and I never get to play. I hate her! I hate Jonathon. And I hate you!

A tear rolled down her cheek. She brushed it away as she plodded, one step after another up the stairs, but others followed. Finally, halfway between the second floor and the third she paused to mop at her face with the hem of her shirt. But for some reason, her eyes just kept burning. She sniffed hard—and erupted into violent coughing. The smell—the burning food smell—was so strong it was choking her.

No—not a food smell. *Smoke.*

Smoke was drifting up the stairwell, reaching with ghostly tentacles, spreading like fake, stage fog, the kind that comes from dry ice. She could hear something now, too—a faint, far-off crackling sound.

Fear came first. It spiked through her like a lance, pinioning her to the spot. Paralyzed, unable to breathe, she closed her eyes tightly and clamped her hands over her ears, trying to shut out the screams. *Momma! Jonathan…Chrissy! Where are you? Momma!*

But the screams were inside her own head.

She never knew how she'd come to be there, but suddenly she was running down a hallway, hammering on doors with her fists and screaming, *"Fire!* Fire—get out! You have to get out!" Screaming until her throat was raw. Screaming and banging until doors opened to angry faces…slowly comprehending faces…frightened faces. And in the midst of that chaos, her mind was rejecting it all, insisting with the adamance of a stubborn child, *No—no, this can't be happening. It can't be happening, not to me!*

Angrily now she herded them down the hallway toward the stairs—children and old people, some half-dressed, some crying…some too dazed to even be scared. Inwardly raging, she felt almost glad to have an excuse to scream at someone, a reason to vent her fury at the Fates who would play such a cruel joke on her. *Not me! Why is this happening again…to me?*

The understanding came to her gently, more like a sunrise than a thunderclap. The screams and shouts and poundings faded and she entered a strange kind of calm, almost like a dream. *Of course you, Joanna. Of course you.*

In the dream she heard whispers, voices from the past. Doveman's voice, saying, "…Look in the place where I was when I lost it." She'd come full circle, Joanna had. The Fates had brought her back to the place where she'd lost herself, twenty-five years before. For reasons she couldn't begin to understand, she was being given another chance. A chance to find Joanna.

On the second floor the smoke was thicker. Doors were opening even before she got to them, people finally roused by the commotion, coming out to see what was going on and meeting with the black, choking cloud.

"Get down!" Joanna screamed at them. "Stay low, but hurry! Get out! Run!"

Down the stairs she went, elbowing people aside, stumbling, half falling, lungs screaming for air. It was her nightmare come to life—the blackness and choking smoke…the colors of fire, flames licking up a door frame, hissing across the ceiling…and a strange keening sound that she realized finally was coming from her own throat.

From somewhere nearby she heard glass breaking. People were all around her, pushing past her, some crying and choking, others eerily silent, all running, running for the front door and the clean clear air outside. She kept trying to make headway in the opposite direction, certain there must be someone else left inside, certain that only she could save them. But as in her nightmare, no matter how hard she tried, her legs would not propel her forward. She felt herself being carried along with the crowd, helpless as a leaf in a torrent.

Then she was outside, moving like a sleepwalker through the crowd of people that had gathered in the street…dark shapes with shocked faces, eyes staring past her at the smoke that had begun to billow from broken windows. Somewhere in the distance sirens wailed, getting louder, coming nearer. Someone clutched at her arm and she jerked around, startled and uncomprehending.

A woman stood there, arms wrapped protectively around the baby clinging in terror to her neck. The woman was shouting at her, her face contorted with anguish and fear, screaming words Joanna couldn't hear. The noise and the wailing of the sirens filled her ears, filled all the space inside her head. Clapping her hands over her hears, she bent her head close to the woman's and shouted, "What?"

"It's Michael! I can't find Michael! I don't know what happened to him—I thought he was right *there*. Oh, Lord—Oh, Jesus…I don't what I'll do if anything happens to him. First his momma and now…"

Michael. The little boy whose mother had died. The child she and Ethan had spent the day with Saturday, in the park. The child who had stood in front of his mother's apartment and gazed up at her with lost, golden eyes. She remembered the feel of his small hand stealing into hers, felt it so vividly she looked down and was surprised not to see him there.

She clutched the woman with both hands just as the sirens yelped and died, so her voice grated loud in the comparative silence. "You think he's still in there?"

The woman's head bobbed frantically. "He mighta went to his old place—I know he had the key. He'd do that sometimes, when he was missin' his momma bad. It's the first one you come to, right at the top—"

But Joanna was already running, pushing through the crowd with her panther's stride, making for the cracked concrete steps that would take her back into the burning building. Back into Hell. Back into her own half-forgotten past.

Ethan unbuckled his seat belt and hitched himself forward. "What's going on? Why are we stopping?"

Tom Applegate shrugged. "Can't see, sir. An emergency of some sort—they've got the street blocked off."

"Some kind of mess up ahead," Rupert Dove muttered, tapping his gnarled fingers on one bony knee.

Ethan demanded harshly, "Can't we get through some other way?" Urgency jumped and twitched in all his muscles; he felt a tightness in his chest and a churning in his belly he couldn't explain, except that he knew he had to see Joanna—or Phoenix, or whomever she decided she wanted to be; it no longer mattered to him, and he wanted, *needed,* to tell her that—*now.*

Tom lifted a hand from the steering wheel in a gesture of helplessness. His eyes met Ethan's in the rearview mirror— steady, uncompromising but not without compassion. Staring back at him, Ethan knew what he had to do. Without a moment's hesitation, he reached for the door handle.

"You ain't goin' without me," Rupert Dove wheezed as he pushed his own door open. Ethan heard the old man's raspy breathing close behind him as he wove his way between idling cars, wading across the streams of headlights and through clouds of engine exhaust. Just as he reached the sidewalk, Tom Applegate pushed past him, swearing, to take his customary place in the lead. Behind them in the clogged street, horns began to bleat futilely.

Two blocks farther on they found the street filled with fire engines and police and EMS vehicles. Beyond the police barricades shadowy figures were going efficiently about their business in a world turned chaotic, moving quickly, shouting orders, wrestling equipment, or bending quietly over silent shapes huddled on stoops and curbs. Outside the barricades people stood clumped together in groups, holding each other, some weeping, some just staring at the frantic scene with dazed and empty eyes.

With Tom running interference, Ethan pushed his way through the crowds and vehicles. He spotted Kenny Baumgartner near an EMS wagon and waved at him as he approached one of the cops manning the barricade. "I'm a doctor," he shouted. "I can help."

The cop looked over at Kenny, who yelled, "It's okay, he's a doctor. Let him in." He shifted the barricade enough to let Ethan through, then moved to block Tom Applegate and Rupert Dove when they would have followed.

"They're with me," Ethan said, but Tom already had his I.D. out.

"Where he goes, I go," the Secret Service agent said flatly. The cop gave the I.D. a glance, then looked up...and up...at Tom's impassive face, and moved aside. He looked as if he wanted to step in again when Rupert Dove moved to follow in Tom's wake, then thought better of it and waved him on through.

Ethan waded toward The Gardens through a swampy quagmire of déjà vu. Had it been so short a time since he'd been here? A few days that seemed like hours—or a life-time. It seemed the same to him in so many ways—the darkness, the aura of tragedy and disbelief and shock—and yet so much was not the same. Then he'd been one of the shadowy figures going about his work with detached calm, his emotions safely shut away in the protected Eden of his quiet place. Now he was one of *them*—the shattered and frightened ones, caught unawares by capricious disaster, his emotions all out in the open, unshielded, unguarded and unprepared. *Joanna...Joanna...* His fear for her was like a beast, tearing at his insides. It would not listen to arguments and reason. No use telling it she might not be here at all, and that if she had come, in all likelihood she'd have es-caped the building along with everyone else. On some prim-itive level of awareness he knew. *He knew.*

A baby's crying penetrated the worry that cloaked him, and then a woman's voice, bright and shrill with hysteria. It seemed somehow familiar to him. Focusing on the sound, he saw a woman clutching a sobbing, hiccuping baby, strug-gling in the determined grip of a paramedic. A new fear joined the beast already gnawing at his insides as he rec-ognized Michael's aunt, Tamara.

He had no memory of how he got to her, only of touching her arm and finding it dangerously cold and clammy. He joined the paramedic in trying to get her to sit down on the steps of the EMS truck, but she turned on him, clawing blindly at his shoulders, her voice shredded, made almost inaudible by her terror and grief. "Oh, God—Michael's in there. Michael's in there. She went after him, but they ain't come back. Oh, God—somebody go—"

"She? Who went after him? *Who?*" His throat brought up the words, and it was like coughing up glass.

"I don't know her name..." Tamara's knees were buckling. As Ethan and the paramedic eased her and her baby to the ground, she gasped out, "She was with y'all the other day when you brought Michael—"

Ethan turned blindly—and ran straight into a solid wall named Special Agent Tom Applegate. Breathing hard through his nose, he said flatly, "I'm going after her."

The Secret Service man's voice was just as unequivocal. "Sir, the only way you're going in there is over my dead body."

Something primitive leaped inside Ethan's chest. Adrenaline surged through his muscles. His fists curled. The next thing he knew he was caught in a viselike embrace, and his arms were pinioned to his sides. Near his ear Tom's quiet voice, breaking a little, was saying, "Sir, I'm sorry...I can't let you go in there. You know I can't. I'm sorry..."

Seconds passed. Ethan's sanity balanced on a razor's edge. Then a long quivering breath dragged agonizingly through his chest. "All right," he breathed. "All right..."

"Sir, let the firefighters do their job. They'll find her. If she's in there, they'll do everything they can to bring her out."

But will it be in time? Will everything be enough?
"Yeah...okay. All right..."

The bands around him eased. He drew another excruciating breath; his heart was racing, every beat torture. Dazed and shaking like a sleepwalker woken up too suddenly, he pulled away from the Secret Service man and looked around. But it was another few seconds before he was able to make full sense of his surroundings, and when he did, realization slammed him in the chest. Pivoting, he clutched a handful of Tom Applegate's shirt.

"Where's Rupert Dove?"

There were some advantages after all, Doveman thought, to being old. Old age made a person invisible, especially to the young. Young folks concentrating hard on doing a worrisome and difficult job paid no mind to an old black man— not until it was too late. He heard the shouts that followed him up the steps of the corner row house, but he paid them no mind. Then he was inside the burning building, and couldn't hear them, anyway.

The noise of the fire filled his ears, filled his head, filled his mind, suffocating thought. Ahead of him through the swirling, billowing smoke, he could see the stairs. Pulling the tail of his shirt over his face, he focused on them, held his breath and began to climb.

He knew just where she'd be. He'd spotted that third-floor window, the first one on the side, the one with the crumpled ledge and the remains of a broken balcony hanging off the bricks. The one where that boy's poor momma had died. Doveman knew his Joanna. If she'd gone after the boy, that's where she'd look for him. If she was alive, that's where she'd be.

And she *was* alive, Doveman was sure of that. The Lord wouldn't have brought her all this way to take her now, not when she was so close to the Promised Land....

Momma? Where are you? It's dark, and I'm scared. I can't see you, Momma...

I'm here, baby. Put out your hand...see? Just hold on to me. Everything's going to be all right...

"Momma? *Momma!*"

"It's okay, baby, I'm coming," Joanna shouted. Coughing racked her again as she crawled along the floor, feeling her way through the choking darkness, but it was mixed now with sobs of sheer relief. "Keep calling, Michael. Keep calling so I can find you…"

"Mom-*ma!* I can't *see* you!" The voice was closer now. And angry rather than afraid.

"I'm coming, Michael, I'm coming…" And all at once she could see him, over by a window—a dark head-shape in a backward baseball cap, silhouetted against the flashing lights from the emergency vehicles outside. "Here I am, Michael, I see you." And she was laughing…coughing, choking and laughing with relief and joy. "Put out your hand, see? Just hold on to me. Everything's going to be all right…" She felt a hand creep into hers, like a little lost thing seeking shelter. She reached out, and a pair of thin arms wrapped themselves around her neck. A cheek came against hers, leaving it wet with tears. "It's okay," she croaked, patting the child's shaking back. "Okay."

Trying to peel the boy's arms from her neck was like bending wire. "Michael, now listen," she said firmly. "We have to crawl now, okay? Like this…and hold your breath as long as you can—like when you swim underwater. Okay? Let's go…"

But out in the hallway the smoke was thicker, taking up all the space, even down near the floor. Michael began to whimper. "I can't breathe…I can't…*breathe!*"

Joanna tried desperately not to breathe. Then she was desperate to breathe, and found that she couldn't. It was just like her nightmare—there was no air for breathing.

With her last ounce of strength she gathered Michael into her arms, lurched to her feet and staggered toward the stairs. Darkness closed in, and she was falling…falling…

Then…as in her old nightmare, just when she was sure the darkness would take her forever, she felt strong arms around her, and a cracked voice murmuring comforting words in her ear: "It's okay, baby-girl…you gonna be all right now. Doveman's got you under his wings…."

Ethan was standing on the edge of the chaos, hugging himself and shivering in the muggy night, hearing his teeth chatter as he stared through glittering, flickering patterns of light and darkness. When a cry went up from someone in the moving crowd of emergency personnel, he started upright, his body tensing as if it had received a powerful jolt of electricity. Cheers followed, and a smattering of applause, and the crowd surged forward as one body toward the entrance of the burning building. Ethan felt himself moving with them, with no idea how he'd come to be.

A small cluster of people had appeared at the top of the steps, seemingly disgorged from the doorway along with billows of smoke and the snapping, creaking, cracking sound of collapsing timbers. A strange-looking assembly it was—two firefighters in breathing masks and full protective gear supporting one elderly man, who held cradled in his arms a woman—who carried in *her* arms a child—and all of them barely recognizable, covered from head to toe with soot.

As paramedics rushed forward to relieve the exhausted firefighters of their burden, Ethan struggled to join them.

"Please," he croaked, looking into Tom Applegate's eyes.

The Secret Service man hesitated only a moment, then nodded and let him go.

He got to Joanna just as a paramedic was fitting an oxygen mask over her mouth and nose. She struggled against it, eyes blazing like pieces of a sunny day in her blackened face, until Ethan, down on one knee beside her, laid a restraining hand on the paramedic's arm. She spoke to him, then, in a voice like blowing sand, and he had to lean down close to hear.

"Help...them. Doveman...."

Something fierce and bright exploded inside him. It rushed through his chest and exploded from his lips in a sound—not words, just a gust of breath, as if someone had punched him hard in the stomach. He felt himself shattering, saw his heart and soul and every preconceived notion he'd ever had of goodness and character and courage and strength lying in glittering shards all around him. For the first time in his life he felt that he was seeing things clearly, all those things and one more: *Love*. There they were, all laid out before him in one ravaged, smoke-blackened face. Joanna's face.

"Doveman..." she whispered again, pleading.

"I will, I promise," he said, forcing the words through the terrible ache inside him.

He nodded to the paramedic, who replaced the mask. Joanna's eyes drifted closed.

Dragging in great gulps of air, Ethan surged to his feet. He stood for a moment, swaying slightly, trying to slow the frantic pace of his heart, trying to orient himself in a world that seemed suddenly to have spun out of his control. The only concrete thing in his life just then was the woman lying at his feet. The only thing he knew for certain was that leaving her just then was the hardest thing he'd ever done.

He touched the paramedic's shoulder and croaked, "Take good care of her." Then he went to find Michael and Rupert Dove.

Michael he found with no trouble. All he had to do was follow the racket, because his aunt Tamara was hovering over the paramedics who were trying to tend to him, sobbing and scolding at the same time with the shrill ferocity of overwhelming maternal relief. "Boy, what were you *thinkin'?* I'm gonna skin you alive—what am I gonna do if you get killed? What's your momma gonna *think?* Don't you *ever* do that again, you hear me?"

Ethan stopped long enough to assure both himself and Tamara that the boy's condition was far from life-threatening, which in the latter case took some doing. It was only when she realized who she was talking to that she finally stopped her agitated pacing to whisper, "Dr. Brown…he's really gonna be okay? You sure? Praise God, he's gonna be okay…" Then she sank to the curb and began to rock herself and her baby back and forth, back and forth, crying in soft, exhausted whimpers.

"Where's the other one?" Ethan quietly asked the young female paramedic who was checking Michael's vitals. "The old man—the one who brought them out."

The paramedic jerked her head. "Over there, last I saw."

"Thanks…"

In a quiet eddy behind an EMS wagon he found a little knot of people working in grim and frenzied silence. Wading through them, he crouched over the still body of Rupert Dove. "What've we got?" he asked hoarsely.

Kenny Baumgartner glanced up at him and pulled the stethoscope out of his ears. "Lost him once," he said tersely. "He's back now, though. We're 'bout ready to roll."

Ethan nodded. "Let's go."

Kenny gave him a surprised look as he got to his feet. "You coming along, Doc? I didn't think this was your night—"

"I'm coming," said Ethan softly. He looked down at the haggard and blackened face of the old piano man, mostly hidden now behind the oxygen mask. "You know who that is?"

"Well," said Kenny, "I hear he's one helluva hero."

"Yeah. He's also Rupert Dove."

"The *Doveman?* You kiddin' me?"

Ethan shook his head. "We're not losing him." He felt calm in his mind for the first time since he'd climbed out of the dark sedan back there in the street, and filled with a tense resolve. This was a battle he was used to, a battle he was trained to win. A battle he was determined to win. Because there was just no way in hell he was going to let the Doveman die. Not here, and not now.

Not until Joanna'd had a chance to say goodbye.

"No, sir," Kenny said, "not if I have anything to say about it. Okay, guys, let's move!" Moving in perfect sync, the team of paramedics popped the gurney and rolled it to the wagon.

Just as they got there the sky opened up the way it can do sometimes in the east, in June. The rain fell straight down, heavy and hard, with a rushing sound like the beating of wings.

Ethan sat in a hard plastic chair and watched her sleep. He'd lost track of what time of day or night it was, or how long he'd been there. Outside, beyond the hospital walls, the world waited; word had gotten out that the rock-and-roll icon known as Phoenix and her legendary piano man Rupert Dove had been injured in a row house fire, and that the president's son was somehow involved.

In here, though, all was quiet. The hospital went about its business as usual; routine noises faded in and out of his awareness, like the ticking of a clock.

He hadn't been able to take his eyes from her face, still a dusky-gray from the residue of smoke they hadn't quite gotten washed off, but with a lovely pink glow showing through, her hair splashed like spilled ink across the pillows and down over her neck and breasts, a spiderwebbing of it clinging to the dampness of one cheek like a fine filigree of black lace. He'd been able to find again the endearing little flaws he'd noticed that first day, the first time he'd seen her in person—the tiny lines near her eyes, the smudges, deep purple, now, the sprinkle of freckles across the tops of her cheeks—and had memorized them all. He wondered if he would ever again be able to close his eyes and not see her face in every detail…so vulnerable and unguarded…just like this.

He'd been expecting her to look different, as if his thinking of her as Joanna Dunn instead of Phoenix would have changed her in some fundamental way. It had taken him a while, sitting here alone with her, but it had finally come to him that she was who she had always been. That it was *he* who had changed. Though she was the one lying helpless in a hospital bed, it was he who felt stripped naked…he who was vulnerable and unprotected.

He'd accused her of hiding her true self with her disguises, but now he wondered if he'd been doing the same thing himself, all his life. His childhood shyness had grown into reserve, then hardened into detachment masquerading as quiet self-confidence. But what if all it had really been was another kind of mask—what was it she liked to call it? *Protective coloring?* Yes…protective coloring, a way of camouflaging his feelings to keep them safe from the terrifying dangers of involvement.

And now he'd lost that protection. Here he stood, all out in the open, soft and squishy as one of those sea creatures that sheds its shell and then has to wait for the new one underneath to harden. Except that he was very much afraid his shell was never going to grow back, that from now on he was going to feel like this—desperately fragile, vulnerable and afraid. Was this what it was like to love someone? He wondered if he would ever feel safe again.

Tearing his eyes away from her face, finally, he reached for her hand and raised it to his lips, then simply sat and gazed at it. They'd made an effort to clean it up some, he noticed, but grime still lingered around the short, unmanicured nails, making it seem more than ever like the hand of a child—a grubby one, now. Slowly, he raised it again and pressed his lips to the palm. Then he folded it into a fist and enclosed it in both of his. Bowing his head over his clasped hands, he closed his eyes and silently spoke the words he knew he'd never be able to say to her out loud. *Please...hold me. Protect me. My heart is here, now...in your hand. I've placed it in your keeping.*

"Jeez, Doc, am I that bad off?" Raspy as a file, her voice scraped across his raw and tender nerves. Speechless, shot through with adrenaline and shaky as a newly awakened child, he held on to her hand like a burglar caught with the goods. Her smile quirked sideways; her eyes regarded him calmly, shining like broken pieces of sky. "What are you doing, *praying?*"

On the last word she erupted into racking coughs. Ethan rose and, relinquishing her hand, picked up a basin from the tray beside her bed. He held it for her until the spasms had subsided, then said calmly, "Not praying—just...thinking."

"Oh, yeah? What about?" Her sideways glance seemed wary.

He didn't reply, and after taking sips of water from the straw he held for her, she wiped her mouth with the back of her hand and lay back on the pillows with an exhausted sigh. A moment later, though, she sat up again, her eyes going wide. "Oh, God—are they all right?" Her voice was a painful croak. "They are, aren't they? That little boy—"

"Michael's fine—he's going home later today."

"Doveman?" And her face was suddenly still, her eyes stark with fear. She'd already read the truth in his.

"He's been waiting for you," Ethan said gently. "I'll take you to him now."

The wheelchair made whispering sounds on the smooth hospital floor. To Phoenix the sounds seemed like voices just out of earshot, voices of people she'd loved...and lost.

She felt chilled...stone-cold. And more frightened than she'd ever been in her life.

The chair paused at a doorway. Beyond a half-glass partition she could hear the quiet beeping of monitors, see a nurse moving about with efficient and soundless steps. Of the person who lay on the bed, she could see only one hand, lying stark and black as a gnarled old tree root against the pristine white. When the chair moved forward again she reached out a hand and clutched at the door frame, stopping it.

"I can't," she whispered fiercely. "I *can't.*"

Ethan's hand lay gently on her shoulder; as if she were drowning and he'd thrown her a life preserver, she grabbed at it and held on. "He's not in any pain," he said softly.

Pain? But what about me? I feel like my heart's being torn out through my throat. A sob spiked through her and emerged as a faint, desperate laugh.

After a moment she nodded and the chair began to move, though she still clung like a child to Ethan's hand.

"But it's hard, so hard to say goodbye..."

It's what happens between hello and goodbye that matters, baby-girl...

"Hey, Doveman, how're y'doin'?" Her voice sounded loud and harsh, like a sputtering chainsaw. She reached for the hand that was lying on the sheets and took it in both of hers. It felt cool and papery...almost weightless.

His eyes opened about halfway and focused on her. "Hey, baby-girl," he whispered. His lips curved in a smile.

There were fewer tubes than she'd have expected, but the doc had told her what that meant. Doveman was DNR—Do Not Resuscitate. Because he had end-stage lung cancer and wouldn't have lived much longer anyway, even if the smoke and heat from the fire hadn't destroyed what was left of his lungs. Doveman was dying, and he hadn't told her.

She felt herself being buffeted about as if by cruel, freezing winds. She felt herself breaking apart inside, shattering into a million tiny pieces.

It's okay, baby-girl...ol' Doveman's got you under his wings.

She heard herself whimper like a lost child, "Doveman, don't go..."

"Got to, child. It's like I told you. It's time..."

"I won't let you go!" The child was angry now, railing futilely against that over which she had no control.

His chuckle was a soft whiskery noise, like dry leaves rustling. "These ol' lungs been shot for years...wouldn't a' had much longer anyway. This is a good time to go...now I know you gonna be okay..."

"Okay! How can you say that?" How would she ever be okay again? "What will I do without you?" She was trembling...desolate. Closing her eyes, she held his hand against her cheek and felt it grow wet with her tears. Frail and lost, she whispered, "Who's going to sing to me when I have my nightmares?"

For a few moments the silence in the room was broken only by the beeping of the monitor, while Doveman's tired eyes looked past Joanna's bowed head and straight into Ethan's. Then, with a tremendous effort he croaked, "Can you sing, boy?"

Ethan, knowing exactly what was being asked of him, didn't hesitate. With a fierce and protective resolve burgeoning inside him, he nodded. "Yes, sir, I can."

"There, you see?" Gently withdrawing his hand from Joanna's, he placed it on her head as if he were bestowing a blessing...then let it slide down to her shoulder, where it covered and briefly squeezed Ethan's. "You got nothing to worry about..." His eyelids drifted closed.

Joanna gave a little cry and clutched at his hand. Gently, as he might have touched a newborn baby, Ethan stroked her hair. He said, "He'll sleep now..."

"I'm not leaving him." Her voice was hard, breaking. She looked up at Ethan with tear-silvered eyes…then took a deep breath and wiped a cheek dry before she quietly added, "I want to stay."

Ethan nodded, but he couldn't bring himself to leave her. He stood beside her and gently stroked her hair while she held on to her old piano man's hand.

It was only later, when the line on the screen had gone flat and the beeper sang its sad one-note farewell, that she finally said it:

"Goodbye…."

Chapter 13

Back in her room, Joanna sat staring at the narrow white bed, the head cranked up and the covers rumpled, just as she'd left it. Now it looked to her like the set from a TV hospital show; except for the wheelchair under her and Ethan's hands on her shoulders, nothing seemed real. The bed was a movie prop, made of cardboard and tissue paper; it would collapse if she tried to sit on it. The window was just a painted rectangle on a cardboard wall.

"Take me home," she whispered.

Ethan's hands moved on her shoulders, massaging gently. They slipped alongside her neck, holding her in warmth and safety. The thumbs softly rubbed the edges of her jaws. And she sat rigid while peppery tears stung her nose and eyelids, filled with such sorrow...for *him*. He didn't know—how could he?—that every place he touched her, meaning only tenderness and comfort, ached so savagely she could scarcely bear it.

Leaning close to her ear, he said quietly, "There's a

pretty big crowd of reporters out there. Are you sure you feel up to it?''

Desperately, she shook her head. ''Tom and Carl could get us around them, couldn't they?''

He was quiet for a moment. Then... ''I imagine they could. You'll need some clothes. Wait here...''

He left her then, taking with him all that was alive and real in her existence...as if the screen had suddenly gone blank and the sound had been turned off. She sat motionless, unaware of the passing of time, feeling nothing at all except emptiness. Thinking maybe this was what death would feel like....

Then Ethan was there again, and when she saw him her heart gave a painful leap, as though it had been jolted back to life with a new and unfamiliar rhythm.

''All arranged,'' he said, sounding slightly out of breath. He was dressed in hospital scrubs, and held out another set for her. ''Protective coloring...'' His grin was crooked. ''We can thank Ruthie Mendoza for these.''

''Ruthie...?''

''Father Frank's sister—helps out at the clinic. She's a nurse here. Do you think you'll need any help putting them on?''

Deep inside the frozen crust that encased her, she felt prickles and stirrings of...could it be jealousy? Sexual possessiveness...territorial pride? To her it was like sensation returning to numbed limbs, reassuring her that she was alive...that she *would* feel again.

''I can manage,'' she said, when what she really meant was, *I need you...please help me...don't go away and leave me again...*

Ethan nodded. ''I'll be right outside here.''

He went out and quietly shut the door behind him, then leaned against it, breathing carefully, almost guiltily, as if he feared she might hear the ragged stutter of it...the runaway stampeding of his heart. He hadn't known how much it was going to hurt, seeing her like this. He hadn't known what it was going to be like, hurting *for* someone. These were new feelings, and he hadn't learned what to do with them yet. He wondered, as he had before, if this was what it was like to love someone. And what on earth he was going to do if he'd fallen in love with Phoenix.

Then the door opened and she stood there, shapeless in green surgical scrubs, with her signature hair hidden under a cap and her perfect oval face pale with exhaustion and smudged with smoke and grief. And he knew it wasn't a question of *if*.

"Ready," she said breathlessly. "Which way to the gauntlet?"

"Uh-uh—I have a secret exit," he said, and smiled, wondering if she'd remember. But if she did, she was too preoccupied to smile back.

As he led her down through the bowels of the hospital, through echoing concrete stairwells and corridors where pipes ran along the ceiling and the air was thick with formaldehyde, he thought about that time, the first day he'd met her. Thought about what a short time ago it had been, and how much things had changed since then. One thing, though, remained the same—he still felt completely out of his league...in over his head. What, he wondered, *does* a man do when the woman he loves has been dealt a killing blow?

In the basement, in the secret place where the coroner's vans parked when they came to pick up bodies, the dark sedan waited, quietly idling. Tom Applegate held the door for them, then got into the front seat. Carl Friedenburg's eyes met Ethan's in the rearview mirror.

"Where to, sir?"

Before he could say anything, Joanna's hand clutched at his arm, desperation in her grip. "Take me home with you," she said in a raspy, panicky undertone. "I can't go back there—to the loft—not tonight. I don't want to be alone..."

He nodded. There was a vast lump in his throat. To Carl he said quietly, "Just take us home."

Phoenix sat hunched and withdrawn as the car rolled through silent early morning streets, still glistening from the previous evening's rain. Ethan didn't even try to talk to her; he had no idea what to say. He'd never felt more helpless, more frustrated in his life. He felt she needed him—*knew* that she needed him, and that he was failing her miserably. He was a *doctor,* for God's sake. He'd been trained to heal people. But no one had taught him how to heal a broken heart.

Secure inside his own apartment building, he said good-night to Tom and Carl and climbed the stairs with Phoenix beside him. He kept one hand deferentially on her elbow, exactly the same way he'd have touched his sister, or Dixie, if they'd come to pay him a visit. But never for his sister or stepmother would his heart have pounded so, or frustration sizzle like acid below his breastbone. Never for them or anyone else had he felt jangled and jerky like this, as if there were a loose connection somewhere between his nerves and muscles.

He closed and locked his apartment door, shutting them in together, then turned, pulling off his surgical cap. "Are you hungry?" he asked. He could heard his jaws creak with tension.

She shook her head, and he was utterly at a loss—until he saw that she was shivering. This, at last—a physical symptom—was something he knew how to deal with.

"How about a shower?" he suggested gently, and was pleased beyond measure when she whispered, "Thanks... that'd be nice."

"I'll see if I can find you something to put on. Would

sweats be okay?'' He had quite a few of those—probably even some that were clean.

Again he was delighted with her murmured acquiescence. He led her into his bedroom, grateful for the embarrassment he'd suffered the last time he'd brought her here, which had prompted him to tidy up some—he'd even, praise God, made his bed. She stood silently while he collected clean sweats from a drawer and towels from his closet, nodded when he showed her where the shampoo was, if she wanted it. He felt positively masterful when he found her a new, unopened toothbrush. It was a feeling that lasted exactly as long as it took him to say, ''Well…if you need anything else, let me know,'' and walk out of the bathroom and close the door.

Then he knew with absolute certainty that he hadn't given her anything even close to what she needed.

He hovered nervously until he heard the water running in the shower, then for something to do, went out to the kitchen and filled a tea kettle with water and put it on the stove. Hot cocoa, he thought—or maybe herbal tea. That would be better this time of night than coffee.

While he waited for the water to boil, he puttered around in the living room…debated putting on music and decided against it. Changed out of his borrowed scrubs and put on sweats and a T-shirt instead. The tea kettle whistle rose to a crescendo and as he went to turn off the stove, he checked the time on the stove top clock. Fifteen minutes. She'd been in there fifteen minutes. And he could still hear the shower running. He wouldn't have thought he had that much hot water.

Heart pounding, he went into the bedroom. The only sound from the bathroom was the steady shushing of water hitting tile. Leaning close to the door, he called, ''Joanna? Everything all right in there?''

There was no answer. But now he could hear something

else—a very small sound, like a bird...or a kitten. His heart shot into his throat. He knocked, then called again, "Joanna—you okay?" He pounded on the door. Tried the knob. Found it unlocked. "Joanna? I'm coming in..."

The air in the bathroom was cool and wet, like a jungle in the rain. The fog that had collected on the mirror and shower door was already condensing, beginning to run in little rivers down the glass. Through the dimpled door glass he could see a small shape, darker than the tile...

"Oh, God—" He felt as though the top of his head was coming off. As if he could plunge through walls. Wrenching open the shower door, he fumbled with the faucets, shutting off the water.

She was huddled on the floor in the far corner of the shower, knees pulled up to her chin, hands covering her face, her hair streaming over her and plastered to her body like seaweed...sobbing...brokenly, heartrendingly, like a child.

A strange quietness came over Ethan then...a new kind of quietness that was altogether different from his old retreat to a place of peaceful solitude. There was nothing solitary about this quietness, but there was peace. The sweet and tender peace that comes with confidence...with certainty...with knowing at last exactly what it was she needed. And with knowing at last that, of all the people in the world, *he* was the one who could give it to her.

He took a towel from the stack he'd given her, shook it out and stepped into the still-dripping shower. Crouching beside her, he wrapped the towel around her. Then he lifted her tenderly into his arms and carried her to his bed. And all the while he was murmuring to her, crooning soft reassurances as if she were a frightened or injured animal.

His gentle voice...words she didn't really understand...seeped into her tormented mind and spread like oil. His arms felt warm and sturdy around her...she liked the strong, reassuring thump of his heartbeat against her cheek. She liked the way he smelled. And, oh, he felt good...so good. Now, everywhere he touched her, that part of her seemed to hurt a little less.

Sodden on the outside, inside her head—her throat, her eye sockets—felt hot and dry. She was tired of crying. She didn't want to cry anymore. But every time she thought of anything—anything at all—and even now she could feel fresh shudders building—she started all over again.

"Hold me," she whispered fiercely, gathering handfuls of his sweatshirt into her fists.

"I will," he promised, rocking her tenderly. "I am."

But it wasn't his gentleness she wanted now. She wanted oblivion, craved it like some powerful, mind-numbing drug. Pulling herself up in his embrace, she pressed her damp face into the curve of his neck, opened her mouth and tasted his salty-sweet skin. She shivered at the tickle of his beard on her cheek. Grew hot inside at his thundering heartbeat, the soft intake of his breath. Her fingertips found his beard...played in its softness...then moved on to his lips, stroked them lightly, teasingly, sensitizing them...preparing them for hers.

Hot all over inside, she heard his intake of breath become a growl, and then her name. *"Joanna..."*

He knew what was happening, of course he did. Knew that what she was doing was filling a fundamental human need, obeying an instinct as old as time—attempting to vanquish death by creating new life. And he had no thought at all of denying her. Sometime later, he thought he might feel ashamed of himself, but just then it seemed to him the only possible thing to do. That was his last rational thought before her lips touched his.

A moment later he knew how desperately he'd been craving the taste of her. He knew she must have been in his dreams, when he'd woken up itchy and feverish and swollen with unfulfilled desire. Knew she'd been just behind his thoughts every waking moment, like a sprite playing peek-aboo, playing havoc with his concentration, popping up un-expectedly to give him a breath-stopping vision of her lush, sensual mouth, lips curved in a sardonic smile...

So, he opened to her...felt her lift herself and with one hungry surge, come inside him. She wanted the lead and he gave it to her with all the generosity of spirit that was his nature, holding nothing back. His breath scalded his throat; groans that formed deep in his belly somehow fought their way through his chest to mingle with her tigerish little growls. Desire exploded inside him and scattered sparks through all his muscles. His skin ignited.

The towel fell away, forgotten. His hand found and filled itself with her breast...but at the first brush of his fingers on her cold-tightened nipple she gasped...first arched against him, pushing into his hand...then tore her mouth from his and instead pulled his head down, her fingers weaving themselves though his hair as she lifted herself to meet him.

The sound she made when he lowered his mouth over the jewel-hard tip was heart-wrenching—a whimper, sharp and bright as crystal breaking. Hearing it, love and passion came together inside him for the first time in memory, forming a tenderness so intense and so vast it filled every corner of his being, and his throat and eyes with tears. Quaking inside, he held himself still...save for his tongue, which gently...so gently laved her nipple to melting softness. And for his hand...which, usurped, went searching, skimmed down the sensitive sides of her waist, her hip, the gentle concavity of her stomach, to find the nest of damp curls between her thighs. Lightly, he rubbed her legs with long, easing strokes until she opened to him...then brushed the silky insides of her thighs with his fingertips...nested the damp mound at their apex in his palm.

At first, as before, she gasped and pushed into his hand, hungry…demanding…shivering in anticipation. Then, as before, she twisted away from him with an inarticulate little cry. Her hands clutched at his shoulders with an urgency he heard a moment later in her hoarse and guttural "No!"

Before the meaning of that could penetrate the delirium of his thoughts, it came to him that she was tearing frantically at his T-shirt, trying to pull it over his head while at the same time pushing on him, bearing him down. Understanding came. Laughing softly, he drew off his shirt in one swift motion and lay back on the bed, drawing her with him.

She was amazed by the way he seemed to know just what she wanted—and gave it to her. And touched beyond measure by the easy unselfishness of his giving. As impatient as she was, as brittle with desire, the quick but careful way he prepared himself for her was a revelation. And as she came astride him and felt the first bright shock of penetration…then the slow, sweet filling…that hard and shiny ribbon of desire inside her somehow became entangled with something softer…a delicate fluttering streamer of feeling, gossamer as spiderwebbing, lovely as a butterfly's wing. As she moved over him, rocking her body with his, the two coiled and danced through her consciousness, becoming so inextricably knotted she couldn't tell, finally, one from the other. Hopelessly tangled, she began to feel clumsy, shaky, out of control.

"Easy…" he murmured, smiling up at her. His hands ran up and down her sides…then around to her back, dipping under the wet-silk fall of her hair to cup her buttocks as he set himself deep inside her.

She felt her body coiling…bracing…and tears rushing up in her throat. She gazed at him, defiance of the tears blazing hot and fierce in her eyes…

It came so suddenly…her eyes bright as chips of sky one moment…the next dissolving in misty rainbows. She swayed, and he drew her down onto his chest, her body wrapped in the webbing of her hair, quaking and trembling, release mixing with sobs. Swiftly then, while she clung to him, her body still hot and pulsing, he drove himself into her and gave her his own completion like a gift...a sweet shuddering rapture that was like nothing he'd ever known....

Gradually, he understood that she was crying. Not the sobs of reaction to overwhelming climax, but deep, wrenching, grief-stricken sobs. He didn't try to stop her tears, nor did he feel any remorse, understanding that tears were a necessary antedote to grief, and a prerequisite for healing. Instead, he wrapped her in his arms and warmed her with his body while he stroked her back and murmured reassurances into her damp hair.

"Sorry," she croaked, when the weeping had subsided into exhausted snuffles, sounding grumpy in her self-disgust. "I thought I was done with that. I really *hate* to cry."

"Why shouldn't you cry?" Ethan said matter-of-factly— a trifle gruffly. "You've lost someone you care about very much."

She didn't say anything for several minutes. Then, in a careful whisper, lest she bring forth the lurking sobs again... "He was...the only person in this world who loved me. Now he's gone. And now there's...no one."

"That's not true." He paused, his hand still moving up and down her back. And then he softly said it. "*I* love you."

He couldn't have been more surprised when she rolled away from him, as suddenly and violently as if he'd turned into something monstrous and vile right there in her embrace. Crouched on her knees just beyond his reach, she snatched up the forgotten towel and drew it jerkily around her.

"Well," Ethan said mildly, as his heart banged without mercy against his ribcage, "I had hoped for a little different reaction."

She snorted, but said nothing, concentrating instead on knotting the towel above her breasts. She couldn't look at him, couldn't see the hurt in his eyes that he tried so hard to hide with that quiet, gentle way of his.

"I do, you know. I shouldn't think that would come as much of a surprise. Men must fall in love with you all the time."

She did look at him then—as penance, perhaps, for the pain she was causing him. "They do," she said evenly. "I suppose I just never cared before what happened to any of them. I guess I thought they got what they deserved."

"Oh—" and his lips twisted into a droll little smile "—and what's the terrible penalty for loving Phoenix? Do I turn to stone? Oops—no, that's Medusa."

She snorted and looked away again. Turning sideways to him, she settled herself cross-legged and began to gather her hair into her hands. "You just…shouldn't," she said, mechanically twisting it into a rope. "I'm not very loveable."

"Don't you think you should let me be the judge of that?" His voice sounded almost amused…but she hadn't missed the burning brightness of his eyes.

"You don't know who I am," she mumbled, hating what she was doing to him. Hating herself.

"I know you better than you think I do," he said, and something in the softness of his voice made her turn to look at him. Her heart lurched…stumbled and ran away from her, leaving her cold…cold as ice. Her face must have gone sheet-white, but he went on anyway, in that same gentle way. "Your mother's name was Rachel. You had a twin brother named Jonathan, and a little sister named Chrissy. They died in an apartment house fire when you were nine."

Chapter 14

Her lips felt as if they'd been sculpted of ice. Numb. "How did you...how long have you—"

"I just found out yesterday. I went to your studio to talk to you, but you weren't there. Doveman told me...a little more. We put it together, where you must have gone. That's why we were both there...at The Gardens...the fire."

A choking blackness crawled into her throat. Desperately she swallowed, fighting it down. "Then you—" She swallowed again, and croaked, "Then you know..."

"I know that you were a child...a little girl...and that you suffered a terrible, terrible loss. And then, to compound the trauma, you were put into foster care, probably without proper treatment for post-traumatic—"

But she was shaking her head wildly, and when she spoke, her voice sounded like an intractable child's. "No—but you don't know what I did. You don't know!"

"What don't I know?" She looked stubbornly away from him—again like a child. He cajoled her like one. "Come on…you can tell me. You can, you know. Whatever it is, it can't make me think less of you.''

"Oh, yes, it will."

He smiled. "Now, what can a nine-year-old child have possibly done that could be so terrible?"

"Something…"

"How terrible? Big black ugly terrible? Or little mean red terrible?"

She threw him an angry look that dissolved into bleakness, and he recognized the look as the one he'd seen that day in the park beside the basketball courts, the one that looked like rain was falling somewhere behind her eyes. She looked down at her hands, knotted in her hair. Pulled in a shuddering breath. "Momma sent me to the store," she said softly.

"That's why you weren't there. But—"

She held up a hand, stopping him. "I was angry. I didn't want to go—I don't know why, I was in the middle of something, probably. But I was mad because I always had to be the one to do everything—run errands, take care of the baby, do the chores. Jonathan was always sick—he had asthma, I think. Sometimes he even had to go to the hospital. So I was always the one Momma called on when she needed help. That day I was supposed to get milk for Chrissy and some medicine for Jonathan. Momma told me to come right back, and I promised her I would. But—" she paused to draw another quivering breath "—I was feeling angry and resentful and rebellious. I remember thinking 'I hate you! I hate you all.' I don't know if I said it out loud…" Her voice broke.

Ethan held himself still. The urge to gather her into his arms burned in every muscle, every fiber of his being. But after a moment she went bravely on.

"Anyway, I got the things like I was supposed to, but then, instead of going right home like I'd promised, I stopped to listen to some men playing music. There were two of them, and they were always there on that corner— one played a guitar and the other one had a banjo. They'd play and sing, and people would put money in the guitar case that was lying open on the sidewalk. I used to love to listen to them, but Momma didn't like me to. So, that day I did it anyway, because I was mad at her. And I got so caught up in listening to the music, I just…lost track of time…until I heard the sirens. They came right up the street, getting louder and louder, until I thought my ears were going to burst. The engines went right by me, with this big wind. Screaming…screaming. And for some reason, I just…ran. Ran after them. I ran and ran as fast as I could, but by the time I got there…'' She choked, and a sob gusted from her, shaking her like a powerful wind.

Ethan reached for her and gathered her in, encompassing her jutting legs and stiff, unyielding body, and arms that tried to fend him off. Little by little, coaxing and insisting, he drew her close against him. Molded her quaking body to his. "You were a *child*," he whispered brokenly. "You were nine years old. What could you have done? If you'd been there you'd only have died in that fire, too."

But she was shaking her head, wildly, insistently. "No— no, if I'd been there, I'd have *saved* them. Don't you understand?" She drew back and looked at him, touching his soul with her wounded eyes in the same way, he realized now, she'd been touching him with her music all those years. "Jonathan was sick—he'd been in bed. Chrissy was little—not even three. Momma couldn't carry them both! If I'd been there like I promised, I could have helped. I could have gotten them all out—I know I would have saved them…I would have saved them…."

He had nothing to say to her; the enormity of the burden she carried on her soul, had carried for so many years, utterly defeated him. He could only hold her…stroke her and caress her, trying so hard to tell her with his touch what he couldn't possibly in words…pleading with her silently to lay her terrible burden down, or if she couldn't do that, at least to let him help her carry it.

"It didn't work, you know," he murmured when she'd quieted, his voice thickened slightly, as if he were drunk.

"What?" It was a croak, defiant and angry, making him smile.

"Your terrible sin. It only made me love you more."

Her reply was a hopeless-sounding whimper. But he felt encouraged when she lay quiet, peaceful in his embrace, as if she'd found a home there. And a little while later he heard the cadence of her breathing grow deep and even, and still later, a faint but unmistakable snore.

Dawn was breaking when she began to stir and whimper in her sleep. He remembered then what Doveman had told him about her nightmares…remembered the lullaby she'd played on his guitar…remembered her grief-stricken, *Who's going to sing to me…?* Remembered Doveman's words: *Can you sing, boy?* And his own response: *Yes, sir, I can.* So that's what he did, brokenly, stroking her hair while his lashes grew wet with his own tears:

"Hush little baby, don't say a word, Papa's gonna buy you a mockin'bird…"

Phoenix woke to an unfamiliar sound: a man was singing in her shower. No—not her shower, she remembered; the doc's. *Ethan's shower…Ethan's bed.*

A sneaky little sense of well-being crept over her in the instant before she remembered exactly how and why it was she'd come to be there. Before she remembered that Doveman was dead, and that Ethan Brown loved her. Two more tragedies she was responsible for causing—two more items to add to the ever-growing list of her sins.

Defiantly, knowing herself to be damned already, she

threw off the bedspread that had been folded over her and tiptoed into the bathroom.

Ethan had his eyes closed when he felt the sudden rush of cool air and an instant later the silky slide of her arms coming around him...the exuberant press of her body. The bar of soap he was holding slipped from his hands, in much the same way his heart had just slalomed out of his chest and into his belly. Turning in her slippery embrace, he found her mouth there, hungry and waiting, and sank into it with a laughing, good-morning growl.

"Feeling better this morning, are we?" he said when he surfaced for air.

"Mmm...I had a very good doctor." Her hands were busy...busy.

"Yeah, well...keep in mind, I don't hand out this particular prescription to just anybody." Breathless, he caught her hands and brought them together, pinned between their chests, stifling her protest with his mouth.

Her protests grew in volume, threatening insurrection when he reached behind him and turned off the water. He recaptured her rebellious hands, and, laughing, gave her excuses about winding up in traction, and running out of hot water. But the truth was, he'd had a lot of time last night to think about the implications of what had happened to them. Singing away her nightmares and holding her while she slept, it had come to him that the road ahead of him wasn't going to be an easy one. Finding Joanna had been the easy part. Loving Joanna, he now realized, had been a given all along. *Healing* Joanna, now—that was the real challenge. He knew his job as healer had just begun. He very much wanted to get it right.

Standing dripping on the rug in the middle of the bathroom, he took a towel and mopped water droplets from her face and his while she sipped them thirstily from his chest. With the air chilling their skin and tightening her breasts, raising her nipples to rosy nubs, he turned her to face the mirror. He held her tightly with one arm across her hips, her buttocks cool and firm against him, and with the other hand reached with the towel to wipe away the condensation from the mirror. Eyes half-closed, she leaned her head back against his shoulder and moved sinuously against his body, testing its heat and hardness.

Desire coiled like a python in his belly, but he held her still and kept his voice gentle as he asked her, "Do you know why I fell in love with you?"

Staring dully at their blurred reflections, she made a soft, snorting sound and shook her head. He let her look for a long time, then lifted his hands to frame her face. The perfect oval gazed back at him, lovely as a cameo, black-fringed eyes like tiny pools, reflecting a summer sky. Lightly he brushed her cheeks with his fingertips…traced the lines of her jaw…her nose…her lips. She gave a sad little sigh and closed her eyes.

"Not this," he whispered. "Or this…" His hands skimmed downward over her throat…briefly cradled her breasts…stroked the taut planes of her belly, the subtle curve of her hips. "You are beautiful…so incredibly beautiful. But that's not why I fell in love with you. Here—shall I show you why?" He took her hand and led her out of the bathroom, and she followed silently, stumbling a little like a just-woken child.

He led her through the bedroom and into the living room. Standing in front of his stereo, with her close against him as they'd been before, he reached with one finger and pressed the power button. Music poured from the speakers and filled the room, wrapping itself around them. Phoenix's music.

She started and tensed against him. "Hush," he murmured. "Listen…"

"Newspaper says…
  'House Burns, City Woman Dies.'
  Paper never says
  'City Woman Dies…Someone Cries…'"

"That's you," Ethan whispered. He laid his hand gently over her heart. "That came from the real Joanna…the one that's in here." He turned her to face him, his love for her burning hot in his cheeks, stinging in his eyes…thickening in his voice. "I've loved you for years…."

She didn't speak or move, just stood there and looked at him with tears streaming down her cheeks. He took her face in his hands and tenderly brushed the tears away with his lips…then carried the sweet-salt taste of them to her mouth. He kissed her for a long time, deepening slowly, like the ripening of fruit in a hot summer sun. Then he took her back to his bed and made love to her the same way, cherishing her with his mouth, his body, and his healer's hands.

He came into her slowly, gently…filling her with himself, with all the love that was inside him…fitting them together so sweetly, so perfectly, that it was hard to tell where he left off and she began…then rocked them together as one being, so that when their explosions came the shattered pieces might reform as one inseparable whole.

She wept again, but softly…and this time, when he told her he loved her, she didn't pull away.

She wept often, in the days that followed, and Ethan didn't try to prevent or stop her tears. It was necessary, he told himself. Healing.

He did wish, sometimes, while he was making love to her, that she would look into his eyes and smile.

She stayed with him from the night of Doveman's death until the day of his funeral. She made all the arrangements herself, some by telephone, some in consultation with the other members of her band. Ethan's living room had become their meeting place, with the grudging consent of the Service—after Ethan had appealed personally to his father, through Dixie, of course. He got used to coming home from the clinic to find his apartment throbbing with music—or arguments—and every space strewn with instruments, bodies, and take-out food containers.

The arguments were mostly about details. Everyone agreed that the services would be simple; that there would be music—lots of music; that in keeping with the traditions of Doveman's New Orleans jazz beginnings, there would be a procession through the streets. The media would have to be accommodated—there was no getting around that. It would be managed, somehow. Everything would somehow be worked out. On one point, though, Phoenix was adamant. Rupert Dove's remains would be cremated; she hadn't decided yet what to do with his ashes, but she was certain of one thing: there would be no internment. A Dove, she said, did not belong in the ground.

The day of the funeral dawned cloudy, threatening rain, but it had all blown over by the time the procession wound its raucous and joyful way through the streets, past The Gardens, past the clinic, to St. Jude's Church. During the service, which Father Frank conducted, Phoenix and the band played and sang for the select few invited guests inside the church. Among the songs performed was Rupert Dove's last composition, the hauntingly beautiful, "Hard To Say Goodbye."

After the service, Tom and Carl took Ethan and Phoenix back to his apartment. When, with the door closed and locked behind them, Ethan turned and found her standing tense and still in the middle of his living room, holding the small rosewood box containing Rupert Dove's ashes in her hands, his heart began to pound. He knew before she said it, in her raspy, Phoenix voice.

"I have to go."

He made himself calm and still as she, willing himself to numbness. "I suppose you do."

"There are so many things I have to do—the album…the tour. We're way behind schedule as it is." Her eyes clung to his, begging him to understand.

He went to her and put his hands on her shoulders…brushed his fingers up and down her arms. "I understand," he said, then bent and kissed her. Her mouth quivered. His throat ached.

She pulled away and would not meet his eyes. "I don't know how long I'll be gone…where I'll be…what I'm going to be doing. I'll call you…."

"Well, I'd hope so." His smile felt as if it had been carved in his flesh with a knife. He wanted to beg her to stay just a little longer, make love to her one more time, so unforgettably she'd have to change her mind about going. Instead, he said, "I'll get Carl or Tom to run you home."

While he was doing that, she went into the bedroom to gather her things. She came out carrying the small sports bag she'd collected from her loft, containing her toiletries and not much else. He walked her down the stairs and out onto the row house steps, where Tom was waiting for them. The dark sedan was at the curb, door open, engine idling.

"Take care of yourself," he said huskily.

"You, too." She went down the steps and crossed the sidewalk. At the car, she paused and looked back at him. "I do know one thing I'm going to be doing." Her eyes shone at him like distant water through trees.

"What's that?" He could barely breathe….

"Finding Joanna," she said. She got into the car and the door closed, leaving him gazing at his own reflection in the tinted window.

But she didn't say it, he told himself. *She didn't say good-bye.*

It wasn't until he was back in his own bedroom and found the little rosewood box sitting on his dresser that he started to breathe again...that his heart stopped bludgeoning him, and the knife wound in his belly began to heal. He knew for certain then that she'd be back. She'd left Doveman's ashes in his care.

Though there were times, during the next few months, when he wondered. She did call a few times, but the conversations felt stiff and artificial, the way people talk when there's someone else in the room. He told himself he had to be patient, that he had to give her time. That she would come to him when she was ready to accept his love, and that it would be pointless for her to come any sooner. But there were times he wondered if he was even alive in her absence. As if she'd taken his heart and soul with her, and left only *his* ashes behind.

He kept busy with the clinic and his ride-alongs, spent time with friends. Now and then he'd catch a glimpse of Phoenix when she appeared on some news show or other, being interviewed about her new album, the upcoming tour, the title of which was being kept a closely guarded secret. He didn't know what was worse—seeing her like that, a small flat picture, so empty of life, so far away, or not seeing her at all. When things seemed loneliest, when he thought it most likely he'd never see her again any other way, he reminded himself of two things: the rosewood box, and the fact that she'd never said goodbye.

She came back on a late afternoon in early autumn. The only warning he had was a phone call from Tom. A terse "Sir, you have a visitor."

He barely had time to get to the door. He opened it and

she burst through and hurled herself into his arms, laughing and kissing him until he couldn't breathe. Probably wouldn't have been able to anyway, with his heart in his throat, and joy and relief and desire and love taking up all the room in his chest.

"My God," he whispered when he could, "is it really you?"

"It's me—Joanna. I swear it is. Oh, God, and I have so much to tell you. But—" she danced away from him, vibrating with excitement "—there's something we have to do—right now…" And she crossed the room with her panther's stride and disappeared into his bedroom.

Before he could even begin to think whether or not it was sex she meant, she was back, carrying the rosewood box. She grabbed at his hand, pulling him toward the door. "Come on—quick, before it's too late…."

"There…" Joanna stood back and linked her arm through Ethan's. She gave a sigh—of acceptance, of completion—and then there was only silence as they stood together gazing at the box, nestled in the maze of construction like a single blossom in a patch of thorns.

Behind them the sun was setting, casting long purple shadows across the site where The Gardens had once stood, and where the foundations of a new apartment complex were now taking shape. Tomorrow the cement trucks would arrive to pour the last section, the front of the main building, including the entryway. The forms stood empty, waiting. It was there that Joanna had placed the box containing Rupert Dove's ashes.

A short distance away, Secret Service Special Agents Tom Applegate and Carl Friedenburg waited with backs discreetly turned, watching the street with their customary vigilance, forcing the ever-present photographers to keep a respectful distance.

Nearby, a sign proudly announced this as the "Future Site Of Rupert Dove Apartments." The name of the construction company was prominently displayed, along with a telephone number for rental information—although at least half the units had already been promised to the former tenants of the Gardens, who were being temporarily housed at the expense of the Phoenix Corporation. Also on the sign was an artist's rendering of the completed complex, and the words, "Funding for this project provided by the Rupert Dove Foundation—A nonprofit organization dedicated to the reclamation and restoration of the quality of human life..."

"I thought you said he didn't belong in the ground," Ethan said as the shadows merged into lavender twilight.

"Not in the ground." Joanna's head moved against his shoulder. "In the building...in the foundations. Right here by the entrance, where he can watch over the people who live here...you know...keep them safe."

Ethan said nothing for a moment, while he weighed risks, pride, and hope for the future. His lifelong habit of shyness and reticence limited his response to a soft "What about you?"

Her head came up and her eyes met his, catching the last of the light like the glimmering of moonlight on water. "I don't need him anymore," she said. "Now I have you."

Ethan's chest filled with the sweetest, most beautiful ache as he lowered his head to kiss her...and heard her whisper at last, "That's what I wanted to tell you. I love you, Doc."

Neither of them paid the slightest bit of attention to the distant click and whir of cameras.

Epilogue

The spotlight grew from a pinprick to a golden pool on the darkened stage. The screams of the capacity crowd rose to deafening cresendo when Phoenix stepped into the light.

She stood alone, holding only a microphone, wearing a simple white gown, with her black hair tumbling in a silken fall to the backs of her thighs. There was no band, no elaborate costumes, no laser lights. This was the long-anticipated concert tour—the one billed as "Joanna Dunn: Phoenix Unveiled."

A hush gradually descended on the arena as she spoke a few words of introduction and dedication. Then, in that profound and vibrant silence she began to sing…without accompaniment, in her famous Phoenix voice, husky and cracking with passion…but softly now, like a mother singing to her infant child:

"Hush little baby, don't say a word…Momma's gonna buy you a mockin'bird…"

Smiling with pride, aching with love, Dr. Ethan Brown stood and watched his wife from the shadows offstage, well out of the limelight. Which was just where he wanted to be.

* * * * *

Two down, one to go!
Watch another member of the next generation
of Browns—this time cousin Rose—find love
where she least expects it, in The Seduction of
Goody Two-Shoes...coming in July 2001
only from Silhouette Intimate Moments.

Hard To Say Goodbye

Music by Rupert Dove. Lyrics by Joanna Dunn.

Entrances are hard, hard, hard,
  Full of butterflies and fears;
Exits are easy—take your bows
  And listen to the cheers.
Being born looks hard
  Though who can remember?
Dyin' looks easy...
  Close your eyes and go to sleep forever.

  But if it's harder to come than to go...
    Why's it so much harder to say goodbye than
hello?

Love affair begins and it's so easy...
  Hello slips by like petals on the river flow;
But the river rolls on, it don't go back,
  And how are we to know what lies
  where the river meets the skies?
And when it's time to say goodbye
  Might as well tear out pieces of your heart
  And throw 'em on the water...
It's that hard, so hard to say goodbye.

Silhouette

INTIMATE MOMENTS™
and
BEVERLY BARTON
present:

THE PROTECTORS

Ready to lay their lives on the line, but unprepared for the power of love

Available in March 2001:
NAVAJO'S WOMAN
(Intimate Moments #1063)
Heroic Joe Ornelas will do anything to shelter the woman he has always loved.

Available in May 2001:
WHITELAW'S WEDDING
(Intimate Moments #1075)
Handsome Hunter Whitelaw is about to fall in love with the pretend wife he only "wed" to protect!

And coming in June 2001, a brand-new, longer-length single title:
THE PROTECTORS: SWEET CAROLINE'S KEEPER

Sexy David Wolfe longs to claim the woman he has guarded all his life—despite the possible consequences....

Available at your favorite retail outlet.

Silhouette®
Where love comes alive™

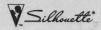

LINDSAY McKENNA

continues her most popular series with a brand-new, longer-length book.

And it's the story you've been waiting for....

Morgan's Mercenaries:
Heart of Stone

They had met before. Battled before. And Captain Maya Stevenson had never again wanted to lay eyes on Major Dane York— the man who once tried to destroy her military career! But on their latest mission together, Maya discovered that beneath the fury in Dane's eyes lay a raging passion. Now she struggled against dangerous desire, as Dane's command over her seemed greater still. For this time, he laid claim to her heart....

Only from Lindsay McKenna and Silhouette Books!

> "When it comes to action and romance, nobody does it better than Ms. McKenna."
> *Romantic Times Magazine*

Available in March at your favorite retail outlet.

Silhouette®
Where love comes alive™

If you enjoyed what you just read,
then we've got an offer you can't resist!

Take 2 bestselling
love stories FREE!
Plus get a FREE surprise gift!

Clip this page and mail it to Silhouette Reader Service™

IN U.S.A.	IN CANADA
3010 Walden Ave.	P.O. Box 609
P.O. Box 1867	Fort Erie, Ontario
Buffalo, N.Y. 14240-1867	L2A 5X3

YES! Please send me 2 free Silhouette Intimate Moments® novels and my free surprise gift. Then send me 6 brand-new novels every month, which I will receive months before they're available in stores. In the U.S.A., bill me at the bargain price of $3.80 plus 25¢ delivery per book and applicable sales tax, if any*. In Canada, bill me at the bargain price of $4.21 plus 25¢ delivery per book and applicable taxes**. That's the complete price and a savings of at least 10% off the cover prices—what a great deal! I understand that accepting the 2 free books and gift places me under no obligation ever to buy any books. I can always return a shipment and cancel at any time. Even if I never buy another book from Silhouette, the 2 free books and gift are mine to keep forever. So why not take us up on our invitation. You'll be glad you did!

245 SEN C226
345 SEN C227

Name		(PLEASE PRINT)	
Address		Apt.#	
City		State/Prov.	Zip/Postal Code

* Terms and prices subject to change without notice. Sales tax applicable in N.Y.
** Canadian residents will be charged applicable provincial taxes and GST.
 All orders subject to approval. Offer limited to one per household.
 ® are registered trademarks of Harlequin Enterprises Limited.

INMOM00 ©1998 Harlequin Enterprises Limited

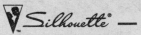

#1 *New York Times* bestselling author

NORA ROBERTS

brings you more of the loyal and loving,
tempestuous and tantalizing Stanislaski family.

Coming in February 2001

The Stanislaski Sisters

Natasha and Rachel

Though raised in the Old World traditions of their
family, fiery Natasha Stanislaski and cool, classy
Rachel Stanislaski are ready for a *new* world of love....

And also available in February 2001 from
Silhouette Special Edition, the newest book in the
heartwarming Stanislaski saga

CONSIDERING KATE

Natasha and Spencer Kimball's daughter Kate turns her
back on old dreams and returns to her hometown, where
she finds the *man* of her dreams.

Available at your favorite retail outlet.

Silhouette®
Where love comes alive™

Visit Silhouette at www.eHarlequin.com

PSSTANSIS